REUNION

REUNION

Michael Jan Friedman

POCKET BOOKS
New York   London   Toronto   Sydney   Tokyo   Singapore

POCKET BOOKS, a division of Simon & Schuster Inc.
1230 Avenue of the Americas, New York, NY 10020

This book is published by Pocket Books, a division of Simon & Schuster Inc., under exclusive license from Paramount Pictures.

ISBN: 0-671-74808-4

First Pocket Books hardcover printing November 1991

10 9 8 7 6 5 4 3

POCKET and colophon are registered trademarks of Simon & Schuster Inc.

Printed in the U.S.A.

For Uncle Leslie, never forgotten

Acknowledgments

Books like these don't get published without the help of a lot of people. I hope you'll indulge me while I take the time to thank them.

First and foremost, there's my wife, Joan—the guiding light assigned to me in this particular lifetime. For six months, every time I got up from the word processor at the end of a long day, she asked me the same thing: "Is it good? Is it *really* good?" Not that I'd ever let a book out of the house until I was happy with it. But if I'm ever tempted, it's good to know that Joan will be around to set me straight.

You don't know what it's like to work with a cranky kid running around the house. Fortunately, neither do I. Though you're too young to read this, Brett, I want you to know how much I appreciate your very unchildlike cooperation. And also the occasional hug.

Special thanks to my mom and dad. No explanation needed.

Joseph Critelli, an old friend from my wild high school days, helped me out with my subspace mechanics and the physics behind Phigus Simenon's favorite pastime. It was sort of funny hearing something learned and logical coming from a man who used to leap out of moving cars for the hell of it. Hey, Joe—this time I had one and the wheels stayed *on*.

To David Stern, Star Trek editor at Pocket Books, two grateful nods—one current and one belated. The belated one is for the job Dave did on my last two books, *Fortune's Light* and *Legacy,* which wouldn't have been nearly as good if not for Dave's tireless (and eventually maddening) requests for expanding one point or another. Hell of a job, big guy. The other nod is for all the work Dave's *going* to put into this book, Lord help me. You see, I'm writing these acknowledgments *before* I get Dave's response to the book, while I still *like* him.

Then there's Kevin Ryan, Dave's assistant and a terrific editor in his own right. Kevin had the unenviable task of

ACKNOWLEDGMENTS

helping me piece together a chronology of events for the Next Generation cast—without which none of the flashbacks and historical references could have been written. Also, if you like the description of Jack Crusher's heroic demise . . . you've got Kevin to thank for it. If you hate it, you can blame it on me.

And of course, no set of acknowledgments would be complete without an expression of gratitude to Gene Roddenberry. Picard and company are *his* children; I'm only a Dutch uncle who gets to take them to the circus now and then.

Honorable mentions . . .

Bob Greenberger, Star Trek editor at DC comics. A seemingly normal person if you saw him on the street, Bob's one part Trek encyclopedia, one part juggler (if you don't know what I mean, you've got to see him at the office) and one part plain ol' nice guy. Whenever I couldn't get hold of Dave or Kevin for a point of information, I called on Bob—and he never disappointed me.

Dr. Seth Asser of the University of California at San Diego and Dr. Keith Ditkowsky of Long Island Jewish Hospital in New York, who continue to serve as my braintrust for things medical.

Karen Haas, a former Star Trek editor and the woman who helped me sell my first manuscript.

Lorraine (alias Susan), Lori and Lee, Lois and Cliff, Carol and What's-his-name, Patti and Marc and all the kids: Fara, Eric, Amy, Craig, and Matthew.

Carrie Anderson, whose warmth has been a welcome addition to our home.

The New York Yankees, who every day give me more reason to prefer the future to the present.

CHAPTER 1

In the dream, he was on a crowded shuttlecraft.

They had left the *Stargazer* behind—a hulk, crippled in the encounter with the Ferengi at Maxia Zeta. Somewhere ahead—*weeks* ahead—was Starbase 81.

But there was no trace of the desperation they'd felt during the battle. No trace of the sorrow for lost comrades that had hung over them like a cloud.

Instead, there was an air of optimism. Of camaraderie, as there had been on the ship when it was whole. He looked around at the faces—familiar faces. Gilaad Ben Zoma, his first officer, dark and handsome, confident as ever. Idun Asmund, his helmsman, tall and pristinely beautiful as she bent over the shuttle's controls. "Pug" Joseph, his security chief, characteristically alert, ready for anything.

And another—a face that he was gladder to see than all the rest.

"Jack," he said.

Jack Crusher turned his way. He indicated their surroundings with a tilt of his head. "A little snug in here, isn't it, Jean-Luc?"

"That's all right. It won't be forever."

The other man quirked a smile, brushing aside a lock of dark brown hair. "I guess not. It'll only *seem* like forever."

It was so good to see Jack sitting there. So *very* good.

"You're out of your mind," someone rasped.

He turned and saw Phigus Simenon, his Gnalish head of engineering. As usual, Simenon was arguing some point of science or philosophy with Carter Greyhorse, the *Stargazer*'s towering chief medical officer.

"If it's by definition the smallest thing possible," the Gnalish went on, "how can there be anything smaller?" His ruby eyes were alive with cunning in his gray, serpentine visage.

"Easy," Greyhorse answered, the impassivity of his broad features belying the annoyance in his deep, cultured voice. "You take it and cut it in half." Easing his massive body back into his seat, he raised his arms. *"Voilà,* you've got something even smaller."

"Can't be," Simenon argued. "By definition, remember, it's the *smallest—*"

The Gnalish was interrupted by Cadwallader, their slender, girlish communications officer. She placed her freckled hands on the combatants' shoulders. "Could you keep it down a bit, fellas? Some of us are trying to sleep back here, y'know. Thanks *ever* so much."

Chuckling, the captain returned his attention to Jack. "What will you do when you get back? Take a leave for a while?"

His friend nodded. "I want to see Beverly. And my son. He's probably grown six inches since I last saw him." A pause. "Ever think about having a family, Captain?"

2

"You know me, Jack. I'd rather be boiled in oil than dangle a baby on my knee. Scares the—"

Suddenly, he remembered something. It chilled him, despite the closeness of the quarters. "Jack . . . you're not supposed to be here."

"No? You mean I should've taken one of the *other* shuttles?"

"No." He licked his lips. "I mean you're dead. You died some time ago—*long* before we lost the *Stargazer.*"

Jack shrugged. "I can go if you like—"

"No. Don't. I mean—"

But it was too late. His friend was moving away from him, losing himself in the crowd aft of the food processor.

"Don't go, Jack, it's all right. I didn't mean to send you away—"

That's when Jean-Luc Picard woke up.

The air in his cabin was cold on his skin. He wiped his brow and felt the perspiration there.

"Damn," he breathed. Just a dream.

Nothing like his tortured dreams of Maxia Zeta, inflicted a few years back by the Ferengi DaiMon Bok. No, this had been different, but in its own way just as frightening.

Nor did it take a ship's counselor to figure out why he'd happened to have the dream *now.*

Beverly Crusher was halfway across sickbay when she realized she had no idea where she was going.

Out of the corner of her eye, she saw Doctor Selar, her Vulcan colleague, watching her from her office. Crusher could feel an embarrassed blush climbing up her neck and into her face.

Think, Beverly, think. You were late for—

Suddenly, she snapped her fingers and started walking again. On the way, she glanced at Selar.

The Vulcan was still watching her. Crusher smiled.

Being Vulcan, Selar didn't smile back. She just returned her attention to her desk monitor.

Breezing into the examination area, Crusher saw that Burke was already waiting for her. She nodded by way of a greeting.

"How's it going?" he asked her.

"Not bad," she told him. "Care to lie down for a minute?"

Sitting down on the biobed, the security officer swung his legs up and leaned back until he was directly under the overhead sensor bank. As Crusher consulted the readings that were displayed at eye level, she found herself remembering again . . .

"Doctor Crusher?"

Snapping out of her reverie, she looked at Burke. "Mm?"

"I don't want to rush you, but I'm due to start a shift in ten minutes."

How long had she been staring at the bio-readings? She didn't dare ask.

The security officer smiled. "Listen, it's all right. I don't blame you for being a little distracted. Hell, even *I'm* excited about all those *Stargazer* people coming on board—and I don't even know any of them."

Crusher took a breath. "Actually, I don't know them either. Except one, of course. You can get up now— you're as fit as they come."

As Burke swiveled into a sitting position, he looked at her. "You don't know them? But I thought—"

He stopped himself short, realizing that he might be

4

intruding, but the doctor supplied the rest: *I thought your husband served with them.*

"I heard about them," Crusher explained coolly. "But I never met them face to face."

Burke nodded. "Right. Well, thanks. See you in a few months."

"In a few months," she echoed, as he walked off toward the receiving area.

Leaning against the overhead sensor bank, she buried her face in the crook of her arm. *Damn,* she thought. Why did they have to pick *this* ship?

Will Riker sat down at his personal terminal, took a deep breath, and called up the ship's "visitor" file.

He had been looking forward to this for days. And not because one of his duties as first officer was to keep track of all personnel boarding and disembarking from the ship. The *Enterprise* was about to play host to Starfleet legends—*living* legends—and Riker wanted to know everything there was to know about them. The thousand and one other matters that had been cropping up and demanding his attention lately would just have to wait awhile.

Now, let's see, he told himself, scanning the list of names on the brief menu. The one he wanted to see first was at the bottom—of course. He called up the relevant subfile.

Name: Morgen. Affiliation: Starfleet. Rank: Captain. Homeworld: Daa'V.

The full details of Morgen's career in Starfleet since his graduation from the Academy twenty-one years before came up on-screen.

The record bore out what Riker had heard over the years about Captain Morgen of the *Excalibur.* That he was an even-handed leader. That he brought out the best in his people. That he was militarily brilliant, diplomatically adept, and personally charming.

Not unlike his mentor, Jean-Luc Picard.

Now Morgen was leaving the service that had benefited so much from his presence to discharge another set of responsibilities—as hereditary leader of the Daa'Vit. He was returning to the planet of his birth to assume the throne in the wake of his father's death.

And bringing with him an honor guard—seven Starfleet officers with whom he'd served on the deep-space exploration vessel *Stargazer*. It was a Daa'Vit custom for a returning prince to be surrounded by his closest companions. And despite the friendships Morgen had made on the *Excalibur,* he had selected his fellow officers on the *Stargazer* to stand by him at the coronation ceremony.

It was quite a tribute to those individuals. And to the esprit de corps that had characterized Picard's old ship.

Chief among the honor guardsmen was Picard himself, Morgen's first captain. The others comprised the remainder of the visitors' roster.

He returned to the menu. Some of the names were as familiar to Riker as Morgen's—Ben Zoma, for instance, the captain of the *Lexington,* and First Officer Asmund of the *Charleston.*

The others were somewhat less well known to him, but their names still seemed almost magical. Professor Phigus Simenon. Dr. Carter Greyhorse. Peter "Pug" Joseph. All of them had been part of the *Stargazer's* historical mission—and, just as important, all had lived to tell the tale.

Riker leaned back in his chair and, not for the first time, wondered what it had been like to serve under the captain in those days—on a vessel like the *Stargazer,* whose mission carried her into uncharted space for years at a time. And beyond that, what it had meant to *lose* that ship, in the Federation's first fateful brush with the Ferengi.

With all of Picard's surviving officers scheduled to board the *Enterprise* over the next couple of days, the first officer would never have a better chance to find out.

Going to the top of the list this time, he called up another subfile.

Asmund, Idun . . .

Captain Mansfield of the U.S.S. *Charleston* sat on the edge of the *s'naiah*-wood desk. It was as uncomfortable as it looked, what with all the savage iconography carved into it. He frowned.

"Idun," he said, "if you'd like to talk about it . . ."

His first officer, who had been staring out the viewport, turned to face him. She was a handsome woman—he couldn't help but notice that. Tall and slim and blond, with eyes the elusive color of glacial ice. Deep, dark . . .

Enough of that, he told himself. *She's your exec, for godsakes. And even if she wasn't, what would she see in an old warhorse like you?*

For the four hundredth time, he put his libido aside. After all, there was something troubling her. If Asmund needed anyone, it wasn't a lover. It was a friend.

"I am all right," she told him evenly. But her eyes said that she was lying.

He sighed.

For six of the eleven years he'd been captain of this ship, Idun Asmund had been his second-in-command, and a damned good one at that. She'd never given him any reason to regret his having taken her aboard.

But he knew of the doubts people had had about her. After that terrible incident on the *Stargazer* . . . what was it? Two decades ago now? For a time, it had haunted her. Kept her from advancing through the ranks as quickly as she should have.

And her manner didn't help any. *Brusque. Icy,* even, some had said. But underneath, Mansfield had sensed a good officer. He'd taken a chance on her—and was glad of it ever since.

"I know you," he said. "You're nervous. And I think we both know why."

"No." She folded her arms across her chest. "I am surprised."

"That Morgen would want you to be with him at a time like this?"

"Yes. After what happened . . . I don't think he said two words to me. Then came Maxia Zeta and . . . well, frankly, I thought I'd never see him again."

"Maybe this is his way of making amends for all that. You and your sister were different people—vastly different, as it turns out. Can it be he's finally figured that out?"

Idun's eyes blazed momentarily. "He is Daa'Vit. When it comes to blood feuds . . ."

"He might not be the same person you knew back then," suggested Mansfield. He looked at her. "People can change a lot in thirteen years. Especially when they've spent half of them in a command chair." He cleared his throat. "Take me, for instance. I wasn't always an iron-willed dictator, you know."

Idun scowled. "He is Daa'Vit. That will not have changed."

"At least try and go in with an open mind," he

pleaded. "Remember—you'll be seeing other familiar faces as well. Surely they didn't all treat you as Morgen did."

Idun thought about it. "No," she conceded. "Suppose there are *some* I would like to see again."

"There you go. That's the Idun Asmund that I know." He grunted. "And don't worry about us. We'll just go off and risk our lives somewhere while you take your grand paid vacation."

Her brows knit. "Captain, I can still decline this. Here *is* where my priorities lie."

"It was a *joke,* Idun. Just a joke."

She relaxed again. "Of course it was," she noted.

He chided himself for joking about duty with her. When one had been raised by Klingons, one didn't take such things lightly.

Pug Joseph was just where Erwin expected to find him—sitting by himself in the corner of the lounge. *He does too much of that lately,* the *Lexington's* first officer told himself. *No wonder he's getting into trouble.*

As Erwin approached, Joseph turned around. His expression said that he wanted to be left alone. Then he saw who it was, and his features softened.

"Commander. To what do I owe this visit?" he asked, grinning.

The first officer turned his resolve up a notch. There was something about Joseph that made it very difficult to be stern with him. Maybe it was the man's resemblance to Erwin's brother's boy, who had died in a skirmish with the Tholians. After all, Joseph had the same close-cropped sandy hair, the same upturned nose. Or was it that no-nonsense attitude, a throwback to the first rough days of interstellar flight, that made him so endearing? The quality that, years earlier in his stint on the *Stargazer,* had earned Joseph the nickname "Pug"?

No matter. Erwin had promised himself he wasn't going to leave it alone this time. He wouldn't be doing anybody any good by ignoring the problem.

The first officer pulled up a seat and leaned close to Joseph. "I'll *tell* you what you owe this visit to. I just got a subspace message from my pal Marcus—on the *Fearless?"*

Joseph's grin started to fade. "Oh," he said.

"You know what Marcus told me," Erwin went on. "Don't you?"

The other man nodded. "Something about a little disagreement, I bet. One in which his man got the worst of it." The grin started to reassert itself. "You should've seen my right hook, Commander. I haven't lost a thing."

With an effort, Erwin frowned. "Fighting," he said, "at *your* age—and you a security chief, no less!" He shook his head disapprovingly. "It's a disgrace, Pug. It's got to stop."

Joseph looked at him. "You should've heard what he said about the *Lexington,* sir. About the captain. And about *you."*

Erwin stiffened. He came *that* close to asking what the man had said. But he restrained himself. "I don't care what anyone said about anyone else. We're supposed to be adults, responsible people—not children who start brawling at the drop of a hat."

The security chief sighed and looked away. "I hear you, Commander."

"That's not good enough," Erwin told him. "Look, you're an officer of this vessel. I want you to *act* like one." He leaned back and pulled down on the bottom of his tunic. "Is that clear?"

The security chief saw that Erwin wasn't kidding. "It's clear," he said.

"Good. And you needn't worry—the captain won't get wind of this. Just as he hasn't gotten wind of the other reports I've received." The first officer paused. "But it's the last time I cover up for you, understand? The last time."

Joseph seemed contrite. Reaching over the table that separated them, Erwin clapped him on the shoulder. Then he got up and made his way to the door.

It wasn't easy to keep from looking back, but he managed. As the lounge doors opened and he emerged into the corridor beyond, he breathed a sigh of relief.

He'd been pretty harsh—maybe harsher than necessary. But this time, Erwin was worried. Marcus had made it sound like more than a brief exchange of haymakers. Considerably more.

Of course, the message in the subspace packet couldn't actually come out and say anything; otherwise, it might have come to the attention of someone inclined to handle it more *officially*—someone like Captain Ben Zoma. But if Erwin read correctly between the lines, Joseph's opponent had taken a *vicious* beating. It was a miracle the man hadn't pressed charges.

The first officer shook his head. "Vicious" wasn't one of the words he'd ever associated with Pug Joseph. If things had gotten that far out of hand, his little reprimand had been long overdue.

He could only hope it would have the desired effect.

"I have the *Excalibur* on long-range sensor scan," reported Worf.

The captain couldn't help but notice the note of anticipation in the Klingon's voice. "Excellent, Lieutenant. Give them our position."

"Aye, sir."

Picard took in the bridge with a glance. Data was intent on his Ops console; likewise, Wesley at Conn. Everyone, it seemed, was going about his business with clockwork efficiency.

If they showed any emotion at all, it was excitement; they were upbeat about the imminent arrival of their captain's old comrades.

There was no trace of the trepidation Picard himself was feeling.

Fortunately, he had gotten quite good over the years at keeping his feelings under wraps. On the outside, he was his normal self—composed, focused, in charge. It was only on the inside that anything was amiss.

The dream of Jack Crusher still haunted him. *Still,* after all this time.

He remembered the lesson they taught at the Academy—the one that was supposed to put the loss of crewmen in perspective. It sounded as hollow now as it had then. *A starship captain makes a hundred decisions a day, and a goodly number of them involve the well-being of part or all of his crew. . . .*

For a while immediately afterward, Jack's death had cost him his confidence—caused him to second-guess himself. And for even longer, it had left a gaping pain of loss.

Because the victim of his decision wasn't just another crewman. He was a *friend.* And at that stage in his career, Picard had never before lost a friend.

Certainly, he had lost others since. Vigo and the others

at Maxia Zeta. And Tasha—dear, fierce Tasha. But the first, as the expression went, was the worst.

Perhaps he should have expected this. With his *Stargazer* officers converging on the *Enterprise,* was it any wonder that Jack was on his mind? Or that his memories would manifest themselves in dreams?

And that was all right—as long as it didn't affect him the way it had once. As long as it didn't in any way jeopardize the safety of those for whom he was *now* responsible.

He resolved that it would *not.*

"Captain?"

He turned and looked up at Worf. "Lieutenant?"

"I have a response from the *Excalibur.* It seems that Captain Morgen would prefer to beam over without any preliminaries."

Picard smiled tautly, nodded to himself. "That sounds like Captain Morgen," he said. "Inform him that I will attend his arrival."

Worf took a moment to send the return message. "Done, sir," he said finally.

"Thank you, Mr. Worf."

Rising, the captain made for the turbolift.

CHAPTER 2

"**A**dmiral?"

"Yes?"

"The *Charleston* has arrived, sir. Commander Asmund is beaming down now."

"Thank you, Mr. Marcos. Please see to her wants. I'll be by to meet her shortly."

Vice-Admiral Yuri Kuznetsov cursed softly under his breath as he pulled up his swim trunks. *Yet another of these* Stargazer *survivors,* he mused. And if she was anything like the first two, it was nothing to look forward to.

Look on the bright side, he instructed himself. *It's only for another couple of days. Then the* Enterprise *comes and takes them all away, and you never have to put up with them again.*

Truth be told, Dr. Greyhorse wasn't so bad. A little too serious for Kuznetsov's taste, a little too intellectual. Carrying on a conversation with him was like talking to a machine. But from what he understood, these were personality defects that ran rampant at Starfleet Medi-

15

cal. And if they were disingenuous, they were also tolerable.

It was the Gnalish, Simenon, that really jump-started Kuznetsov's reactors. Not only was he opinionated, self-centered, and domineering . . . he also brought out the worst in Dr. Greyhorse. Since their arrivals, which were almost simultaneous, the two had done nothing but butt heads on every subject in creation. No doubt, at some level they *enjoyed* their bickering. But listening to it was driving Kuznetsov up a wall—and then some.

He grabbed a towel, closed his locker, and padded barefoot across the synthetic tile floor. He could almost feel the temperature-controlled water leeching away his frustration.

It was his responsibility to entertain Greyhorse and the Gnalish—Starfleet Command had made that plain enough. They didn't want *anything* to go wrong with Captain Morgen's return to Daa'V. With the Romulans an active threat again, the Daa'Vit Confederacy was too valuable an ally to take chances with—and if the *Stargazer* people were important to Morgen, that made them important to the brass back on Earth.

But it was 0600 hours—long before he was scheduled to go on duty. For a little while, anyway, he could relax.

As Kuznetsov approached the locker room exit, he had a premonition. A nagging *something* at the back of his consciousness.

In fifteen years of active service, he had learned never to ignore his feelings. So it was with some trepidation that he stepped forward, triggering the entry mechanism.

The doors slid apart silently. The pool sprawled before him, its blue depths lit from below.

And among the shifting light shadows floated Phigus Simenon, former chief engineer of the *Stargazer*. Noticing Kuznetsov's entrance, the Gnalish looked up, his slitted ruby eyes evincing amusement.

"Ah," he said. "Admiral. So good to see you." He raised his tail out of the water languidly, then let it submerge again. His scaly gray body gleamed in the bluish light. "Care to join me?"

My God, thought Kuznetsov. *Is there no escape?*

Morgen had served aboard the *Stargazer* for only nine years, but it seemed like much more. His presence was such that when Picard recalled his decades-long foray into deep space, he could swear that the Daa'Vit had been at his side from the first to the last.

Apparently, Morgen felt much the same way, or he would not have honored his *Stargazer* crewmates by asking them to be his honor guards.

But as the transporter platform became host to the Daa'Vit's reassembling molecules, Picard wondered how much Morgen had changed in other respects. After all, the last time he'd seen him, the Daa'Vit was still a junior-grade lieutenant. Now he was a captain—a peer. And more than that—Morgen was only days away from ruling one of the Federation's most powerful allies.

Then again, this prodigious fate had always been in the cards for the Daa'Vit. And he had never tried to gain special treatment because of it. Nor had he let it temper his sense of humor—a caustic wit that was apparently typical of his race.

Ensconced in a shaft of blue light, Morgen began to take on shape and substance. Picard recognized the features—long and angular, with jutting cheekbones

17

and wide, deepset eyes. Fearsome-looking by human standards. And his protruding collar and hip bones only reinforced that impression.

Transporter Chief O'Brien made a final adjustment to his controls and completed the process. Morgen's eyes, a fiery yellow that contrasted with the green tint of his skin, came alive at the sight of Picard.

"Captain," he said.

"Ens—er, *Captain* Morgen." Picard frowned. "Forgive me. Old habits die hard."

"No need for apologies," said the Daa'Vit. As always, his tone was subdued, almost conspiratorial. "Not between you and me."

And in that moment, Picard realized that *nothing* had changed about Morgen—nothing significant, anyway. It was like old times again. True, this was not his ensign standing before him—but neither was it the head of a powerful empire. It was simply *Morgen.*

Stepping down off the platform, he extended his hand. Picard grasped it.

"This *is* how you humans greet one another—isn't it?"

"Yes," Picard smiled. "I am glad to see your years in Starfleet have produced *some* cultural improvements."

The Daa'Vit smiled back, obviously delighted. "Pitifully few, I'm afraid."

Picard chuckled. He was tempted to clap his former officer on the shoulder. "It *is* good to see you, Morgen."

The Daa'Vit looked around. "And where is the full-dress review appropriate for a guest of my stature?"

"Indeed," said Picard, "I have assembled my officers —though not here, and not in full dress. Rather, they await you in our Ten-Forward lounge—an environment

18

I thought better suited to your . . . er, grave and formal demeanor."

Morgen looked at him askance. If he didn't know the Daa'Vit so well, he might have been alarmed by the intensity of the scrutiny. "Do I detect a note of sarcasm, Captain?"

Picard shrugged. "In all our years on the *Stargazer,* did you ever *once* know me to be sarcastic?"

"Come to think of it, no. But then, I wasn't wearing all those pips on my collar then—and you *were."*

Picard grunted. "Strange. I don't believe I can remember that far back." He straightened his tunic and gestured in the direction of the exit. "Come. Let's see if we cannot refresh my memory in Ten-Forward. There are some people there who are eager to meet you."

Morgen inclined his head. "Agreed."

So much for melancholy, the captain told himself as they exited the transporter room with a nod to O'Brien. Seeing the Daa'Vit seemed to have cured him of it for the time being.

He was even starting to look *forward* to the remainder of this mission.

"Damn," said Geordi. "Seems like just a few years ago I was sitting in command class, listening to stories about the *Stargazer* and its valiant crew of deep-space explorers—and before you know it, they're going to be walking around in these very corridors, just like regular people. Hell, one of them's here already."

Walking beside him in the long, curving corridor, Worf scowled. "It is a problem," he rumbled.

Geordi looked at him. "A *problem?"* he echoed. "How so?"

His companion cleared his throat. "The dignitary we have taken aboard—Morgen. He is . . . Daa'Vit."

The Klingon appeared to think that that was explanation enough. But Geordi still didn't get it. He said so.

Worf's scowl deepened. He turned to the chief engineer without breaking stride.

"The Daa'Vit," the Klingon explained, "were the enemies of my people for more than three hundred years. We have licked each other's blood from our fingers."

Licked each other's . . . ? Geordi hoped that that was just a *figurative* description.

"Shortly after the Federation allied itself with the Empire, it entered into a similar arrangement with the Daa'Vit Confederacy. . . ."

The Klingon stopped himself as a couple of female ensigns approached from the opposite direction. The women nodded as they went by, and Geordi nodded back.

Not until the ensigns were well out of earshot did Worf continue—and then only in subdued tones. "The Empire had been wed to the Confederacy without its consent. Tempers ran high among my people."

Geordi could only imagine what *that* was like.

"In the end, however, the Romulan threat induced the Empire to keep its ally. And to tolerate its *ally's* ally." Worf grunted. "Since that time, no Klingon has attacked a Daa'Vit or vice versa. But then"—he paused significantly—"no Klingon has stood face-to-face with a Daa'Vit in that time."

Geordi was starting to see. "You're concerned that when you see our guest, your instincts will take over."

The Klingon looked at him. *"My* instincts?" He made a derogatory sound. "I am talking about *his* instincts."

Geordi smiled. "But Morgen was the captain of a Federation vessel for six years. Surely, he had dealings with the Klingons at *some* point."

"Possibly," conceded Worf. "But not *face-to-face.*" He paused again. "You must understand—the Daa'Vit are a *barbaric* race."

The chief engineer found the choice of words interesting. If the Daa'Vit were barbaric by *Klingon* standards . . .

"There is no telling how he may react."

Geordi nodded. "And you can't exactly stay away from him. Not when it's your job to provide security for him."

"Precisely."

Geordi thought for a moment, his excitement about meeting the *Stargazer* crew pushed aside for a moment. "You know," he said finally, "maybe you *do* have a problem."

Riker looked around Ten-Forward and smiled. There was a feeling of history in the air.

Though their group was a small one, seated at a single unobtrusive table near one of the observation ports, it had drawn the attention of everyone in the room.

The reunion between Morgen and Captain Picard had not failed to live up to Riker's expectations. The Daa'vit was every bit as charming as he had heard, and a hell of a raconteur to boot. The first officer—and everyone in the lounge, it seemed—couldn't help but be enthralled by him.

"Believe me," said Morgen, considering the glass of synthehol on the table before him, "I am far from eager to leave Starfleet. I have grown to love the starspanning life." He raised his eyes, glancing at Riker, Picard, and

21

finally Troi before continuing. "But my father's passing has left a gap in the government that must be filled. As crown prince, it falls to me to fill it—and within the allotted time, as you are no doubt aware, or the throne will pass to someone else."

"Manelin was a good man," observed the captain. "I was sorry to hear of his death."

The Daa'Vit shrugged. "He was old. He was in pain. Better that he died when he did, with a few shreds of dignity left to him, than to drag it out any further."

It was a sobering thought. Riker saw Troi's brow crease slightly, no doubt in empathy with Morgen's discomfort.

"Of course," the Daa'Vit went on, "I don't wish to make it seem that I am complaining. If one must abandon a captaincy in Starfleet, ruling a confederacy of planets is not a bad alternative."

They all smiled. But Riker knew that Morgen's remark wasn't from the heart. He himself wouldn't have traded places with any monarch in the galaxy—and he was only a first officer.

"My only regret," said Morgen, "is that I could not approach Daa'V on the vessel I commanded. Now, *that* would have been *something.*"

The captain grunted. "Yes—something *dangerous.* I haven't forgotten your descriptions of Daa'Vit politics, my friend. Starfleet knew what it was doing when it offered you the *Enterprise* for your return."

Morgen smiled a thin smile. "Perhaps *some* Daa'Vit take their politics too seriously. I will concede that much. But the necessity of bringing a Galaxy-class vessel into play . . ."

"The Federation," said Riker, "values you too much to take any risks, sir."

The Daa'Vit eyed him. "Values me as *what?* A skilled officer in which it has a massive investment? Or the ruler of a confederacy whose friendship is strategically important?"

"Perhaps both," the first officer suggested.

"And does it really matter?" the captain asked, cutting into the subtly rising tension.

Morgen leaned back in his chair, his angular features softening again. "You're right. It *doesn't* matter. No doubt, I should be flattered that the flagship of the fleet has been deployed for my homecoming." He considered his glass from a fresh perspective. "And if nothing else," the Daa'Vit went on, "this gives me a chance to see old friends." He gazed meaningfully at Picard. "It will be a reunion of sorts, won't it? Who knows—maybe the last chance we'll all have to be together again."

The captain shrugged. "One never knows—though I would not be surprised." He met Morgen's gaze. "All the more reason to enjoy each other's company while we can."

The Daa'Vit nodded, turning to Riker. "A wise man, your captain."

Riker chuckled. "We like to think so."

Wesley Crusher made the necessary adjustments on his control panel, and the Constitution-class vessel *Lexington* jumped up two levels of magnification on the forward viewscreen. A moment later, the ship's image was supplanted by that of its commanding officer, a dark, lanky man with graying temples.

"This is Captain Gilaad Ben Zoma." He smiled. "You must be Commander Data. I have heard a lot about you—and not just from your captain."

Wesley turned in his seat to look back at the command

center, where Data was seated in the captain's chair. The android seemed pleased by the recognition.

"I *am* Commander Data," he said. "It is my pleasure to invite you aboard the *Enterprise.*"

Wesley studied Ben Zoma carefully. Up until now, he had met only one person who'd served with his father aboard the *Stargazer*—Captain Picard. And the captain wasn't always the easiest person to strike up a conversation with.

But for the next few days, there would be *seven* other people who had worked alongside Jack Crusher—and Captain Ben Zoma, the man on the screen, was one of them.

Not that it was likely he'd have much of a chance to speak with any of the visitors. No doubt, they'd all want to reminisce about old times. Besides, these were important people. They probably wouldn't have much time for him . . .

"I accept your invitation," replied Ben Zoma. "There will be three of us altogether." The man had an infectious charm about him, an affability. "Oh, and Commander . . . If you will humor me, I would like to *surprise* Captain Picard. So it will not be necessary for you to alert him as to our arrival."

That caught the android off balance. "This is most irregular," he said.

"Granted," said the captain of the *Lexington.* "But I would appreciate it nonetheless." He paused. "Would you feel better if I couched my request in the form of an order? You can hardly disobey the instructions of a superior officer—providing you have no standing orders to the contrary."

Data took a moment to mull it over. "I have no *orders* as such, Captain. However—"

"Then it's settled."

The android was still perturbed—but he no longer had any choice in the matter. Ben Zoma had seen to that. "As you wish, Captain" was all he could get out.

Interesting guy, Wesley mused. A different style from Captain Picard's, for sure.

Wesley assumed the conversation was over, and was turning his attention back to his Conn board, when he noticed Ben Zoma looking at *him.*

He returned the man's gaze—an eerie feeling, considering people on the viewscreen usually ignored anyone outside the command center. He'd almost forgotten he was even visible in some of these transmissions.

"And you," said Ben Zoma, "must be Wesley Crusher."

The ensign felt the heat of embarrassment climbing into his cheeks. He cursed inwardly.

"Aye, sir."

The captain of the *Lexington* nodded. "Without question, your father's son." The skin around his dark eyes crinkled. "I look forward to meeting you as well."

Wesley straightened eagerly. His heart was pounding in his chest, and all he could think of was to repeat his earlier response: "Aye, sir."

Then Ben Zoma's image blinked out, and once again the ensign found himself staring at the lines of the *Lexington.*

Riker happened to be facing the door, so he was the first to mark the trio of unfamiliar faces as they entered the lounge. He was on the verge of saying something about them when he observed the gesture of the dark-skinned man in the lead—a finger planted vertically across his lips.

Seeing the captain's pips on the man's collar, Riker kept his mouth shut. Nor did any of his companions take note as the newcomers wound their way among the intervening tables.

It wasn't long before the dark man was directly behind Picard and Morgen, a mischievous gleam in his eye. He paused there, savoring the moment. Finally, he spoke. "Damn. I'd heard the two of you had aged, but the stories didn't say just how much."

As recognition set in, Picard declined to turn around immediately. He looked at Morgen. "Just remember," he said, "it was *you* who invited him."

The Daa'Vit nodded. "In a moment of insanity," he said, straightfaced. "One that I am already beginning to regret."

"Liar," said Ben Zoma as they got up to face him. "You've missed me like crazy—both of you have."

He took their hands—first Picard's, then Morgen's. Riker found himself smiling.

"You haven't changed," observed Captain Picard. "Still the same old Gilaad Ben Zoma."

"I can attest to *that,"* said one of the other newcomers, stepping up alongside the dark man. A lieutenant commander, Riker noted, though she didn't look old enough to have come that far. Her freckles and tousled strawberry-blond hair gave her a girlish sort of appeal— but not the air of authority one generally associated with high rank. "That is, I *could* attest to it," she amended with a hint of an Australian accent, "if not for the fact that Captain Ben Zoma is my commanding officer."

"Cadwallader," said Picard. He took her hand. "Still keeping this madman in line, I trust?"

She nodded. "It's a tough job, but someone's got to do it."

26

"Don't make it sound like you do it alone," said the third arrival. A stocky, almost squarish man, he evidenced a slight limp as he came closer. "Security is something of an adventure on the *Lexington*—to say the least."

Riker tried to imagine the *Enterprise* officers talking about their captain that way. And to his face! But then, he knew from experience that not all ships were run the same way—and when formality was suspended to a degree, it didn't necessarily mean that the crew was any less efficient. It was just a matter of each captain's individual style and preference.

Apparently, however, Ben Zoma wasn't *quite* as liberal as first appearances indicated—because he stifled his companions with a glance. Then, turning back to his fellow captains, he said: "Don't listen to Commander Cadwallader—*or* Mr. Joseph. They've never had it so good in their lives."

Joseph—the stocky man—looked sceptical. The woman just smiled. And not a bad smile at that, Riker mused.

"I am glad you could come," Morgen said. *"All* of you."

"You couldn't have kept us away with phaser cannons," said Joseph.

"Please," said Picard, "pull up a chair, won't you? And I will try to forget that you bullied your way aboard behind my back."

Once they were all seated, Picard made the introductions. "Commander Riker here is my first officer. Troi is our ship's counselor."

"Something we could have used on the *Stargazer*," Ben Zoma pointed out. He smiled at Troi. "Of course, someone of *your* beauty would be welcome anywhere."

27

The Betazoid took the compliment in stride. She smiled back.

"Captain Ben Zoma," Picard continued, "besides being one of the galaxy's great flatterers, was my first exec. We served together for twenty years, if you can bring yourselves to believe that."

The dark man shook his head. "I can scarcely believe it myself."

Picard indicated the woman who had come in with Ben Zoma. "Tricia Cadwallader. The best damned communications officer a captain ever had—back in the days when there *were* such things as communications officers. Today she's the second officer of the *Lexington.*"

Riker nodded by way of a greeting. It caught her eye, and for a moment she lingered on his gaze. Then she turned to Troi.

"Pleased to meet you," she said.

"Likewise," the ship's counselor replied.

"And last—but certainly not least—" Picard resumed, "security chief Peter Joseph—though we all know him as Pug."

The reasoning behind the nickname was self-evident. Joseph resembled nothing so much as a bulldog.

"The genuine article," the security chief quipped. "Accept no substitutions."

There was laughter all around at that, and when it quieted, Riker took the opportunity to raise his glass. "I'd like to propose a toast. To Captain Morgen. May his reign be a long and fruitful one."

There were sounds of agreement—not only from their own table, but from a number of others around them.

"And," added Morgen, "to the former officers of the *Stargazer.* May they never forget how fortunate they were to have served under the legendary Jean-Luc Picard."

As the others drank, Picard grunted. *"Legendary?"* he repeated. "I'm not *old* enough to be *legendary."*

As Troi approached the bar, Guinan shook her head in motherly fashion.

"You're a trooper," she told the empath.

Troi smiled. "What do you mean?"

"What do I *mean?* Counselor, you've spent the last five *hours* listening to *Stargazer* stories. And now that the *Lexington* contingent has joined us, you'll probably be in for *another* five hours' worth." Guinan grunted. "In my book, that's being a trooper."

"Oh, come on," Troi said. "I *like* listening to those old stories. Apart from their entertainment value, they give me insights into the captain that I've never had before. I can understand a little better how he became the person he is." She glanced at the table she'd just come from, where Ben Zoma was recalling some incident involving a shuttle and a pair of Grezalian ambassadors. "You know, it's funny. I get the feeling that Commander Riker and myself are being shown off in a way—almost as if we were his children." Troi paused thoughtfully. "Which is not so difficult to comprehend, I suppose. Captain Picard never had any offspring of his own. Why *shouldn't* he think of us as his children?"

"Actually," Guinan responded, "I think he considers you *all* his children—not only you and Commander Riker, but Morgen and the *Stargazer* people as well. And he's pleased that all his children are enjoying an opportunity to get to know one another." She shrugged. "It just seems a little barbaric for you to have to force yourself to stay awake."

29

"I am *not* forcing myself to stay awake," the empath protested. Then, noting the way Guinan's mouth was curling up at the corners, she added: "Besides, I can't let the older kids have *all* the fun."

Guinan looked past Troi. "Uh-oh. Don't look now, but one of the older kids is hitting the sack."

The counselor turned and saw Joseph getting up from his chair. He said something under his breath, got a round of laughter for his trouble, and gave the group an old-fashioned salute. Then he made his way to the exit.

When Troi turned back, she looked thoughtful.

"What?" probed Guinan.

The empath raised her eyes. "Mr. Joseph—Pug, they call him. He's not quite as happy as the rest of them. Oh, he *seems* to be, on the outside. But inside, he's—" She paused, trying to translate perceived emotion into words —not always an easy task. "Bitter," she said finally.

"About what?" asked Guinan.

Troi shook her head. "I don't know. I'm not a telepath, remember? But I can guess."

Guinan leaned forward over the bar. "I'm listening," she said.

"When the *Stargazer* set out," said the Betazoid, "Joseph was the chief of security. Cadwallader was a junior-grade communications officer, Morgen was an ensign, and Ben Zoma was the first officer. Obviously, they've all moved up—Morgen and Ben Zoma to captaincies, and Cadwallader to lieutenant commander. But Pug is still security chief. No change in rank or function."

Guinan nodded. "No wonder he's bitter."

"And particularly so toward Cadwallader. From what I gather, he took her under his wing when she joined the *Stargazer*. Treated her like a kid sister."

"And then she grew up and left him in the dust." She flicked her finger at a tiny piece of napkin left on her bar. "But then, that must be fairly common in Starfleet. Not everybody is moving-up material."

"No," said the counselor. "But that doesn't make it any easier on the ones who are left behind."

"Mom?"

Beverly Crusher jumped at the sound. She looked up from her desk, saw that it was only Wesley. Her heart pounding, she tried not to show how badly he'd startled her.

"Mom, are you feeling all right?" asked Wesley, entering her office. Unlike her, he was still in uniform.

She smiled. "Of course I'm all right. Why shouldn't I be?"

He shrugged. "I heard that Captain Picard had assembled some of his officers in Ten-Forward. You know—to meet the *Stargazer* people. And I knew you weren't on duty, so . . . if you're feeling okay, why aren't you there? In Ten-Forward, I mean, with everybody else?"

Crusher sat back in her chair. "That's a good question, Wes."

The boy—she would *always* think of him that way, she couldn't help it—regarded her with a lack of understanding. "I don't get it," he told her. "Don't you *want* to see Dad's old friends?"

She shrugged. "Yes and no."

The lack of understanding deepened. "Why the *no* part?"

The doctor sighed. "This may sound strange, Wes, but I've come to terms with what I knew of your father. With the Jack Crusher I knew. And *loved*." Another sigh. "I don't know if I want any *new* memories. Not if they're going to make me start mourning him all over again."

Wesley started to say something, thought better of it. "Mom," he went on finally, "this isn't like you. You're not the kind of person who backs off from things."

"From most things, no." The doctor found she couldn't look at him, so she looked at her desktop monitor instead. She didn't blame him for being surprised at her. To tell the truth, she was surprised at herself. "From *this* thing . . . I don't know. It's hard to explain."

Silence. An uncomfortable silence—for him, no doubt, as well as for her. But she didn't break it.

In the end, it was Wesley who took the initiative. "I suppose," he said, "you've got the right to do what you want." There was a hint of pain in his voice; maybe someone else wouldn't have noticed it, but *she* did. "If it doesn't bother Captain Picard, maybe it shouldn't bother me either. But I intend to get to know these people— that is, if they let me."

Her heart went out to him. "Wes . . ."

"I don't *have* your memories, Mom. I've got to find out all I can about him. And if it makes me start missing him again, then I'm willing to pay that price."

It hurt to hear him say that. "You do what you have to, Wes. Just forgive me if I don't feel the same way, all right?"

The pique cooled a little inside him. Not all at once, but it cooled.

Just like Jack. *Slow to hurt, slow to heal.* Wasn't that one of his favorite expressions?

"Look," said Wesley, "I didn't mean to say all that. Maybe it's not my place."

"You can say anything you want to me, Wes. *Anything.*"

"But it doesn't mean you'll agree with me."

"It's not a matter of agreement. It's . . ." She shook her head ruefully, at a loss for words.

He came around the desk and took her hand. She looked up at him.

"Try to understand," she said.

"I will," he assured her.

Then he left, and she drew up her knees and hugged them as hard as she could.

CHAPTER 3

"Thank you for having us," Asmund told Vice-Admiral Kuznetsov.

He smiled at her. "The pleasure was all mine, Commander."

Walking up ahead of them in the corridor, Simenon and Greyhorse were at it again, having found some new subject to work over. Kuznetsov never thought he would be saying this—not even to himself—but he had grown fond of the engineer and the doctor in comparison to the way he felt about Idun Asmund.

Not that she was rude, like Simenon. Nor was she annoyingly intellectual, like Greyhorse. Far from it— her comments were simple, down to earth. And certainly, she was wonderful to look at.

But, strange to say, she *scared* him—and had from the first time he met her. Of course, in the beginning, he couldn't understand why.

Then he'd inadvertently walked in on her exercise session. Exercise *indeed*. It looked for all the world as if she were fighting for her life—and enjoying every second of it.

"Sorry to interrupt, Commander. I didn't know you were in here."

"That's quite all right, sir. I was almost finished anyway."

She brushed aside a lock of blond hair, wet with perspiration. Breathed through her teeth, like . . . like what? An animal?

"Er . . . those knives . . . they're very unusual."

The blades were razor-sharp, the handles savagely carved. Made of some wood he'd never seen before—and the workmanship was so intricate, it looked like the things were writhing in her hands.

"Yes—they are unusual. They're Klingon-made."

"Oh. I see."

Later on, he'd taken a closer look at her file, and discovered why she had such an affinity for things Klingon. As children, she and her twin sister had been the only survivors of a Federation colony disaster on the planet Alpha Zion. As luck would have it, the Klingons intercepted the colony's distress calls and reached it before Starfleet could—no doubt hoping that there would be Federation technology there worth raiding.

Apparently, there wasn't. Just a couple of towheaded five-year-olds, sunken-cheeked and huddled against the elements.

Normally, it would have been unthinkable for a Klingon to take pity on a human. But after what the Asmund twins had gone through, it was obvious that they were made of sterner stuff than most Homo sapiens. Their courage was something the Klingons could not ignore—nor could they leave them there in the ruins, counting on Starfleet to arrive before the girls died of starvation or exposure.

The captain of the Klingon vessel packed the humans

aboard his ship. He brought them back to his sister and her husband, who were childless, giving them the option of keeping them—or disposing of them as they saw fit.

They kept them—and raised them as Klingons. Apparently, the training took, if Asmund's exercise session was any indication.

Twice a survivor, Kuznetsov had mused upon finishing her file. First Alpha Zion, and then the *Stargazer.* Somehow, he wasn't surprised.

But something was still gnawing at him—still bothering him. What? For lack of any other options, he called up her *sister's* file—and realized where he had heard the name Asmund before.

How could he have forgotten? The incident had brought the Federation *this* close to losing the Daa'Vit as allies—maybe even starting a war.

Idun had never been linked with what her sister did. Her slate was clean.

But they were *twins.* Was it possible that she hadn't *known* about her sister's plan? Hadn't even suspected?

That question had kept Kuznetsov up late the last few nights. And given him another reason to be scared by her—though in some ways it was even less rational than the first.

Up ahead, Simenon and Greyhorse turned and entered the transporter room. A moment later he and Commander Asmund followed them in.

The transporter technician was waiting patiently for them. She smiled cordially at Kuznetsov; he smiled back.

He wondered if his relief was evident in his expression—though at this point, he hardly cared. The important thing was that he was getting rid of them—*all* of them.

* * *

Beverly Crusher had managed to keep to herself up until now, leaving little opportunity for her to run into the *Stargazer* people. But she was forced to abandon that policy when they reached Starbase 81.

After all, she had worked closely with Carter Greyhorse for most of the year she'd spent at Starfleet Medical. They'd become more than colleagues; they'd become friends. And he'd been sensitive enough not to bring up more than a passing reference to her late husband, once he realized she didn't want to talk about him.

So how could she snub him now by not attending his arrival? It would have been worse than bad manners. It would have been a breach of professional etiquette.

And if there was one thing of which she would *not* be found guilty, it was a lack of professionalism.

The doctor repeated that to herself as she stood beside Captain Picard and watched the last of their guests materialize. Under O'Brien's expert touch, the shafts of shimmering light coalesced into flesh and blood.

Greyhorse wasn't difficult to discern from the other two. His towering height, black eyes, and blunt Amerind features set him apart right away. And as if that weren't enough, the medical blue of his uniform stood out in stark contrast to the garb of his companions.

Crusher stepped forward. "Carter," she said, her smile coming naturally.

He clambered down from the platform and took her hand. She felt tiny beside him—she'd forgotten about that.

"Beverly. So good to see you." Greyhorse's voice was as dry as ever, but she knew him better than to be offended. Deep down, he was a warm, even affectionate person.

"Good to see you," she told him.

The captain was exchanging pleasantries with the others. After a moment or two, he turned to Crusher and touched her arm.

"Dr. Beverly Crusher, my chief medical officer . . . this is Commander Idun Asmund of the *Charleston.*"

The blond woman had a small Starfleet-issue pack slung over one shoulder—a little unusual; ship's stores could reproduce any personal effect a passenger desired. But then, some effects were more personal than others.

Asmund extended her hand and they shook. She had quite a grip.

"And *this,*" said Picard, indicating the third member of the party, "is Lieutenant Commander Phigus Simenon, once my chief engineer and currently an instructor at Starfleet Academy."

"And not dead *yet,*" said the Gnalish, "contrary to popular belief—and the fervent hopes of my students." He smiled, his bright-red serpentine eyes slitting even more than usual as he extended his hands palms downward. His stooped posture made it necessary for him to crane his neck to look up at her—a gesture that would have been awkward, not to mention painful, for a human. Of course, Simenon was decidedly not human.

Crusher returned the greeting as best she could, extending her hands in the same manner. The Gnalish seemed to approve.

"Not only beautiful," he told the captain, "but respectful as well."

"I've been to your world," explained the doctor, taking the compliment in stride. "It was part of my training in xenobiology."

"I gathered as much," said Simenon.

"No doubt," said Picard, "you'll want to join the

others. They're in our Ten-Forward lounge." He looked at Crusher. "In fact, one might say they're *commandeering* the lounge, and have done so for the last two days."

Greyhorse grunted. "Sounds about right," he remarked.

"To the lounge, then," said the Gnalish. "But only on one condition."

The captain became mock-serious. "And that is?"

"That afterward you take me to your engineering section. And leave me there with someone who knows a driver coil from a magnetic accelerator."

Picard nodded gravely. "I think we have *someone* like that. I'll see what I can do."

The Gnalish harumphed. "You mock me, Captain." He appealed to Crusher. "Imagine—ridiculing someone of *my* advanced years."

The doctor found herself smiling. Perhaps Wesley wasn't entirely wrong.

Both Simenon and Asmund had heard her last name, but neither had made the least mention of Jack. And Simenon seemed like the kind of person she'd like to know better.

She still wasn't about to invite them to her room for a party. Or, for that matter, join them in Ten-Forward. Not yet. But she made a promise to herself—and to Wes—that she'd be a little less of a hermit.

At Tactical, Worf noted the intercom activity a fraction of a second before they heard the voice on the bridge.

"Commander?"

It was O'Brien down in Transporter Room One.

Data sat up just a little bit straighter in the captain's chair. "Yes, Chief?"

O'Brien frowned. "Sorry to disturb you, sir. It's probably nothing, but . . . well, one of our guests—Commander Asmund—brought aboard some rather unusual cargo."

"Can you be more specific?" asked the android.

A pause. "Some kind of *knives,* sir. I can't tell you much more about them, except . . . I think they've got a sort of ceremonial look to them." Another pause. "I would've said something to the captain himself when he was here, but Commander Asmund *does* have top-security clearance, and I didn't want to embarrass anyone."

Worf grunted. Ceremonial knives? That *was* unusual.

Data rose and started to circumnavigate the command center. "Please make your scan available to the Tactical station," he told O'Brien.

"Aye, sir," came the response.

A fraction of a second later, the image appeared on one of Worf's monitors. And a fraction of a second after that, Data was standing beside him, looking it over.

The android's brow creased ever so slightly. He turned to the Klingon. "You are the weapons expert, Lieutenant. Have you ever seen specimens of this sort?"

Indeed he had.

Worf nodded. "Mr. O'Brien is right. They are ceremonial knives." He frowned as his eyes traced the familiar serration pattern. *"Klingon* ceremonial knives. My brother showed me a pair just like them when he was on the ship."

Data nodded. "I see. Then that explains it."

Worf looked at him. "It *does?"*

"Certainly. They must have been a gift from her parents."

41

The security chief's confusion only deepened. "I do not understand," he confessed.

Data stared at him. Then comprehension dawned. "Did you not know that Commander Asmund was raised in the Klingon Empire?"

He might as well have told Worf that they were headed for the heart of a supernova. It took the Klingon a moment to recover.

"No," he said finally. "I did *not.*"

But that would be rectified as soon as his shift on the bridge was over, and he had a chance to access the necessary information. Worf did not like mysteries— particularly when they hit so close to home.

Guinan was swabbing down her bar with a damp towel when Pug Joseph approached her, glass in hand. He smiled.

"We're keeping you busy, aren't we?"

It was an understatement. Now that the Gnalish and Dr. Greyhorse had arrived, the party was *really* in high gear—though the other newcomer, Commander Asmund, had declined to join them.

Guinan shrugged, returning the smile. "That's what I'm here for."

Joseph placed an elbow on the bar and leaned over in a conspiratorial sort of way. "Tell me," he said. "Do you have anything a mite stronger than this Ferengi bug-juice?"

She looked at him. "That's the first time I've ever heard synthehol referred to as Ferengi bug-juice. Very colorful." Her smile deepened. "In any case, the answer is no. I can offer you a beer, if you like. But the strongest drink we serve in Ten-Forward is synthehol. In fact, I'm a little surprised at the question. I thought synthehol was the strongest drink served in *all* ship's lounges."

"Well," said Joseph, "that's the way it's supposed to be—*officially,* that is. But, y'see, we bend the rules a little on the *Lexington.*" He indicated Ten-Forward with a tilt of his head. "Of course, we haven't got anything nearly this fancy on our ship. But we give a man freedom of choice—if you know what I mean."

Guinan nodded. "I know exactly what you mean, Mr. Joseph. But I'm afraid that doesn't change anything on *this* vessel. As long as I'm in charge of the Ten-Four lounge, there will be nothing harder than synthehol served here. Keeps the repair bills down." She paused. "But how about an ice cream soda? I can whip up one of those in a flash—and no one has to be any the wiser."

Joseph scowled. "You're breaking my heart, you know that?" He held up his glass. "Look. I can go back to my quarters and fill this with the finest Maratekkan brandy." He jerked a thumb over his shoulder. "But that would mean I'd have to drink it all alone—when some of my closest friends in the world are sitting right there." He gave her his best cherubic look. "Now, normally, I could see your point. Hell—you don't want everybody drinking the good stuff, or what would happen in an emergency? But under the circumstances—these *special* circumstances—I think even the head of Starfleet would look the other way and pour me something interesting."

Guinan sighed. "You're a tough man to reason with, Mr. Joseph."

"That's what they tell me," he said.

"And I must say, you've got a point there. You *could* simply go to your cabin and drink anything you wanted."

"It takes an astute person to put matters in their proper perspective," he encouraged.

"But it strikes me that you might want a *real* drink a little too *much.*"

His expression hardened a little. "Eh? What d'you mean?"

Guinan resumed her swabbing of the bar. "Just this— that if I had a problem, I wouldn't keep it to myself. Especially when there's someone willing to hear about it. Maybe even help me with it."

"Are you saying that I'm an alcoholic?" His eyes blazed. "There are no such people anymore—haven't been for some time, in case you hadn't heard."

"They're rare, all right," she agreed. "But they do pop up occasionally. Even aboard starships."

Joseph's features went taut—so taut they looked painful. For a moment, Guinan had the uncomfortable feeling he was going to reach across the bar and grab her by the front of her garment.

But it never happened. Gradually, the fury in his eyes cooled.

"Thank you anyway," he told her, putting his glass down on the bar. "I guess I'll just have to seek my comfort somewhere else."

She watched thoughtfully as he left Ten-Forward.

Riker, like everyone else at the table, was listening to Ben Zoma's yarn.

"And then," said Ben Zoma, turning to Troi, "your captain here had the gall to ask the Clobatians if he could *drop them off* somewhere."

Troi smiled. "Did he really?"

Picard shrugged. "It seemed like the only humane

thing to do. Without our help, they would have frozen to death."

Simenon snorted. "Naturally. You blew up their shuttlecraft."

"A last resort," countered Morgen. "As you well know, Phigus. If the Clobatians had returned to their mother ship before *we* returned to the *Stargazer* . . ."

"We never would have caught up with them," finished Cadwallader.

"Exactly right," said Greyhorse.

"And with the phasers they'd stolen," Riker added, "they would have held the key to our weapons technology."

Morgen nodded approvingly. "You have a better appreciation of the situation," he told the first officer, "than *some* of us who were *there.*"

Picard grunted. "At least *someone* understands the subtleties of command."

Riker chuckled. "Thank you—both of you. But I'm afraid I'm going to have to take my appreciation and understanding and pack them off to the bridge right now. I believe Mr. Data's shift ends in a few minutes."

As he stood, Cadwallader got up as well. "That reminds me," she said. "I'm supposed to meet Lieutenant Worf—for a tour of the communications system."

"Communications?" echoed Greyhorse. "You're a second officer now. A generalist."

Cadwallader winked at him. "You know what they say, Doctor. Once a communications officer, always a communications officer." She looked at Riker. "You *did* say you were headed for the bridge? That's where my tour is supposed to begin."

"Then," said the first officer, "it would be my pleasure to show you the way."

Cadwallader inclined her head. "How gallant of you."

"Nice ship you've got here," Cadwallader remarked as she and Riker stepped out into the corridor.

He nodded. "Thank you." He paused, trying to be diplomatic. "Although to be honest, our communications system isn't a great deal more advanced than the *Lexington*'s."

She smiled. "I know. I get a kick out of *any* system. I wasn't entirely kidding when I said I was still a communications officer at heart."

A couple of security officers passed by, going the other way. Riker acknowledged them with a nod.

"You know," he said, "for a moment there, I thought you were going to say 'kid.' As in 'a kid at heart.'"

Cadwallader laughed. "That too. In fact, I'm sure most of them think of me that way—as 'the kid.' I was pretty young when I beamed aboard the *Stargazer*."

He glanced at her. "I know. Nineteen, wasn't it?"

She grinned. "How did—oh. I guess you've been doing your homework."

Riker smiled back. "I guess I have. Let's see. Hometown: Sydney, Australia. Graduated from Starfleet Academy with honors. First assignment as ensign on the *Goddard*. After a year, you came to the *Stargazer*, where you served until the Maxia Zeta incident. Three years as lieutenant jay-gee on the *Victory*, and another three on the *Thomas Paine*—where you distinguished yourself by saving your captain's life on not one, but two occasions. When Captain Ben Zoma was given command of the *Lexington*, he offered you a promotion if you'd come aboard as his second officer."

She looked at him suspiciously. "You've got quite a memory, Commander."

"Will," he told her.

Cadwallader laughed. "All right. Will it is. But tell me—do you memorize all your visitors' bios the way you memorized mine?"

The turbolift was just ahead. As they approached, the doors opened to accommodate them. They stepped inside and the doors closed again.

"Main bridge," said Riker.

"You haven't answered my question," she told him.

He returned her gaze. "The truth?"

She thought about it for a moment. "No."

"In that case," he said, "yes, I *do* memorize them all that way."

She laughed. He found it infectious; a moment later he was laughing too.

"You're a very charming man," said Cadwallader.

"Some times more than others."

She eyed him. "Nonsense. I bet you were charming the day you were born." She looked at the cciling. "Let's see . . . in Valdez, Alaska, wasn't it? Graduated from the Academy with *high* honors. Served as ensign on the *Zhukov,* lieutenant jay-gee, and later full lieutenant on the *Potemkin.* Three years as second officer on the *Yorktown* and two more as first officer on the *Hood.* Most recent assignment, of course, the *Enterprise*—where you've become known as one of the top officers in the fleet. Credited with almost single-handedly stopping the Borg invasion."

Riker's smile broadened moment by moment. "I guess," he said when she was finished, "I'm not the only one around here with a good memo—"

Before he could complete his sentence, the turbolift

doors opened onto the bridge. Worf, Data, and half a dozen other officers were looking in their direction.

Riker cleared his throat. He considered Cadwallader, who obviously enjoyed having taken him by surprise.

"Carry on, Commander," he told her.

She nodded. "Aye, sir."

And as he made his way to the captain's chair, she headed for Tactical—where Worf's replacement had already arrived.

CHAPTER 4

Geordi knew he was a little early for his Engineers' Meeting, but that was all right. It would give him a chance to get his thoughts in order.

The meetings were informal, and purposely held as far away from engineering as possible. Their original inspiration had been the incident with Broc—with Barclay. (Even now he had to be careful not to refer to the man by that silly nickname.) Geordi had realized that he didn't know some of his people as well as he should—hence, a weekly off-duty coffee get-together, which would give everybody the chance to let off steam without worrying about offending a superior officer. At the Engineer's Meetings, there was no such thing as rank—everybody was on an equal footing.

As the lounge doors opened, Geordi noticed that there was someone already inside—a tall, rather alluring-looking woman he was sure he'd never seen before, wearing a cranberry-red command tunic. She stood with her back to him, gazing out the observation port at the streaking stars.

One of the captain's friends, Geordi concluded. Entering the lounge quietly so as not to disturb her, he couldn't help but stare a little—and not just because she was one of the *Stargazer* people. He'd seldom seen a woman so well put together.

What's more, she was all by herself. Seems sort of lonely, he thought.

Or maybe not. Maybe she *wanted* a little solitude.

If he'd known in advance that she was here, he would have changed the location of the meeting. Lord knows, he told himself, there are plenty of other lounges on the *Enterprise.*

Geordi frowned. The least he could do was warn her that the lounge was about to be invaded. Coming a little closer, he cleared his throat. No reaction. Maybe she hadn't heard.

Walking the rest of the way across the room, he tapped her gently on the shoulder.

Before he knew what was happening, he found himself draped backward over her knee—looking up at her savagely clawed fingers as they hovered mere inches from his face. As he found her eyes, he saw a deadly hostility in them—a gleam that under other circumstances he might have called *murderous.*

Quickly, the hostility died. *"Qos,"* the woman breathed, mortified. Her cheeks burned a bright red.

Qos?

Lowering her hand, she helped Geordi get back on his feet. "I'm sorry," she said. "I didn't hear you come in. And—" She shook her head. "Please forgive me."

"Sure," he told her, grinning—trying to salvage what was left of his machismo. "No problem. I shouldn't have surprised you like that." Smoothing out his tunic, he held his arms out. "See? Good as new."

She didn't grin back. "There's no excuse for this. It's just that I was trained, early on, to—"

"It's all right," he assured her. "Really." He held out his hand. "Geordi LaForge, chief engineer."

She grasped it—more firmly than he expected. Though after what had just happened, he probably shouldn't have been surprised.

"Idun Asmund," she responded. "First officer of the *Charleston*. One of your captain's guests."

"I gathered as much," he told her. "You don't normally see too many command uniforms around here."

"No, I don't suppose you do."

Just then, Duffy and DiBiasi walked in. When they saw Geordi's companion, they stopped dead in their tracks. Apparently, she was every bit as striking as his VISOR had led him to believe.

"That's what I wanted to tell you," Geordi explained. "This place is about to become lousy with engineers. We're having a meeting, sort of—though you're invited to sit in if you'd like." He glanced at Duffy and DiBiasi. "I'm sure no one would mind."

"Thank you," said Asmund, "but no. I was just about to be going anyway," she lied.

Geordi shrugged. "Suit yourself. See you around, then."

She nodded. "Yes. See you around."

As she crossed the room, neither of the newcomers could take their eyes off her. "My God," said DiBiasi once she was gone. "Who *was* that, Commander?"

"No ranks here," said the engineering chief, "remember? And as for who she is . . . she's one of the *Stargazer* officers. You know, the bunch serving as Captain Morgen's honor guard."

Duffy grunted. "Some guys have all the luck."

"Hey," DiBiasi chimed in, "I thought all the captain's friends were in Ten-Forward. What's she doing *here?*"

Geordi shook his head. "I guess that's *her* business," he said. Suddenly, he saw those clawed fingers again—hovering like a hunting bird, ready to tear him apart. Shuddering, he put the image from his mind. "Come on. Let's get some coffee."

Beverly tucked one leg underneath her and sat down on her bed. Opening the box of audio modules, she picked one out at random.

How long had it been since she'd listened to Jack's old tapes? A year? Two? Had she played them at all since she'd come aboard the *Enterprise?*

She looked at the module in her hand. Reading the stardate, she decided that the message was about sixteen years old—which meant she would have received it on . . . where? Delos Four? Yes—Delos Four. Unbidden, memories flooded her mind like gentle rains.

Rain. She chuckled. It hadn't rained more than a dozen times during her entire internship in the Mariadth Valley, though the Delosians said that it rained there all the time. Of course, when one was as long-lived as the Delosians were, and used to places where it didn't rain at all, a dozen times in four years may have seemed like "all the time."

Her mentor, Dalen Quaice, had called Delos Four "the hottest, driest place in the galaxy." She could see him bent over a zaphlid-calf, innoculating it for scale-fever and complaining about the heat. "It's unbearable, Beverly. Have you ever been to Vulcan? No? Well, it's pretty dry there too. But this place makes a Vulcan desert look like a rain forest."

And without Jack it had seemed even drier, even more barren.

Taking a deep breath, Beverly slipped the tape into the mechanism next to her bed and waited for Jack's voice to emerge from the speakers. When it did, she was surprised at how young he sounded.

"Hi, honey. Greetings from the *Stargazer,* where we're wrapping up with the Mandrossa—*still.* It turns out that their negotiation protocols are a lot more complicated than those of other races we've encountered; even establishing an agenda for further contact has kept us here for weeks. In the end, though, I think it'll be worth it. The Mandrossa are way ahead of us in genetics, and we can teach them a few things about immunology. The way it looks, both parties will benefit from the relationship.

"Unfortunately, speaking of relationships, this puts off my shore leave awhile longer. But be patient. I can't wait to see you and little Wes. By my calculations, he ought to be about up to my waist now. Just big enough to swing my old baseball bat—you know, the one I got when I was a kid. Do you think I can teach him to hit in five days? I'm certainly going to try.

"As for you, my love . . . I have a little excursion in mind. You see, Pug Joseph was on Delos Four a while back, and he's been regaling me lately with stories about this place he rented in the mountains. Not necessarily the kind of stories you'd tell your grandmother, but then, that's Pug. Anyway, I did some research, and it appears his love nest is still around. What's more, it's supposed to be beautiful there. Seems like as good a way to get reacquainted as any—and Wes won't miss us overnight. Especially if he ends up getting a baby brother—or sister—out of the deal.

"Not too much else to tell you. Cad had a birthday, Morgen was promoted to lieutenant jay-gee and—oh, Greyhorse says he'll be glad to answer any questions you have about being a doctor aboard a starship. His main advice is to avoid any vessel that has a Gnalish aboard— his words, not mine.

"I guess that's it. Give my love to Wes and I'll see you soon, I hope. I mean, how much longer can these negotiations go on? We already hold the Federation record. Miss you."

Crusher took a deep breath, let it out. Stopping the tape, she had the mechanism eject it and replaced it in the box.

Then she began putting herself in a more professional frame of mind. She was due in sickbay in a few minutes.

Stopping at the entrance to the holodeck, Worf turned to the group that was trailing behind him.

"This," he said, "is a holographic environment simulator. Known in the vernacular as a holodeck."

The Klingon scowled. Why, he wondered, has this task fallen to *me?*

He had asked the captain the same question a couple of hours earlier.

Because, Mr. Worf, you have proven to be an expert guide. Commander Cadwallader said your tour of the communications system was nothing short of breathtaking.

Breathtaking *indeed.*

Worf considered his audience. Dr. Greyhorse and Morgen seemed interested. However, Ben Zoma was more intrigued by the shapely technician checking the disposal unit down the corridor.

The Klingon cleared his throat. It immediately had the desired effect, as Ben Zoma's attention was returned to him.

"Sorry," said the captain of the *Lexington*. "By all means, carry on, Lieutenant."

"We have four such facilities on the *Enterprise*," continued Worf, as if he'd never stopped. "All four are on deck eleven. In addition, there are smaller versions—*personal* holodecks—scattered throughout the ship."

He tried to avoid the Daa'Vit's gaze—but it was not entirely possible. After all, he *was* standing square in the center of the group.

"I have a question," said Greyhorse.

Worf turned to him, relieved—even though he had to look up at the man, and he wasn't used to looking *up* at people. "Yes, Doctor."

"Is it true that the holodecks are used for exercise regimens? Jogging and so forth?"

The Klingon nodded. "They can be. Of course, the areas in the holodecks are finite. One cannot jog very far without reaching the wall. However—"

"However," Greyhorse interrupted, "the electromagnetic fields that make up the ground underfoot flow in a direction opposite that of the runner's progress—acting as a sort of treadmill, and giving the runner the illusion that he or she is moving forward."

The Klingon frowned. "More or less, yes." Obviously, the man was familiar with special field theory. But then, that was not surprising. He was a doctor, and doctors used force fields in any number of procedures.

"But," Greyhorse went on, "what happens if a second participant is placed in the holodeck—one who is stationary? Does the holodeck maintain the illusion of increasing distance between the stationary observer and the jogger? And if so, how is that accomplished?"

Worf grunted. "A good question," he conceded, despite the brusque manner in which it was posed. He approached the computer terminal built into the bulkhead. "And one that is best answered by a demonstration."

Seeking a relatively simple environment for purposes of demonstration, he called up the Ander's Planet program. Instantly, the doors opened on a barren but level stretch of terrain, ruddy with the orange light of twin suns.

"Follow me," he instructed, and entered. The others trailed along behind him, looking around and murmuring appreciatively.

"Ander's Planet," concluded Morgen, "in the Beta Sardonicus system. Correct?"

"Correct," said Worf without actually looking at the Daa'Vit. "I will need a volunteer—to serve as Dr. Greyhorse's jogger."

Ben Zoma raised his hand. "I'm your man. Neither my Daa'Vit friend nor the doctor have stayed in very good shape, I'm afraid. Old age robs some people of their motivation."

"And others of their sense," retorted Greyhorse.

Morgen laughed.

"Where do I begin?" asked Ben Zoma.

"Right where you are standing," said Worf. "But first, let me make an adjustment—so we can all be heard, no matter how far you go."

He looked up at the sky.

"Computer—amplify our voices so that we can be heard throughout the program."

"Done," said a pleasant female voice.

Worf turned to Ben Zoma. "All right," he said. "You may begin jogging. In any direction."

With a last look at Morgen and Greyhorse, Ben Zoma started off. Slowly, at little more than a brisk walk. And as if they were truly on Ander's Planet, he seemed to be getting a little farther away with each step.

Morgen said as much.

"Look back at us," Worf instructed Ben Zoma. "What do you see?"

His voice was like thunder. It seemed to reverberate to the heavens and back, godlike.

The captain of the *Lexington* looked back over his shoulder. "The distance between us is increasing."

"Fascinating," said Greyhorse.

"Actually," Worf told him, "it is quite simple. You see, the illusion created by the holodeck is made up of three components. One is the manipulation of electromagnetic fields you referred to a moment ago. Another is the creation of actual objects, using transporter-analog matter-conversion technology—though these objects must be simple and inanimate. Also, there are devices to simulate sound, smell, and taste, or alternately to dampen those senses. For example, when the illusory source of the stimulus is appearing to recede, like Captain Ben Zoma.

"But the fourth and most important component is visual—a stereoscopic image comprised of polarized interference patterns—"

"Emitted by omnidirectional holo diodes," contributed Greyhorse. "Millions of them, set into the walls."

"Yes," said the Klingon, again doing his best to ignore the interruption. Apparently, the doctor's expertise was not limited to field theory. "The patterns are programmed to intersect at the lens of the participant's eye. So whatever he or she sees appears to be three-dimensional. And as one moves around, the information emitted by the diodes changes, altering the view."

"All well and good, Mr. Worf," said the doctor. "But that doesn't explain how—"

"This is pretty impressive," called Ben Zoma, who now seemed to be twenty meters away. "I'm going to pick up the pace."

And pick up the pace he did. After a moment or two, he was sprinting—going all out. But it did not diminish the veracity of the illusion. From Worf's point of view, Ben Zoma's figure gradually dwindled.

"As I was saying," the Klingon continued, "the diodes dictate what one sees. Not only by creating pure images, but by altering the way one perceives other elements. The electromagnetic fields, for instance. The converted-matter objects. And, of course, *other participants.*"

Greyhorse grunted. "I see. The polarized interference patterns come together to act as a lens—making the moving participant appear farther away than he or she really is."

"Precisely, Doctor."

"And if we were to go running after him," said Morgen, "the treadmill effect would come into play for us too. So we could never close the gap between us unless we put in a lot more effort."

"Or he stopped and allowed us to catch up," suggested Greyhorse.

Worf confirmed it: "That is the general idea, yes."

By then, Ben Zoma must have tired of testing the holodeck's capacity for illusion, because he had turned around and was running back. To his credit, he had yet to break a sweat. His breathing had barely even accelerated.

"I understand," said Morgen, "that holodeck programs may be customized. Even created from scratch."

This time, he was addressing Worf directly. There was no way the Klingon could help but meet his eyes.

Worf could feel the instinctive reaction rising within him. It took an effort to stifle it—to keep it from being obvious.

"That is true," said the Klingon.

Morgen's eyes, bright yellow, narrowed the slightest bit. "Have *you* created programs, Mr. Worf?"

Inwardly writhing under the Daa'Vit's scrutiny, Worf nodded. "I have," he confirmed.

Morgen seemed about to ask something else. But it never came out. For a fraction of a second longer, he regarded the Klingon. Then Ben Zoma had returned from his run.

"Whew," he said, wiping his brow where a faint sheen of sweat had finally emerged. "Not a bad workout." He turned to Greyhorse. "So? Satisfied?"

The doctor looked around, nodded. "Yes," he said. *"Quite* satisfied." He turned to Worf. "Thank you for your patience, Lieutenant."

"It was my pleasure," said the Klingon. He looked up at the sky again. "Save program."

Abruptly, Ander's Planet vanished, leaving in its place the stark yellow-on-black grid of the unadorned holodeck. The visitors took it in, seemingly as intrigued by the naked space as by the illusion. Worf allowed them some time to look around.

Then he indicated the door with a gesture. "This way, gentlemen."

As he exited, he thought he could feel Morgen's eyes boring into his back.

What was the question the Daa'Vit had been about to pose?

In the cavernous engine room of the *Enterprise,* Geordi and Simenon stood side by side, gazing up at the mighty matter-antimatter core. On the catwalk above them, engineering personnel went through their daily diagnostic routine.

The Gnalish grunted. "You know," he said, "I've pictured this a thousand times in my head. Had to, in order to teach advanced propulsion at the Academy." He grunted again. "But seeing it up close . . . for *real*—it's so . . ."

"Impressive?" suggested Geordi.

"Disappointing," finished Simenon. He regarded the *Enterprise's* chief engineer. "It doesn't look a whole lot different from the engine core on the *Stargazer.* Bigger, sure. But when you come down to it, a warp drive is still a warp drive."

Geordi took a second look at his engine room—the heart and soul of the ship, as far as he was concerned. "I guess," he said, "that depends on your point of view."

Just then, the turbolift doors slid apart and spewed out a familiar figure. Wesley crossed the deck as quickly as he could without actually running and came to a halt in front of the two engineers.

"You're out of breath, Ensign," observed Simenon.

"I'm . . . late . . . sir," explained Wesley. He turned to Geordi. "Sorry. Commander Data . . . asked me to make a course change . . . at the last minute and—"

The engineering chief put a reassuring hand on

Wesley's shoulder. "That's all right," he said. "I'm notified about such things, remember? Besides, Professor Simenon just arrived himself."

The Gnalish looked at Wesley askance. "You're not in a hurry to meet *me,* are you?" He leered at Geordi. "Now, *that* would be a refreshing change—a young person actually *hurrying* to bask in my presence."

"Actually," said the chief engineer, "Ensign Crusher here *was* excited about meeting you. Weren't you, Wes?"

Wesley nodded. "I have an interest in warp engineering," he said, having finally caught his breath. "And with all the work you've done in that field . . ."

Simenon dismissed the idea with a wave of his scaly hand. "Nothing at all, compared to those who went before me. My real talent was *hands-on* engineering." He indicated Geordi with a tilt of his head. "What *this* young man does. What I *used* to do," he sighed.

The ensign smiled tentatively. He looked at the Gnalish. "You're kidding, sir—right? I mean, half the advances in the last ten years . . ."

Simenon snorted. "Overrated, I tell you." He turned to Geordi. "Listen to me, Commander La Forge, and listen well. Someday you're going to be faced with a choice like I had—a 'promotion,' they call it. For the good of the service." He poked a finger in Geordi's chest. "Don't do it. Manacle yourself to a monitor. Stow away. *Name of Scaraf*—steal a ship if you have to. You hear me?"

Geordi smiled. "I hear you. But somehow I don't think it's quite as bad as you make it out to be."

Simenon frowned. "No. You wouldn't, I suppose. Not until you've been there." He turned to Wesley. "And *you*—what do you *really* want from me?"

The ensign looked helpless for a moment. Then Simenon put him out of his misery. "You needn't explain," he said. "Even an old cog like myself can figure it out." He seemed to inspect Wesley with fresh interest. "Crusher. As in *Jack* Crusher. Your father, I gather?"

The young man nodded. "Yessir."

"You want to meet someone who served with him— yes? To learn a little more about him?"

Wesley nodded again. "Not that I'm not fascinated by your work," he amended quickly, "because I am. But I guess that's not *all* I'm interested in."

The Gnalish snorted again. "I'd be surprised," he confessed, "if it were any other way." He eyed the ensign. "Then again, I may not be the best person to ask. Certainly, I served with your father—but he was closer with some of the others. Captain Picard, for instance. And Vigo—though he can't help you much, having perished in that nasty business at Maxia Zeta." He paused to think for a moment. "Of course, there's Ben Zoma—he was your father's immediate superior. Cadwallader, I recall, used to trade research monographs with him. And he seemed to joke a lot with Pug Joseph . . ."

A resigned sort of look had come over Wesley's face. Geordi empathized with the young man's disappointment. Apparently, he'd really been looking forward to this opportunity to pump Simenon for some information.

The Gnalish must have noticed the look too, however. Because he stopped dead in his tracks and did an about-face. "On the other hand," he said, "I *do* remember a *few* things about your father. In fact, a particular incident comes to mind . . ."

Wesley smiled.

Without excusing himself, Geordi withdrew and headed for the nearest unoccupied workstation. He had a feeling that Simenon might be a little more open with the ensign if it was just the two of them.

Besides, he had *work* to do.

CHAPTER 5

"Strange," said Picard. "As I recall, Mr. Joseph was always quite punctual."

Standing on the other side of the battle bridge, Asmund shrugged. "Something must have held him up."

The captain frowned. "Apparently." He looked at his former helm officer, and gestured to the captain's chair. "Care for a seat?" he asked.

She shook her head. "No. Thank you." She looked around. "Actually, this reminds me more of the *Stargazer* than anything else."

Picard nodded, leaning back against one of the peripheral station consoles. "I have remarked on that myself, Idun. But then, that makes sense, doesn't it? When we separate the battle section from the primary hull, speed and efficiency are at a premium—just as they would be in a deep-space exploration vessel." He folded his arms across his chest. "There's no room here for the sort of luxury we enjoy on the main bridge."

Asmund went over to the Conn position, leaned over

65

the console, and looked at the empty viewscreen. "I like this better," she said. "Without the luxuries." She ran her fingers over the dormant control panels. "Yes. It feels more comfortable."

Picard watched her. It seemed that she belonged here—much as Worf had seemed to belong here, on those occasions when it had been necessary for him to man the battle bridge.

"And when you separate," said Asmund, "the battle section retains the full range of ship's capabilities? Weapons, propulsion, everything?"

"That's correct," said the captain. "The battle section is equipped with both impulse and warp drive engines, a shield generator, two photon torpedo launchers, and a complete spread of phaser banks."

"And the saucer section?"

"No warp drive. No photon torpedoes. But just about everything else." Picard sighed. "I wonder what Vigo would have said about all this."

Asmund looked back over her shoulder. "He would have wondered why you needed a primary hull in the first place."

The captain nodded. "Or, for that matter, living quarters." He smiled at his own joke.

Idun stared back at him, stony-faced as ever.

Picard looked at her. "Idun," he said. "I don't like to see you acting this way."

"Which way is that?" she asked softly, turning back to the console.

"Like an outsider," he said. "Apart from everyone else."

She sighed. "Captain . . . I *am* apart from everyone else."

He looked at her. "Why do you say that?"

Asmund stood up straight, returned his gaze. "You *know* why."

He smiled gently. "Idun, that was twenty years ago. No one holds that against you."

"That's what Captain Mansfield told me when I received Morgen's invitation. But he—you—you're wrong. Both of you."

"Morgen invited you to be part of his honor guard. Would he have done that if he intended to shun you?"

"Captain Mansfield said that too. But it's not just Morgen. Back at the starbase, Greyhorse was . . . I don't know. *Different.* Not the way he used to be. Even Simenon was . . . distant. Aloof."

"Has it occurred to you that you haven't seen them in almost a dozen years? That they may have changed? That *you* may have changed?"

Asmund frowned. "It . . . occurred to me, yes."

"Nor are Simenon and Greyhorse our two most congenial former comrades. I would not use them as a barometer of how the rest of us feel about you."

She nodded. "Perhaps not." A pause. "With all due respect, Captain, I'd like to talk about something else."

Picard regarded her. He knew that Asmund, like Worf, could not be pushed. She would obey an order, if it came to that. She would go through the motions—but inside she would resist that much harder.

"As you wish," he said finally.

Just then the turbolift doors opened. Turning at the same time, they saw Joseph emerge from the lift.

He grinned sheepishly. "Hi. Sorry I'm late." He looked from one of them to the other. "I didn't miss anything, did I?"

* * *

The guided tour completed, Dr. Crusher sat down at her desk. She indicated the three cabins that comprised the ship's medical facilities.

"Well," she said, "that's what the well-dressed sickbay is wearing these days. What do you think?"

Greyhorse nodded. He seated himself across from her. "Very impressive, Beverly. Not as impressive as your holodecks, but impressive nonetheless." Picking up a tricorder lying on Crusher's desk, he put it through its paces. "A far cry from what we had to put up with on the *Stargazer*. We were lucky if both biobeds were functional at the same time."

She regarded him. "Tempted?"

He looked up from the tricorder. "I beg your pardon?"

"You know," she said. "To ship out again?"

Greyhorse chuckled dryly. "Beverly, there is no sickbay in existence that could tempt me to do that. Don't be deceived by the fact that I signed on with a deep-space exploration ship, where patient care was my first priority. I have always preferred things to people— which is why Starfleet Medical suits me so well. I would rather peer over my morning coffee at a computer monitor than have to deal with something that can talk back."

Crusher looked at him askance. "You mean you don't get even a little twinge now and then? A desire to push out the frontiers?"

"I *am* pushing out the frontiers. I would think you'd know that, considering you pushed them out *with* me for a year or so." He shook his head. "Truth be told, I should have been an engineer—like my father and brothers."

Now that she thought about it, Crusher remembered Greyhorse's saying something about a course in engineering at the Academy—just before he switched over to the medical curriculum, to avoid becoming "just another Greyhorse family robot."

"I don't know what kind of engineer you'd have made," she said. "But you're a damned fine doctor."

He put the tricorder down and met her gaze. "It is very kind of you to say so, Beverly." His eyes narrowed mischievously. "And, I might add, very discerning as well. Now, if you don't mind, could we take in some other part of your ship? I have this premonition that if I stay too long, I'm actually going to have to *treat* someone."

Normally, the gymnasium was quiet at this time of day—which was one of the reasons Riker chose this hour to work out. He was a social enough being in every other aspect of his life, but he'd learned something long ago: If you came to the gym to shoot the bull, all you'd end up exercising was your mouth.

Unfortunately, the gym wasn't as deserted as he would have preferred. As the doors to the room parted, he could hear the sound of heavy breathing, amplified by the echoing gym walls.

Entering, he saw that someone was on the horizontal bar—someone slender and female, her hair bound tightly behind her head, moving too quickly to be easily identified. For a moment Riker stood there, silently appreciating the grace with which each intricate maneuver was performed—not to mention the streamlined form that was doing the performing.

The gymnast, on the other hand, seemed not to have noticed his presence. Nor was that difficult to understand, given the concentration she must have had to apply.

This had to be someone new to the ship, he told

himself. Nobody he knew was capable of *those* kinds of moves.

As he watched, the woman extended herself full-length, swung around the bar a couple of times, and then leapfrogged over it. The momentum she'd built up carried her almost half the length of the gym before she landed on a mat. A little stumble at the end marred what otherwise would have been a perfect routine.

Riker had already begun clapping before he realized whom he was clapping for. Then the gymnast turned around, a little startled—and he found himself staring at Tricia Cadwallader.

"Criminy!" she said, her hand resting on her breast. "You could have let me know you were there!"

He shrugged. "Sorry. I was too dazzled to think straight."

Cadwallader blushed through her light sprinkling of freckles. "I wasn't *that* good. You should have seen me back at the Academy."

Riker tried not to gape at the way she filled out her cutout tank suit. What was it about Starfleet uniforms that made women look like boys? "If I told you," he began, "that I can't imagine you performing any more beautifully *anywhere* . . . it would probably sound like a line, wouldn't it?"

She smiled as she thought about it. "I'm not sure. Why don't you try it?"

He nodded. "All right—I will." He approached her, taking her hand in his, and gazed into her deep green eyes. "I can't imagine you looking any more beautiful anywhere—not at the Academy or anywhere else." He hung on to her hand. It was soft and warm and just the slightest bit damp with perspiration. "How was that?"

Cadwallader's smile became a smirk. "Pretty good—

except you got some of the words wrong. The first time, you said 'performing'—not 'looking.' "

Riker feigned confusion. "Did I? I guess it just came out that way."

She rolled her eyes. "Now, that," she said, taking her hand back with a flourish, "sounds like a line." Crossing the room, she headed for the towel rack.

"Listen," he called after her, "I wouldn't have to resort to such ploys if you'd have dinner with me." His voice echoed from wall to wall.

Cadwallader turned around. "Are you asking?"

Riker straightened. "I'm asking."

She chuckled. "All right, then. But not tonight. I have a prior engagement."

He watched her got to the rack and take down a towel. "Oh?"

"That's right," said Cadwallader, using the towel to dry her hair. "And so do you."

Riker didn't understand. It must have been evident in his expression, because she went on to explain.

"Captain Picard's feast," she said. "Hasn't he told you about it?"

Riker shook his head. "No, I don't believe he has."

Cadwallader shrugged. "It's at 0800 hours. I'm sure he wouldn't assemble all his officers and leave you out." She paused. "Would he?"

"I've been a little busy lately," he said, trying not to sound defensive. "There's probably a message waiting for me in my quarters."

She toweled off some more. "Mmm. Probably. Unless, of course, he means for you to take charge of the bridge then."

Riker couldn't help but smile at the way she was baiting him. "I suppose that *is* a possiblity."

Slinging the towel over her shoulders, Cadwallader headed for the doors. As she passed him, she patted him on the shoulder in a comradely sort of way.

"It's all right," she said, tossing the remark at him offhandedly. "If you miss dinner tonight, you'll just be that much hungrier tomorrow."

Riker watched her go, his smile spreading. He had a feeling he'd be hungry tomorrow no matter *what*.

"And that," Simenon said, standing with Wesley in a corner of engineering, "is how your father and I held off a herd of charging thunalia on Beta Varius Four." He smiled in his lizardlike way, remembering. "If either one of us had panicked and made for the caves, the other would have been trampled—or skewered on the beasts' horns. And more than likely, both would have perished. But by standing back to back, we were able to keep them at bay with our phasers—at least until my transporter chief could beam us back up." The Gnalish nodded proudly. "What's more, we collected the data we went down for, as well as the tissue samples from which new thunalia could be cloned. And, in fact, *were* cloned. If you visit the preserves on Morrison's World, you'll see any number of thunalia roaming the plains—even though Beta Varius Four is now devoid of complex life forms."

Wesley shook his head. "That's great. That's really great. Mom never mentioned that story."

"Your mother may never have known about it," Simenon pointed out. "We were all restricted as to the frequency and duration of our subspace messages. After all, there were hundreds of us aboard the *Stargazer*—all yearning for families and friends—and the subspace equipment was occasionally needed for other matters, mission communications not the least of them. As I recall, your father always had this . . . well, *interrupted* look on his face after a packet went out. As though, given the chance, he would have said a lot more." He harumphed. "Besides, I'm sure he had more personal things to discuss than an encounter with a few dozen predators. Bazzid's bones, we were risking our lives on a different planet each day." He straightened, realizing he might have gotten a little carried away. "Or so it seemed," he amended.

The ensign looked at him. He'd meant to say something about how terrific and how patient Simenon had been. But that's not what came out. What he said was: "Tell me how my father died."

That was the story he *really* wanted to hear—even if he hadn't admitted it to himself earlier. That was the hole inside him that truly needed filling.

Simenon sobered a bit at the request. "There's not much to tell," he said. He shrugged. "Besides, you must already know what happened."

"Only from my mom. And she didn't have much to go on. Just the official report from Starfleet, and whatever Captain Picard told her when he came to the house."

The Gnalish regarded him for a moment, his ruby eyes blinking. Wesley could plainly see the reticence in them. Nor was it difficult to understand.

It was one thing to have to dredge up the memory of a comrade's death. But to have to share it with that comrade's son . . .

"I'll tell you what," Simenon said finally. "Why don't I regale you with that story on another occasion? I *do* have that tour to take, you know." He smirked, abruptly himself again. "Though you're welcome to come along. I wouldn't mind hearing some more about all those contributions I've made to warp drive technology."

Wes smiled back, putting his feelings aside for the time being. "You can count on me, sir."

The Gnalish nodded. "Good. That's what I like about you, Ensign Crusher. You've got a healthy respect for your elders."

The door beeped. Worf turned at the sound.

He did not often entertain guests in his quarters. His preference for solitude was well known, not only among his friends but throughout the entire crew. After all, he was surrounded by humans and other races for most of the day; after hours, he needed time to just be himself. To just be *Klingon.*

Beep. He had not imagined it.

"Come," he said. The door opened.

If it had been Riker, or Geordi, or even Wesley, the Klingon would not have have been all that surprised. They had been here before on one occasion or another.

It turned out to be none of them. In fact, his visitor was the *last* person on the entire ship that he had expected to come calling on him.

"Do you mind if I come in?" asked Morgen.

The Klingon had instinctively recoiled; he forced himself to relax. "Please," he said, expressing the rest of the invitation with a gesture.

His eyes never leaving Worf's, the Daa'Vit entered. Selecting a chair, he folded himself into it.

Worf sat down on the other end of the room. For a moment they just stared at each other.

"You must be wondering why I've come," said Morgen.

The Klingon nodded. "I confess to a certain curiosity."

Morgen grunted. "You Klingons have a way with words. From your lips, even a polite remark sounds like a challenge."

Worf shrugged. "Perhaps it is the way you *hear* it."

The Daa'Vit smiled. "Perhaps it *is*. But then—"

As before, in the holodeck, he seemed to stop himself. To regroup.

"How easy it is," said Morgen, "to get into a war of words." He leaned forward. "Especially when every part of me is repelled by you. Hateful of you."

Instinctively, Worf prepared himself for an assault—visually searching the Daa'Vit for concealed weapons, working out ways in which his posture made him vulnerable.

But in the next moment Morgen leaned back again. "Yet," he went on, "I am an officer in Starfleet—just as you are. We are sworn to stand side by side—not rend each other like beasts. If there is one thing I have learned in my time among humans, it is that prejudice—*any* prejudice—may be put aside."

Worf knew how hard it was for the Daa'Vit to express such sentiments. It gained Morgen a measure of respect in his eyes—if not affection.

The Klingon cleared his throat. "Permission to speak frankly, sir."

The Daa'Vit nodded. "Speak," he said.

Worf eyed his visitor. "I have not always found the same thing to be true. At least not in *my* case. Once, I was asked to save a Romulan's life through an act of brotherhood. I found I could not." He licked his lips. "And I am not sure the outcome would have been any different if the life in question were that of a Daa'Vit."

Morgen regarded him. "Honesty. I appreciate that." He paused. "Perhaps you misunderstand me, Worf. I am not suggesting we become *finna'calar*. What are the English words for it? Ah, yes—*blood brothers*. No, I am not suggesting that at all. But we need not be enemies either." He tilted his head. "You are a warrior. I am a warrior. Surely, there is a common ground on which we may meet."

Worf gathered himself, fighting his instincts. "I . . . would . . . *like* that," he got out.

The Daa'Vit smiled, though there was no humor in it. "Good. I may even have an idea in that regard."

"An idea?" echoed the Klingon.

"Yes. Do you recall what I asked you in the holodeck —if you had created any programs of your own?"

Worf began to see what Morgen was getting at. "Yes," he said. "I do recall. And I said that I *had* created some programs."

"Fit for a warrior, no doubt," said the Daa'Vit.

"I like to think so," replied the Klingon.

"It would be a novelty for a Daa'Vit and a Klingon to fight side by side—instead of against each other."

Worf couldn't help but smile at the thought. As ludicrous as it was . . ."More than a novelty," he decided. "It would be a challenge—one that could only bring honor to all involved." He omitted the last part of his thought: *if it works*.

Morgen nodded. "I agree. When?"

"Tomorrow at this time. I will be off duty."

"Done. Is there anything I should bring? A *ka'yun*, perhaps?"

"Nothing," said the Klingon. "The holodeck will provide weapons."

Gracefully, the Daa'Vit rose from his chair. "I look forward to it."

Worf rose too. "As do I."

Inclining his head to signify respect—another gesture that must not have been easy for him—Morgen took his leave of his new battle-partner.

And the Klingon, watching him go, decided he had much to think about.

CHAPTER 6

Picard stood, looking down the long table at his assembled officers—both past and present. He was glad to note that Idun Asmund was among them, seated between Ben Zoma and Cadwallader. And Beverly as well—though she had been reticent at first, she had apparently managed to overcome that without any encouragement from her captain. He raised his glass.

"A toast," he said. "To those who have served me in such exceptional fashion."

"Here, here," said Riker.

"Jian dan'yu," agreed Morgen, voicing the Daa'Vit equivalent of Riker's acknowledgment.

Everyone murmured their approval and drank—just as their plates were removed and replaced with their main courses by a cadre of waiters. Under Guinan's supervision, of course.

The captain assessed his dinner as it was placed in front of him. The aroma was exquisite, tantalizing. "Manzakini Loraina," he said appreciatively. He looked up at Guinan. "An excellent choice."

Standing discreetly apart from the table, Guinan

inclined her head. "I knew you'd like it, sir," she told him.

"This is an Emmonite dish, is it not?" asked Data.

"That's right," confirmed Troi, who was sitting next to him. "One of the *many* Emmonite dishes of which the captain is so fond." She looked at Picard and smiled.

"Nor am I the only aficionado of Emmonite cuisine," the captain reminded her. "It is served regularly at Starfleet headquarters."

"Is it true," asked Geordi, "that the Emmonites never heard of pasta before they joined the Federation?"

Picard nodded. "*Quite* true. As I understand it, the head of the Emmonite delegation dined at the home of Admiral Manelli—this being a good fifty years ago, of course, when Manelli was in charge of Starfleet. That night, the admiral's wife served linguini with white clam sauce, and the ambassador was so taken with it that he insisted on bringing the recipe back to his home planet."

"I heard he wanted to bring Mrs. Manelli back as well," said Ben Zoma.

Picard nodded. "He did. But that is another story."

Data consumed a forkful of the manzakini, seemed to ponder the experience. He turned to Guinan. "Very authentic," he said. "My compliments to the chef."

Guinan inclined her head again. "Thank you. The food service units will be glad to hear that."

Joseph looked across the table at the android. "You *eat,* Mr. Data?"

Data nodded. "It is not necessary for my survival. However, I have found that in a situation such as this one, it is often distracting to others if I do *not* eat."

"Then you can actually *taste?*" asked Cadwallader.

"Yes," replied the android. "I have the requisite

sensory apparatus. I can even analyze the ingredients. The only thing I cannot do is derive enjoyment from the sensation."

"Too bad," said Morgen. "But then, we all have our limitations."

"Pardon me," said the Gnalish, addressing Worf. "But your Manzakini Loraina looks a little different from mine. It seems to be *writhing*."

"Worf is on a special diet," Geordi jested.

Picard gave his chief engineer a sidelong glance. "The lieutenant has a preference for *Klingon* preparations," he explained, "though he seldom gets them, except on special occasions. This qualifies as such an occasion."

The Klingon looked at Simenon as if he'd been challenged. "It is called blood pie." He pushed the plate toward the Gnalish. "Would you like to try some?"

Simenon swallowed. "No, my boy, I don't think so. I like my food to lie still on my plate. You know—to at least *pretend* it's not alive."

"Actually," said Greyhorse, "blood pie is quite nutritious." He looked around at the surprised expressions of his companions. "I didn't say I had eaten it. Just that it was good for you. That's not a crime, is it?"

Laughter. And from Simenon, a crackling that was as much for Greyhorse's benefit as anything else.

"I have eaten it," said Asmund rather abruptly.

The laughter died down.

"And?" asked Morgen.

Asmund regarded him evenly. "It is not as good as stewed *gagh*."

"Gagh?" asked Geordi, mutilating the word in his attempt to pronounce it.

"Serpent worms," explained Riker. "I've had occasion to try them myself. They are quite . . . filling." He couldn't help but grimace a little at the memory.

"You don't appear to have enjoyed them, Commander," observed Cadwallader.

"It is," said Worf, "an acquired taste. Much like *chicken.*"

"Chicken," Simenon remarked, "doesn't try to eat *you* as you are eating *it.*"

Ben Zoma grunted. "Vigo used to love something called *sturrd.* It looked like a mound of sand with pieces of ground glass thrown in for good measure. And he would down it with half a gallon of maple syrup."

"It was *not* maple syrup," argued Joseph. "It only *looked* like maple syrup."

"Vigo," said Data, who had been taking in the conversation with equanimity. "He was one of your colleagues on the *Stargazer*—one who did not survive the battle at Maxia Zeta."

"That's right," said Greyhorse. "Unfortunately. Vigo was our weapons officer."

Morgen nodded. "And not just any weapons officer. He was the finest Starfleet has ever seen."

"I didn't know Starfleet *had* weapons officers," said Troi.

"Only the deep-space explorers," Picard expanded. "It was an experiment, really. A separation of the ship's defense functions from its security functions. But don't let the terminology deceive you—Vigo did a lot more than look after the weapons systems."

"That's right," said Ben Zoma. He turned to Dr. Crusher. "He also used to thrash your husband regularly at *sharash'di.*"

Beverly smiled. "I think I remember Jack telling me

about that. Though as I recall, it wasn't just Jack he beat. It was *you* too. And a few others."

Ben Zoma laughed. "Now that you mention it, I guess I *was* one of the victims."

"And I as well," said Cadwallader.

"But Jack was Vigo's regular partner," recalled Joseph. "I think they used to play every chance they got. As if Jack couldn't accept defeat—couldn't accept the fact that there was something he couldn't do."

"Not that there was any shame in losing to Vigo," Cadwallader interjected. "He was uncanny. A master."

"Vigo lost only once," said Ben Zoma. He seemed to concentrate for a moment, then shook his head. "Though for the life of me, I can't remember who beat him."

"It was Gerda," said Asmund. "Gerda beat him."

Suddenly, there was silence in the room.

Asmund turned to Data before he could ask. "My twin sister," she explained. "The one who tried to kill Morgen."

Out of the corner of his eye, Picard saw Geordi exchange glances with Simenon. For once, the Gnalish had nothing clever to say.

Picard cleared his throat. The best thing, he decided, was to take the remark in stride. To act as if it were just part of the conversation, and not a complete bombshell.

But before he could open his mouth, Morgen beat him to it.

"What's that expression you humans have? 'Water under the bridge?'" He shrugged—a rather awkward gesture for a Daa'Vit. "As far as I'm concerned, the incident is forgotten." He looked at Asmund. "And forgiven."

The captain breathed a silent sigh of relief. Everyone at the table seemed to loosen up a little.

Everyone except Asmund. *"I* haven't forgotten it," she told Morgen. She looked around the table. "Sorry. I hadn't intended to put a damper on things." She got up. "Excuse me."

"Idun," Picard called.

She seemed not to hear him as she walked out of the room.

Ten-Forward was open around the clock. It had to be. The ship's officers and crew got off duty at various odd hours, depending on their section and individual responsibilities, and nearly everyone felt the urge to unwind in the lounge at one time or another.

And whenever anyone stopped in for a drink and some conversation, Guinan seemed to be there—standing at her usual place behind the bar, mixing drinks and distributing advice in small doses. Of course, that was only an appearance. Guinan slept like everybody else.

Well, perhaps not *exactly* like everybody else. But she slept. So it was unusual that she should have been around during the pre-"dawn" shift when Pug Joseph swaggered into the lounge.

He didn't look very healthy—or very happy. There were faint dark circles under his eyes and a pallor to his skin that told Guinan he'd been drinking more than synthehol. She smiled and prepared herself.

As she'd expected, he made his way to the farthest table from the bar—a small set-up for two right by an observation port. When he pulled out a chair, the legs clattered against the floor; as he lowered himself into it, he did so awkwardly. Then he slumped over the table, turning his head to the observation port—as if he preferred the company of the streaking stars to that of the crewmen who sat all around him.

Dunhill was the waiter assigned to that area. But before he went over to take Joseph's order, he cast a glance in Guinan's direction.

She shook her head slowly from side to side. Acknowledging her silent instructions, Dunhill waited on another table, ignoring the *Lexington*'s security chief. Somehow, though he wasn't looking in that direction, Joseph managed to notice. He turned, straightened, and glared at Guinan through narrowed bloodshot eyes.

Recognizing her cue, she wove her way among the tables, exchanging greetings with those she passed, until she reached the place where Joseph was sitting. He studied her sullenly.

She returned his hard gaze with a more pleasant one. "May I?" she asked, indicating the empty seat opposite him.

His nostrils flared. He shrugged.

Taking that as an affirmative response, she pulled out the chair and sat down. For a moment there was only silence between them—a silence strung so tight that it seemed liable to snap at any time.

Then she spoke. "You know," she said, "you're getting to be quite a regular around here. Aren't there any other parts of the ship you're interested in?"

He chuckled. The sound had an edge to it.

"Not that it's any of your business." He leaned forward, the pupils of his eyes larger and blacker than they had a right to be. "And if I were Morgen or Ben Zoma or—hell, *any* of the others—you wouldn't be mentioning that now, would you?"

"As a matter of fact," Guinan said, "I *would* be."

Joseph sneered, leaning back again. "In a pig's eye."

"I don't lie, Mr. Joseph."

"Uh-huh." He looked at her. "Where did you come from, anyway?"

"You mean what *race?*" she asked.

"That's right. What race."

"An old one," said Guinan. "Old enough to know alcoholism when we see it."

Joseph grunted. "Give me a break, all right? I can hold my liquor."

"No doubt," she answered, though she had lots of doubts. "The question is why you would *want* to."

His mouth twisted into something mean. "I love people like you," he told her. "Crusaders. They always think they know you—know all about you." His voice became menacing. "You don't know *anything* about me."

Guinan stood her ground. "I just might know more than you think."

"Like what?"

"Like you're bubbling over with hate. For others, to an extent—but most of all, for yourself. Because you don't like what you've become. Because you think it could've been different. And because you believe, in the secret center of yourself, that somehow it's all your fault." Seeing him shrink a little from her, she softened her voice. "And the alcohol is the only way you can keep the hate in check. It's the only way you can smile at people and not snarl at them, because if you let them see what's inside you, you know you're going to lose what precious little you *do* have."

Suddenly, Joseph's face was flushed. It took him a few seconds to respond, and when he did, his voice was little more than a rasp.

"You're crazy," he said.

She shook her head. "No. I just come from a very old race."

Gradually, Joseph's confusion dissipated. But it wasn't replaced by anger. Rather, the man seemed on the verge of tears.

"I'm as good as they are," he said. "I'm as good as *anyone.*"

"Of course you are," Guinan assured him. "But now you've got more than a couple of bad breaks to deal with. The *alcohol* has gotten in your way. Can't you see? It's like a jealous lover. It doesn't just console you—it makes sure you stay just where you are. Beaten. Bitter. If you really want to become the kind of person you *can* be, you're going to have to face this—and take care of it."

He looked at the stars again. His face, a portrait of a tortured soul, was reflected in the transparent barrier that separated them from the void. "I—I can't. I just *can't.*"

"You *can,*" she insisted. She sought his eyes, found them as he turned to her again. "I'll help. You hear me, Chief? I can help you."

For a brief moment it seemed Joseph was going to take the first step back. And then, with a pathos that tore at her inner being, he pounded on the tabletop. "No," he got out between clenched teeth. "No. You don't know what I—what it's like. Just—damn it, just leave me alone. You can *have* your stinking lounge."

Shooting to his feet, he glared at her one last time. Then, with all the dignity he could muster, he threaded his way among the tables and left.

Guinan was so busy watching him, she almost didn't see Dunhill's approach.

"Ma'am?" said the waiter.

"Yes, Dunhill?"

"Is everything all right?"

She sighed. "Not exactly." She looked up at him. "But thanks for asking."

The holodeck doors opened.

Morgen nodded approvingly. "I like it," he said.

Worf grunted. "I thought you would."

Before them loomed the remains of a ruined temple, neither distinctly Klingon nor distinctly anything else, but so barbaric-looking that only a Klingon could have invented them. The sky overhead was the color of molten lava; the ground was a dead gray, pocked with steaming, smoking holes.

God-statues stared at them, either from the heights to which they'd been erected or from out of the rubble into which they'd fallen. There were bird cries, savage and shrill, though the birds themselves—a carrion-eating variety—were not evident. Long snakelike things slithered over the crumbled stones, hissing as they went.

Worf indicated the weapons at their feet. Kneeling, the Daa'Vit picked up the one that was meant for him.

"A *ka'yun,*" said the Klingon.

Morgen inspected it appreciatively, testing its balance. He looked at Worf. "Very authentic."

The Klingon shrugged. "There were descriptions of it in the library computer. I merely drew on the data." He bent and picked up his own weapon, a long staff with a vicious hook at one end and a metal ball at the other.

"A *laks'mar,*" noted Morgen. He stiffened a little at the sight. "I am familiar with it. *We* are familiar with it."

Worf decided it would be wise to change the subject.

"This program has two levels of difficulty. I have chosen the second," he said.

The Daa'Vit nodded his approval. "Let's begin."

O'Brien seldom took advantage of the holodecks. It wasn't that he had an aversion to them—just that he liked other sorts of recreation, chief among them being a good, steamy poker game.

Of course, it had been different when he'd first come on board. The holodecks had been a novelty then, and he'd vented his imagination in them. Once he'd constructed a pub in old Dublin, where he'd tossed a few down with his favorite author—a fellow by the name of James Joyce. Another time he'd had dinner with the Wee Folk under the Hill, and let their pipes charm him to sleep.

But after a while the novelty had worn off. The final straw had come when he found himself constructing *poker games* in the *holodecks*—and enjoying them less than the live games he played with the ship's officers.

When he visited deck eleven these days, it was strictly to visit a friend in his or her quarters, or to work up a sweat in the gym. And when he walked past the holodeck panels, it was usually without a second thought.

Except this time. On his way to Crewman Resnick's apartment, he'd seen Worf and Captain Morgen entering holodeck one. And he knew from speaking to Commander La Forge that Klingons and Daa'Vit didn't get along. Hell—Worf had been afraid it might come to blows. Or worse.

But if they didn't see eye to eye . . . what in blazes were they doing in the holodeck together?

In the end, it was more than curiosity that drove

O'Brien to find an answer to that question. It was genuine concern for the Daa'Vit's welfare—not to mention Worf's. And if he didn't exactly feel right checking the computer panel to see what program they were using, he at least felt *justified.*

The panel readout indicated "Calisthenics—Lt. Worf. Level Two." When he saw that, O'Brien thought he understood what was going on.

Klingons were warriors. Daa'Vit were warriors. Yup —it all made sense.

Worf was trying to bridge the cultural gap between them. If they were human, they'd be playing billiards. Or Ping-Pong. But since they were who they were, they were mixing it up with alien monsters instead.

And Level Two—well, that didn't sound so good, but it didn't sound so bad either. After all, Commander Riker had once tried Level One—or so he'd said one night around the poker table.

O'Brien went to see his friend Resnick with a clear conscience. He'd done his part to ensure peace and tranquility on the *Enterprise.*

Responding to the Daa'Vit's request that they begin the exercise, Worf strode ahead into the most congested part of the ruins. Already, he could feel his instincts coming to the fore—his senses becoming sharper, the fire in his blood awakening.

Morgen followed, but at a distance of a couple of meters. A good idea, the Klingon remarked to himself. When things heated up, he didn't want them to become entangled with one another.

The birds shrieked, eager for freshly killed meat. The snake-things crawled. High above them, the heavens rumbled as if with an impending storm.

Movement. Worf saw it only out of the corner of his eye. His first impulse was to attack it, to draw it out.

But it was on the Daa'Vit's flank, not his. If they were to work together, they would have to trust each other. Trust each other's perceptions and abilities.

A moment later, Worf was glad that he had practiced restraint. For if he had gone after the first hidden assailant, he would have been too distracted to notice the second—a powerful, furred being that leapt down at him from one of the god-monuments.

He brought up his weapon just in time to absorb the force of the furred one's downstroke. Recovering, he launched an attack of his own, burying his hook deep in his enemy's shoulder. When the furred one tore it free, Worf used the other end to smash him in the face.

As the furred one sank to his knees, unconscious, Worf allowed himself a glimpse of Morgen's combat. The Daa'Vit was exchanging blows with a horned and hairless white giant modeled after the Kup'lceti of Alpha Malachon Four. No problem there, the Klingon decided.

And whirled in time to face another attacker, who had sprung from behind a ruined altar. This one was broader than the first, squatter, with a black-and-yellow hide and eyes like chips of obsidian. Shuffling to one side, Worf avoided his initial charge. Then, as they faced off again, he caught the being's mace on his staff.

For a moment they grappled, Worf snarling with effort as he tried to gain the upper hand. He could smell his opponent's fetid breath, hear the screams of the carrion birds drawn by the scent of blood. His pulse pounded in his ears, feeding the fires inside him.

Finally, with a mighty surge, the Klingon thrust his enemy back—in the process creating enough space between them to swing his weapon. The metal ball caught the being on the side of the head, spinning him around, sending him sprawling into one of the steaming hellpits. Roaring with pain, he struggled desperately to climb out of the hole. In the end, he failed.

Worf felt a cry of victory burst from his throat, piercing a roll of thunder overhead.

Coiling, wary of another enemy, he caught another glimpse of the Daa'Vit. Morgen was standing over not one opponent, but two—his angular face split by a huge grin, his sword dripping blood.

When he sensed Worf's scrutiny, he whirled and returned it. For a moment they stood there, each fighting the instinct to cut the other to pieces. Straining against themselves, measuring passion against intellect.

Then the battle fury subsided. The moment passed.

"Excellent," said the Daa'Vit. His yellow eyes glinted. "Better, in fact, than I had hoped."

Worf acknowledged the compliment with a nod.

Abruptly, the scene changed. The bodies of their enemies were gone—as if they had never been there at all.

Morgen looked at him. "Something else, Worf?"

The Klingon shook his head. This was not part of his program. It should have ended when they struck down the last attacker.

"Something is wrong," he said out loud.

He didn't have a chance to elaborate. The furred one was descending on him as before, whole again. As Worf leapt backward, a skull-faced warrior—a relic of past programs—advanced from another direction, making his way around a steaming hellhole. And a third opponent, a leathery-skinned, club-wielding Bandalik, was crawling toward him over a slab of stone.

It was happening too quickly. This wasn't Level Two. It was something more difficult.

But he hadn't *programmed* anything more difficult.

"What's going on?" asked Morgen, beset by a second group of antagonists.

"I don't know," said the Klingon. But he wasn't about to risk the Daa'Vit's well-being by subjecting him to a program too fierce for him. And possibly, Worf admitted, too fierce for him as well.

"Stop program," he called to the computer.

It had no effect. His enemies were still converging on him.

"Stop program," he called again.

Nothing.

Off to the side, Morgen cursed. Worf heard the clang of colliding blades, followed by a grunt and another clang.

The Klingon's lips pulled back in fury. This was no joke. Something had happened to the holodeck. It wasn't responding.

Even as he confronted that fact, Skullface swung his ax, meaning to separate Worf's head from his shoulders. The Klingon ducked, slammed his opponent with the ball end of his weapon—then whirled to strike at the oncoming Bandalik.

The blow landed; the Bandalik staggered back. However, the furred one was on top of him now, too close to defend against.

Worf's staff went up, though not in time to keep the furred one's blade from slashing his uniform shirt. There was a hot stab of pain—and the Klingon could feel something warm and wet trickling down the hard muscles of his solar plexus. It smelled like blood—*his* blood.

Hooking the furred one as he had before, he sent him sprawling. But before he could turn and face another adversary, something hit him in the back—hit him *hard*. Gritting his teeth against the pain, the Klingon did his best to keep his feet. But a second blow sent him spinning wildly.

The ground rushed up to meet him, and he found himself at the brink of a steaming hole. A moment later, Skullface was on top of him, bringing his ax up for the killing blow—and Worf had lost his staff when he fell. Still dazed, he forced himself to reach up and grab his enemy's arms.

It worked—but only for a moment. Then his enemy's superior leverage began to take its toll.

As he forced the ax blade down toward the Klingon's throat, Skullface grinned. Behind him, the furred one and the Bandalik looked on eagerly, waiting to finish Worf off if Skullface failed. . . .

Unfortunately for O'Brien, Resnick wasn't home. He called her on the ship's intercom.

"You *did* invite me over?" he asked. "I mean, I wasn't dreaming it, was I?"

Resnick cursed softly. "Sorry, Miles." She apologized profusely for having drawn an unexpected shift in security—and forgetting they were supposed to get together.

"I understand," he told her. "I guess I'll just have to find another way to pass the time."

Making his way back down the corridor, O'Brien passed by the holodecks again—and slowed down. He had nothing else to do, he thought; a visit with old James might hit the spot. As he stopped to see if holodeck one was still occupied, he noticed that Worf's program had escalated to Level Three.

"Hmm," he said out loud. Straightening, he touched his communicator insignia. "O'Brien to Commander Riker."

The response was barely a second in coming. "Riker here."

"O'Brien, sir. I know this is probably none of my business, but I saw Lieutenant Worf and Captain Morgen enter the holodeck together a few minutes ago—to participate in the lieutenant's 'calisthenics' program. And just now I couldn't help but notice that the program had been bumped up to Level Three—"

"Level Three?" Riker exploded. "Turn it off, O'Brien! Turn the damned thing off!"

The transporter chief took a moment to recover from the force of Riker's reaction—but *only* a moment. Then he whirled and pressed the abort program area on the holodeck computer panel.

Nothing happened. According to the monitor, the program was still in progress.

"It's not working, Commander," said O'Brien. He tried to terminate the program a second time, but with no more success. "The program won't abort."

"Damn it," said the first officer. "Riker to bridge—"

That was all O'Brien heard for a few moments. Then the lights went off in the vicinity of the holodecks, and with them the faint hum of the ventilation system.

"O'Brien?" It was Riker again.

"Aye, sir?"

"We've cut power to Deck Eleven. Can you hear anything from inside the holodeck?"

O'Brien listened. His stomach tightened.

"Nothing, Commander."

A muffled curse. "Try to pry the doors open, Chief. There'll be a security team there in a minute or two."

O'Brien tugged at one of the doors, knowing full well that he wouldn't be able to budge it by himself—even with the power shut down. Of course, that didn't stop him from giving it his best shot.

By the time the security team showed up, he'd actually created an opening the size of a hand's-breadth. A familiar face loomed before him as other hands gripped the interlocking segments of the doors.

"Fern," he said, acknowledging her.

Resnick smiled grimly. "Any idea what happened?"

He shook his head. "Just that Lieutenant Worf's in there, and Captain Morgen as well. And they're in some kind of trouble."

He and Resnick strained along with the rest of the security team, but they weren't making much progress. It seemed that the doors had moved about all they were going to.

"Everybody step back," said Burke, the team leader. Waiting a moment while O'Brien and the others complied, he plucked his phaser off his belt, selected a setting, and trained it on one of the doors. Then he activated the thing.

The blue beam knifed out, vaporizing the duranium door in a matter of seconds. As the air filled with steam and the smell of something burning, Burke made his way through the twisted metal remains.

Resnick was right on his tail. And O'Brien was right on hers.

With the power off, the holodeck had reverted to a yellow-on-black grid. There were two figures inside. Both bloody, but both still standing—if barely.

Swaying, panting heavily, Worf waved away Resnick's offer of help. "See to Captain Morgen," he ordered, his voice little more than a rasp.

A couple of security officers approached the Daa'Vit. "No," said Morgen. "Let me be." And promptly fell to his knees.

Burke pressed his insignia. "Sickbay—we need a trauma team in holodeck one. We've got two casualties —one Klingon and one Daa'Vit. *Hurry.*"

CHAPTER 7

"But I feel fine," Worf protested.

"I'm happy for you," responded Crusher, using her tricorder to check the dermaplast patch on the Klingon's back. It was adhering perfectly—a good job, if she said so herself.

"There's really no need for this, Doctor."

She glanced over her shoulder at Morgen. "Another sector heard from."

The Daa'Vit shook his head disapprovingly. "What is it about medical officers?"

"They are excessively cautious," Worf observed.

"To be sure," agreed the Daa'Vit. "No offense, Doctor, but sickbay is the one thing I will *not* miss about Starfleet."

Crusher chuckled. "Listen to you two. One would think you'd been here for days. It's been only a couple of hours." Finished with her examination of Worf's dressings, she moved over to Morgen's biobed.

"A couple of hours too many," complained the Daa'Vit as the doctor positioned her tricorder near his thigh. The gouge there had been deep, but it was healing nicely, with no sign of infection. "You can see we need no further attention."

"I can see," she countered, "that you know nothing about medicine. Or else you choose to ignore what you do know." She moved the tricorder up to Morgen's side, where he'd been badly slashed. "Just because you *feel* fine doesn't mean you *are* fine. Those healing agents and painkillers and antibiotics take their toll. The healing agents in particular—they soak up nutrients like a sponge, leaving just enough for the body's other functions. A little too much physical activity and you'll be flat on your backs, wishing you had enough strength to scratch your nose."

Worf made a derisive sound. "You underestimate the Klingon constitution, Doctor." He considered Morgen. "And perhaps the Daa'Vit constitution as well."

Morgen frowned as Crusher inspected his chest wounds. "Your colleague speaks the truth. Daa'Vit— and Klingons—are tougher than you may realize."

Satisfied with Morgen's progress, the doctor switched off her instrument and closed it up. "I underestimate nothing," she said. "Worf should know that, considering I've been treating him for years now. True, I've never had to medicate him for wounds like *these*—but I think I know a *few* things about Klingon biology." She replaced the tricorder in the pocket of her lab coat. "Now, if you were to say I've never treated a *Daa'Vit,* you'd be quite right. But I've studied up quite a bit on the subject."

"Reading and doing are two different things," Morgen reminded her.

"I agree," Crusher assured him. "That's why I went to

the trouble of speaking recently with a Dr. Carter Greyhorse. You know him? Apparently, he's had some experience treating a Daa'Vit. Naturally, neither of us anticipated any problems, considering the nature of our mission to Daa'V. But he humored me all the same."

Morgen's eyes narrowed. He turned to Worf. "It's a conspiracy."

The Klingon grunted in assent. "No doubt."

Crusher noted with interest the relationship that had developed between the two. Of course, she wouldn't dare point it out to them. That would be the quickest way to destroy it.

Hell of a way to get closer, she thought. If the experience had lasted much longer, it would have killed them.

"In any case," she said, "I've got to go. The captain has called a meeting—you can imagine what it's about."

Worf slid off his biobed. "I should be there."

"No way," the doctor told him. "You'll stay right here. That's an order."

"But I am chief of security. And this is a security matter."

"I don't care if you're the"—she glanced at Morgen— "the hereditary ruler of Daa'V. No one leaves this sickbay until I tell them to. Got it?"

Neither Worf nor Morgen answered—at least, not audibly. But when Crusher left sickbay, she left alone.

Picard was the first to enter the lounge. It was quiet— almost unnaturally so. Outside, seen through the observation ports, the stars bore silent witness to his carefully controlled anxiety. He crossed the room.

Taking his place at the head of the conference table,

gazing at its polished surface, the captain had an over-whelming sense of déjà vu. He could almost feel the years peeling away, the dimensions of the room shrinking . . . faces swimming up at him. Those of Ben Zoma, Simenon, Greyhorse, Idun, Pug and—of course —Jack Crusher . . .

"Is Ensign Morgen all right, Doctor?"

"Fine," said Greyhorse. "He was just a little shaken up."

"And Lieutenant Asmund?" asked Jack.

Picard could feel Idun tense at the mention of her sister—but she gave no other sign of her concern.

"Likewise, Captain. She'll live to stand trial for the attempt on Morgen's life."

"Good. I am glad to hear that she will survive."

He had to be careful what he said. After all, it was Gerda who'd committed the crime—not her twin.

"I've got two men assigned to her night and day," reported Joseph. He glanced at Greyhorse. "The doctor's not pleased about it, but I told him those were your orders."

The captain nodded. "Indeed."

"What about the Klingons?" asked Simenon.

"The Victorious and the Berlin are only hours away," responded Ben Zoma. "They'll be escorting the good ship Tagh'rat to the borders of the Empire, where it will become an imperial matter. But the word from the emperor is that the splinter group will be dealt with harshly. After all, he wants this treaty as much as we do."

"What a damned sorry mess," said Greyhorse.

"Could have been worse," said Jack. "She could have succeeded."

"True," said the Gnalish.

Suddenly, Joseph stood. "Sir," he said, addressing

Picard, "I want to take full responsibility for what happened. If there are any repercussions—"

"We will all assume responsibility," interrupted the captain.

The security chief seemed mute for a moment. He hung his head, and when he spoke again, it was in a softer tone. "It's just that I don't know how this could have happened . . ."

". . . could have happened," said a voice outside the lounge.

Drawing himself up to his full height, Picard saw Riker entering alongside Data. The android's brow was wrinkled ever so slightly.

"It *does* seem highly unlikely," remarked Data.

"What does?" asked the captain.

Both Riker and the android regarded him.

"That what happened in the holodeck could have been an accident," said the first officer.

Data nodded as he pulled out the middle seat on the side of the table facing the stars. "That is correct, sir. It is possible that Lieutenant Worf inadvertently misprogrammed the holodeck, calling for a Level Three scenario to automatically follow Level Two. However, he could *not* have inadvertently instructed it to ignore his command to abort." Seating himself, he went on without pause. "The holodeck computer's mortality failsafe is designed to resist such instructions, to make them difficult for the user to implement—in order to avoid just this sort of occurrence."

Riker sat too—at his usual place, on Picard's left. "Of course, there could have been a malfunction—but you know how rare those are. We check the holodecks on a regular basis. Certainly, we would have caught on to a flaw that profound."

Halfway through Data's observation, Dr. Crusher, Counselor Troi, and Commander La Forge filed into the room. Geordi had something in his hand.

"And even a simple malfunction," said the android, "would not account for Chief O'Brien's inability to end the program from without. That would have depended on a different circuit entirely."

"In other words," expanded the first officer, *"both* circuits would have had to go haywire at once. A pretty big coincidence."

"Yes," confirmed Data. "The only practical explanation is that—"

"Someone tampered with the holodeck circuitry," said La Forge, tossing his burden on the center of the table. It slid a foot or so on the smooth surface before finally coming to a halt. "And that's exactly what happened." As he, Troi, and Crusher took their seats, he pointed to the bundle of wires and small black boxes. "There's the evidence. We found it behind one of the lead panels."

Picard picked up the bundle and turned it over in his hands. "Looks fairly complicated," he concluded.

"It *is,"* said his chief engineer. "Ingenious, in fact. And made from parts one might find around the ship."

"Naturally," said Riker. "A device like that would have been detected in the transport process."

"It appears," said Troi, "that someone among us is out to get Morgen. Or Worf. Or both of them."

The captain felt a muscle in his jaw beginning to twitch. He did his best to control it.

Riker frowned. "Someone was after Morgen once before. On the *Stargazer."*

Beverly turned to the captain. "But that was twenty

years ago. And she was apprehended before she could carry out her mission—wasn't she?"

Picard nodded. "Gerda Asmund was found guilty of attempted murder and remanded to the rehabilitation colony on Anjelica Seven. She spent eleven years of her life there before the authorities judged her fit to rejoin society." He sighed. "Shortly thereafter, she died on a freighter en route to Alpha Palemon. The ship was passing through a meteor swarm when its shields suddenly failed. Gerda was working in the hold; it was punctured, and she was lost with seven others."

"Her body?" asked Riker.

"Never found," said the captain.

"Then she could still be alive," Geordi concluded.

"Not likely," said Picard. "There were no containment suits missing. No shuttle craft unaccounted for."

"Still . . ." Geordi insisted.

Crusher leaned forward. "Captain . . . how much did Idun and Gerda resemble each other?"

It was a chilling thought.

"They were identical," said Picard. "I could barely tell them apart, except for the fact that Idun sat at the helm and Gerda at navigation." He shook his head. "But what you're suggesting seems a bit farfetched." He regarded Troi. "Counselor . . . have you sensed anything to make you suspect Idun is not who she seems?"

Troi shook her head. "No, not really. Just the sort of ambiguities one might expect from a human raised by Klingons." She paused. "Though I must admit, I have had little experience with Idun's sort of mind. There is a discipline there that keeps me from reading her emotions very well."

"What about the transporter?" asked Geordi.

"Wouldn't it have a record of her bio-profile? One we could match with her records?"

"Inconclusive," ruled Crusher. "If Gerda and Idun have the same bio-profile—which has been known to happen with identical twins—then we would have no way of knowing if Gerda beamed aboard in her sister's place."

"They *did* have the same profile," Picard noted reluctantly. "I remember that."

Riker regarded him. "And Idun was at Starbase 81 long enough for Gerda to make the switch." He looked thoughtful, then frowned. "But I have to agree with the captain. We're looking a bit far afield—especially when Idun *herself* has a motive."

"You mean revenge?" asked Troi. "For what happened to her sister?"

"Make that *two* motives," the first officer amended. "I was thinking more along the lines of her completing Gerda's mission."

"Completing . . ." Picard began. "To what purpose, Number One?"

"The same purpose as before," said Riker. "To create a rift between the Federation and the Daa'Vit. To eliminate any need for the Klingons to share a conference table with their old enemies. And with Morgen inheriting the crown of Daa'V, they could hardly have picked a better time to kill him. Not only would the Daa'Vit break ties with us, they'd be thrown into a state of internal disarray."

The captain shook his head. "Idun Asmund has served Starfleet with distinction for more than two decades. She has never given anyone any reason to doubt her loyalties." He straightened in his chair. "When Gerda made her attempt on Morgen's life, I decided that it would be the gravest of injustices to punish Idun for her sister's crime—and I have not changed my mind in that regard. If there is evidence to incriminate her, fine. But let us not judge her on her choice of sibling alone."

"All right, then," said Riker. "What about the others?"

Those at the table exchanged glances. It was not an easy thing to hold up one's fellow officers as murder suspects—particularly when the *Stargazer* survivors had become so well liked. And Picard sympathized; he was no more eager to hear such accusations than his officers were to voice them.

But someone had committed an act of violence on his ship. He could not allow that to happen again.

"Commander Riker asked a question," said the captain. "I want answers." He turned to Troi first. "Counselor?"

The Betazoid sighed. "Mr. Joseph is not a happy man, sir. He is bitter—disillusioned."

"Over his failure to advance his career?" said Picard.

Troi nodded. "Apparently."

"Do you think," asked the captain, "that his unhappiness would manifest itself this way?"

"It is difficult to say. I do not think Joseph resents Morgen in particular. If he has focused his resentment on anyone, it is Commander Cadwallader."

"Then again," said Riker, "Morgen was below him once in the chain of command—just as Cadwallader was."

"And when one is irrational," offered Crusher, "one may lash out at *anyone.*"

Troi shook her head. "Joseph is *not* irrational—at least, not as far as I can tell. But he *is* angry. At times, extremely angry."

Riker indicated the mess of wires and black boxes. "Does he have the knowhow to make something like this?"

"He is not an engineer," said Picard, "if that's what you mean. But security work does involve a knowledge of ship's systems."

"Greyhorse has some technical knowledge," the doctor offered. She shrugged.

Obviously, she did not believe Greyhorse was a viable murder suspect. The captain couldn't exactly blame her.

"What about Simenon?" asked Data, who had remained silent almost from the time he sat down. *No surprise,* thought Picard. Matters of motivation were not exactly the android's specialty.

"He would certainly have the expertise," said Troi. "But does he have a motive?"

"The Gnalish and the Daa'Vit have never been best of friends," Beverly remarked. "I remember Jack expressing some misgivings about Morgen and Simenon serving together."

The captain looked at her. It was the first time she'd brought up Jack's name since the *Stargazer* contingent came aboard.

"True," he said. "On the other hand, there was never any violence between the two peoples—thanks to Federation intervention. Nor did those misgivings ever become material. In fact, Morgen and Simenon always had a healthy respect for each other."

"What about the Daa'Vit angle?" suggested Riker. He looked at Picard. "We know that Morgen has opposition at home. Would his political enemies go so far as to hire an assassin?"

The captain mulled it over. "I suppose it is possible," he conceded. "And the Daa'Vit are sufficiently spread out among the Federation for any one of our guests to have had contact with them."

Riker looked to the intercom grid in the ceiling. "Computer—has anyone in Captain Morgen's escort been to Daa'V?"

The computer responded instantly in a pleasant female voice. "Captain Ben Zoma, Commander Cadwallader, and Chief Joseph visited Daa'V one year ago on the *Lexington*."

"Their purpose?" asked the first officer.

"To deliver medicines requested by the Daa'Vit government."

Picard nodded. Pug on Daa'V, he thought. How could he help but read into the situation? Bitterness often made a man vulnerable. And if the proper incentive was offered into the bargain . . .

No. The captain would not prejudge Joseph any more than he would Idun. Pug had served him well on the *Stargazer;* he deserved better.

And yet, he could not allow his feelings to get in the way of his duty. Picard cleared his throat.

"I must say," he told the others, "it is extremely difficult for me to believe that one of my former officers is capable of murder. I would have trusted any one of them with my life—exactly as I would trust one of *you.*" He considered the device on the table. "But one cannot ignore the facts. We have a dangerous individual aboard —and we must find that individual. *Quickly*—before he or she can strike again."

"I'll organize the security effort," said Riker. "We'll have each of them watched around the clock."

"Good, Number One. But be discreet. Security personnel are not to discuss the matter in public—not even among themselves." He turned to Geordi and then to

Crusher. "That goes for engineering and medical personnel as well. I do not wish to put the assassin on guard."

Assassin. The word seemed so out of place here on the *Enterprise.*

"Counselor Troi," he said, addressing the empath in her turn. "Keep an eye on our visitors. Let me know if you sense any duplicity in them."

Troi nodded. "Aye, sir."

"In some cases, Counselor, you may have to seek them out. We may not have the time to carry on a passive investigation."

She nodded again.

Picard turned to the ship's doctor. "I trust Worf will be up and about soon?"

"I want to keep him—and Morgen as well—for observation overnight. Then they're all yours. But I wouldn't ask Worf to take on anything physically strenuous—not for a couple of days anyway."

That was fine with the captain. What he needed now was the Klingon's *mind*—his training in protecting the ship and its people from calculated harm.

"That will have to do," he said. "When you release him, send him directly to me."

Crusher promised that she would do that.

Morgen shook his head, stalking from one end of the captain's ready room to the other. Dr. Crusher had done a good job; Picard would never have noticed his friend's limp if he hadn't been looking for it. "It is out of the question."

Sitting behind his desk, the human frowned. "It is an eminently reasonable request."

"Not from my point of view."

"I am not asking you to lock yourself in your quarters —only to make yourself scarce."

The Daa'Vit eyed him. "And I categorically refuse."

"Damn it, Morgen. Someone has made an attempt on your *life.*"

"So you'd have me hide from them? Be fearful of them?" He sneered scornfully. "That is not the Daa'Vit way, my friend. I would have thought you'd know that by now."

Picard took a deep breath, let it out. He hadn't expected this to be easy, had he?

"Of course," said Morgen, "you could order me confined to quarters. That is certainly your prerogative." He stopped to face Picard, as if challenging him. "But then, you would be jailing the next ruler of the Daa'Vit worlds."

The captain decided against picking up the gauntlet. He wanted matters to proceed calmly—in an orderly fashion. And arousing Morgen's ire was the wrong way to do that.

Fortunately, a more subtle tack occurred to him.

"I would never think of it," he told the Daa'Vit. "Not even if you were still an ensign, and your crown was twenty years away."

That gave Morgen pause. "That's right," he said finally. "You didn't confine me to quarters then either." He tilted his head. "But then, the killer had already been caught—hadn't she?"

"We didn't know there weren't *other* killers aboard." Picard got up from behind his desk and came forward to sit on the edge of it. "Not for certain, we didn't. What's more, there was the matter of a Klingon escape ship to be reckoned with." He shrugged. "But at the time I was concerned with more than your well-being. I was concerned with your *education.* It occurred to me that if you were to become a Starfleet officer, you had to be treated like one."

Morgen nodded. "I'm grateful."

"You are quite welcome," said the captain. "And my trust was rewarded. Starfleet got itself a fine officer." He looked at the Daa'Vit. "A fine captain." A pause. "That is, before you became a dignitary."

"I beg your pardon?" said the Daa'Vit, his eyes narrowing.

Picard smiled. "Come, Morgen. Admit it. You are, for all intents and purposes, already the ruler of your people. You have left behind your status as a Starfleet officer—in your own mind, if not officially." He held out his hands. "You don't believe me? Recall, if you will, the threat you made a moment ago."

The Daa'Vit regarded him for what seemed a long time. "No," he said finally, his lip curling. "I was speaking in anger. Gods, the very thought of being a *dignitary*—it makes my skin crawl." He looked away from Picard and grimaced.

"Why?" asked the human. "Because dignitaries are notorious for ignoring what we captains know are best for them? Because they insist on endangering their lives for no good reason?" He nodded. "Yes, you are right. Those are things of which you could *never* be accused."

Morgen's head came up and his eyes locked again with Picard's. At that moment he looked like a prototypical son of Daa'V—one whose edges had never been softened by the Federation. Then, slowly, a begrudging smile spread across his face. "You are a master, sir. I salute you." He shook his head appreciatively. "In all that time I spent captaining the *Excalibur,* I never developed that knack you have for making a point."

"Just as well," said Picard. "Then you would have been *completely* insufferable—not unlike Ben Zoma." A beat. "You'll cooperate?"

The Daa'Vit's nostrils flared. "Up to a point," he agreed. "I'll make myself . . . how did you put it? *Scarce?*"

"That is indeed how I put it."

"But if trouble presents itself, don't expect me to run. I am still quite capable of handling myself, you know."

The captain had no doubt of it. "Fair enough," he said.

CHAPTER 8

Troi waited in the corridor outside the doors of Commander Asmund's apartment. Inside, she knew, her presence was being announced by a beeping sound. Nor could Asmund fail to hear the signal; it was audible in every part of her quarters, and the computer had confirmed that she was home.

Of course, the commander could ignore the beeping—indicating that she didn't want to be disturbed. Or she could simply say so via ship's intercom.

The empath was beginning to suspect the first possibility when the intercom suddenly barked out a single word: "Enter."

She gathered herself as the doors opened, revealing one of the apartments set aside for guests. The decor was moderate and subdued—designed more to avoid offense than to delight, since the ship's visitors had such a broad spectrum of tastes and preferences.

In special instances, of course, the apartments were completely redecorated—usually to impress a foreign leader or ambassador with the Federation's respect for other ways of life. The captain's guests, however, had no need of such special treatment. They were all used to Starfleet facilities of one sort or another.

Troi came in and looked around. No sign of Asmund.

"Commander Asmund?" she called politely.

"Be right with you," came the answer from somewhere deeper in the apartment.

The empath nodded, mostly to herself, and took a seat on a small blue couch. Above it was a painting—a replica of Glosterer's famous study: "The Molecular Structure of Certain Amino Acids." She took a moment to appreciate the subtleties of tone and color.

And tried not to reflect on her ambivalence about her mission here.

On one hand, she was doing exactly what she'd aimed for when she set out to be a ship's counselor. She was trying to help an individual who was having problems adjusting to her environment.

And Asmund was certainly having problems. One had only to witness her departure from dinner the night before to know that.

But she was also attempting to pin down a danger to the ship and its occupants. And while this was a part of her job as well, she was more used to gauging murderous intent in outsiders than in fellow officers.

Coming here under the guise of counselor was, in some ways, a subterfuge. A deception, if only by half.

That didn't sit well with her. Her nature was to be sincere, honest. What's more, her effectiveness as a counselor was based squarely on those qualities. If she were to obtain someone's trust, she had to first be confident she was trust*worthy*.

Yet the threat had been so immediate, the evidence so solid that there was a murderer on board, that Troi hadn't protested when the captain asked her to probe their guests' emotions. Nor would she back down now.

"Counselor Troi," said Asmund, bringing her out of her reverie. The woman was standing in the doorway that led back to her sleeping quarters. She was wearing a tight-fitting black jump suit of Starfleet issue; her hair, still wet from the shower, was combed straight back.

The empath started to her feet, and Asmund motioned for her not to bother.

"Can I get you anything?" asked the blond woman.

Troi shook her head. "No. Thank you."

Asmund went over to the apartment's food processing unit. "I hope you don't mind," she said, "if I have something myself."

"Not at all," said the ship's counselor.

With practiced skill Asmund punched in a series of instructions. A moment later a glass of thick dark liquid appeared on a tray, along with a couple of cloth napkins.

At first Troi thought it was a Klingon drink. Then, as Asmund came over and sat on a graceful highbacked chair, the empath got a whiff of it.

"Prune juice," she said.

The blond woman nodded, tucking back a lock of wet hair that had fallen onto her forehead. "You should try it sometime." Taking a sip, she set down the tray and then the glass on the polished black table that separated them.

"Perhaps I will," the counselor agreed, smiling pleasantly.

As they regarded each other, Troi got the same impressions she'd gotten before. Conflicts, uncertainties. The strain of maintaining a façade of humanity when her natural tendency was to be Klingon.

A mirror-image of Worf, she noted, and not for the first

time. One was trying to reconcile his Klingon heritage with his human upbringing; the other was trying to balance her Klingon upbringing with her human heritage.

There was a strange symmetry there. An almost poetic juxtaposition of opposites—what the Betazoid musicians of two centuries earlier would have called *aieannen baiannen.* Literally, *wind and water.*

But Troi had not come here to make esthetic observations. Probing more deeply, she searched for the emotional residue that would normally accompany duplicity in a human—the shades of feeling that would tip her off to Asmund's guilt.

"Tell me, Counselor," said the blond woman. "Why are you here?"

The empath looked her in the eye. "It is obvious that you are having some trouble coping. I was wondering—"

"If there was anything you could do to help?"

Troi maintained her composure despite the interruption. "Something like that. I know how difficult it can be to finally close a wound—and then to have it opened again by people and circumstances."

"Do you, Counselor?" Her voice was steady, giving away nothing. "With all due respect, I doubt it."

"Contrary to appearances," Troi responded, "I have had my share of heartaches. My share of loss. Of pain."

For a fleeting moment, she thought of Ian, and her heart sank. Then she recovered.

Asmund must have noticed her discomfort, because her attitude changed rather abruptly.

"I did not mean to make this a competition," she said. "I apologize." She shrugged. "I have had this conversation twice now—once with my present captain and once with Captain Picard. Both times I managed to convince myself that they were right; both times I made an effort to meet the others halfway. Both times I was unsuccessful." She shook her head. "Then I realized that the problem was not theirs, but mine."

"What do you mean?" asked Troi, though she had a fairly good idea.

"They may have forgiven me my association with Gerda—but I haven't." Asmund straightened in her seat. "How much do you know about Klingon tradition, Counselor?"

"A little," said the empath. "Mostly from my association with Lieutenant Worf."

The other woman stared into her glass. "The ancient Klingons had a law that if a person was not available to be tried for his crimes, his siblings might be held accountable instead." Her voice hardened. "Gerda was my sister. In human terms, I had an obligation to watch out for her. In Klingon terms, it was more than an obligation. It was a *'Iw mir*—a blood-bond."

Troi leaned forward. "Are you saying that you're in some way guilty of your sister's crime? As if *you* had committed it instead of *her?*"

"I know," said Asmund. "The Federation doesn't see it that way. Neither does the human part of me. Over the years, I think, my human self managed to submerge the guilt—the implications of the *'Iw mir.*" She frowned. "I believe, however, that my reunion with my former comrades has awakened my Klingon sense of responsibility."

"And that is why you cannot mingle with them? Because they remind you of the blood-bond?"

"That is my theory. Even if no one else will punish me for Gerda's crime, I will punish myself." She raised her glass and sipped. "What do you think, Counselor? From a professional standpoint, I mean?"

It sounded plausible. Troi was forced to say so.

"As I thought." Asmund put her glass down again and smiled grimly. "So you see, Counselor, I don't need to talk with anyone. I'm quite capable of diagnosing my own problems."

The empath tried to frame her words carefully. "Diagnosis is only the first step, Commander. Now that you know there is something wrong, don't you want to do something about it?"

Asmund stared at her. "From a Klingon point of view, Counselor, it is my responsibility to bear this guilt."

It was a difficult situation. Troi had to concede that.

"Would it hurt," she asked, "if we talked again?"

Asmund thought about it. "No," she said finally. "I suppose it wouldn't hurt."

"Good," said the counselor. "Then let's do that. As often as you like." She returned the other woman's piercing gaze. "And if I do not hear from you, I will take it upon myself to call."

Asmund nodded. "Fair enough."

Troi rose. "I am glad we had this talk." She smiled.

The other woman tried to do the same as she got to her feet—but in all fairness, she wasn't very good at it. Nor did she offer any further expression of emotion—gratitude or anything else—as the empath departed.

Once out in the corridor, Troi took a deep breath and frowned. Again, she had come up hard against Asmund's wall of self-discipline—a discipline born of hiding herself *from* herself. Of course, she had gotten some insight into the blond woman by virtue of their conversation—but nothing she could offer to the captain as an indication of Asmund's guilt or lack of it.

As for easing the woman's pain . . . perhaps she had made some headway there. But not as much as she might have hoped.

All in all, an unsatisfying conclusion.

Riker bit his lip as the doors opened to reveal Cadwallader's quarters. *Come on,* he told himself. *The sooner you get this over with, the better.*

She was sitting by the computer terminal built into the bulkhead, wearing her mustard-and-black uniform. "Hi," she said.

"Hi." He was glad she hadn't changed yet for dinner —particularly when he saw the very feminine green shift folded neatly over the back of a chair.

Cadwallader turned and followed his gaze. "Not very neat," she apologized, "am I? I just can't help it. Leaving clothes all over is my vice."

"Tricia . . ." he began, but she was already up out of her seat and across the room. Picking up the dress, she held it before her. Riker could see that it was translucent in places—all the *right* places.

"You like it?" she asked. "I know it's bad form to show a date your dress before you've got it on, but—" She shrugged. "What can I say? Mum never trained me quite right."

He had known this wouldn't be easy. But he hadn't expected her to be so damned excited—so *vulnerable.*

"Tricia . . ."

She replaced the dress on the chair. "This is appropriate, isn't it? I mean, I've never had dinner in a holodeck. How does one dress for a meteor storm? Or a hot, steaming jungle—"

"Tricia!"

She stopped short, surprised by the tone of his voice. "Excuse me. Did I say something wrong?"

Riker cursed himself inwardly. He hadn't meant it to be like this. "No. It's not your fault. It's just that—" Here came the hard part. "Maybe this isn't such a good idea."

He might as well have told her he was a Romulan in disguise. "I beg your pardon?" she said.

"You know," he told her, "with both of us being officers . . ." It sounded lame and he knew it. But what else could he say?

Certainly not the truth—that she was a suspect in an attempted murder investigation, and that it prevented him from getting emotionally involved with her. If he listened to his heart instead of his head, if he kept on going the way he was going . . . it would be too easy to let something slip, something that would help the assassin achieve success the next time.

Not that he believed *Cadwallader* was the assassin. Far from it. But if Riker let out some detail of the investigation, and she unknowingly passed it on to the guilty party . . .

"Will," she said, "there are lots of officers who have . . . relationships with one another. It's not as if we're even serving on the same ship." She looked at him in a way that made his heart sink. "Or is there some other reason? Perhaps the bit of difference in our ages?"

He steeled himself, shook his head. "No other reason. I like you, Tricia. I like you a lot. But I just don't feel comfortable with . . . with what's happening between us."

She smiled ruefully. "That's too bad," she told him. "I thought—well, never mind what I thought." There was just the slightest trace of huskiness in her voice. "I guess

I'll see you around, then, eh? Maybe in the gym or something."

Riker nodded. "I wouldn't be surprised." And before he could falter—before he could change his mind about the line he'd drawn between his feelings and his duty—he turned and left the suite.

Even after he was outside in the corridor, the doors to Cadwallader's quarters closed behind him, he could see her expression. The disbelief. The disappointment. The embarrassment.

He felt like something one would scrape from the bottom of one's boots.

It was strange. The more time passed without any other incidents, the more it seemed that the sabotage of the holodeck had never taken place.

As Picard looked around the bridge, everything seemed so placid—so orderly. It was difficult to contemplate the possibility of violence in such a setting. Even the viewscreen, with its familiar image of stars stretched into taut lines of light, conspired to create an illusion of stability.

Of course, Picard knew that this was a pitfall he would have to avoid. As much as he wanted to believe otherwise, he knew that someone had attempted to kill Morgen—and perhaps Lieutenant Worf as well.

He could feel the Klingon's presence at the Tactical station—like an anchor in a sea of uncertainty. They hadn't pursued the possibility that Worf might have been the primary target and not Morgen. But then, given the presence of the *Stargazer* survivors, and the fact that the Daa'Vit's life had been threatened once before . . .

Playing devil's advocate for a moment, Picard asked himself if any of his former officers might have a reason for wanting Worf dead. As far as he knew, none of them had ever met him before they'd boarded the *Enterprise*. And the only one who had a reason to hate Klingons was Morgen—the very individual who had shared the security chief's peril in the holodeck.

It seemed far more likely that the Daa'Vit was the intended victim. But just to be sure, the captain resolved to discuss the alternative with Commander Riker. And with Worf himself, naturally, at a—

The captain's thoughts came to an abrupt halt as he felt the ship surge violently beneath him. On the viewscreen there was an accompanying shift—as the dashes of starlight shortened up considerably.

"Mr. Data," he said, "I gave no order to accelerate."

The android had stationed himself at the Conn station for the day to give Solis more practice at Ops. His fingers were fluttering over the controls at a quicker than usual pace.

"Nor did I initiate any change in speed," said Data. He swiveled in his seat to face Picard. "Nonetheless, sir, we *have* accelerated. We are proceeding at warp nine point nine five."

The captain shook his head, incredulous. The *Enterprise's* engines weren't supposed to be *capable* of propelling it that fast—at least, not for more than a few seconds.

"Are you certain?" he asked Data.

The android turned back to his console and checked. "Diagnostics confirm it, sir. Unless the entire computer system has malfunctioned, we are traveling at a rate equal to five thousand ninety-four times the speed of light."

Picard felt a slight queasiness in his stomach as he rose

and approached the Conn station. Normally, he didn't check up on his bridge personnel—particularly Data. But there was nothing *normal* about this.

Sure enough, the monitor showed that they were clipping along at 9.95. The queasiness grew worse. Could this have anything to do with the attempt on Morgen's life?

"How is this possible?" he asked the android.

"I do not know, sir."

One thing was certain—the ship could not be allowed to continue at this speed. Who knew what it would do to the warp engines? The hull integrity? "Slow to warp six again," he instructed Solis. *"Immediately."*

The dark-haired lieutenant looked up at him. "Captain . . . I know this sounds crazy, but the engines are *already* working at warp six. Or at least, what *should* be warp six."

Picard glanced at the viewscreen, as if it could tell him something his officers couldn't. But it yielded nothing of value.

"Mr. La Forge," he called.

"La Forge here," came the response.

"This is the captain. I'm up on the bridge." Picard licked his lips. "Commander, I want you to check on the warp drive—tell me how fast we should be going."

"*Should* be?" asked Geordi.

"There seems to be some question as to our speed," explained the captain.

"Sir, I just *checked* the warp drive. I felt a surge and I wanted to make sure everything was all right."

"And?" Picard prodded.

"Everything seems to be in order. As for how fast we're going . . . let's see." The captain could picture

Geordi checking his instruments. "That would be warp six."

Picard felt his teeth grinding. "Commander, what would you say if I told you we were traveling at warp nine point nine five?"

The intercom system was silent for a moment. "I'd say that's impossible," answered the engineering chief.

"And yet," the captain told him, "our external sensors indicate that we are doing just that. Nor is there any evidence of sensor failure."

This time, Geordi took even longer to react. "You mean we're exceeding top speed—and our engines *aren't?*"

Picard managed to keep his voice free of the frustration he was feeling. "That is how it appears."

"I'll be right there," Geordi told him.

The captain grunted. "Thank you, Mister LaForge." He turned back to Data. "For the time being, Commander, I think it would be wise to drop out of warp altogether."

"Aye, sir," replied the android. With practiced ease, he went through the necessary routine on his board. However, even after Data was finished, Picard could feel the vibration of warp speed in the hull—could see the streaks of light darting by on the viewscreen.

"What is going *on?*" he asked.

"I cannot say," the android responded. "The warp drive has been disengaged. Yet our sensors indicate that we are still proceeding at warp nine point nine five."

The captain felt a muscle in his jaw start to twitch. With an effort, he controlled it. "Then we cannot slow down," he concluded.

It was not a question, but Data answered it anyway. "That is correct, sir."

Picard resolved not to panic—not even on the inside. Geordi would be here in a matter of moments, he told himself. His chief engineer would shed some light on this.

He had damned well better.

CHAPTER 9

With both warp and impulse engines at rest, it was ominiously quiet in engineering. As Geordi entered ahead of Data, two faces turned simultaneously in his direction—those of Phigus Simenon and Wesley Crusher.

"Thanks for being so prompt," he told them.

"What's the matter?" asked Wes.

"Must be something serious," the Gnalish said. "You were up on the bridge for almost an hour."

Geordi nodded. "It's serious all right. That's why I wanted the best help I could get."

He headed for the master situation monitor and pulled up a schematic of the sector through which they were passing. The *Enterprise* showed up as a red blip in the middle of the diagram.

They all came closer to take a look.

"You'll note," Geordi pointed out, "that we're moving pretty quickly—especially in light of the fact that our engines have been turned off."

Data spoke up. "Warp nine point nine five, to be precise."

Both Wesley and the Gnalish looked at him.

"You're kidding," said the ensign.

"I am not capable of humor," replied the android. "As you know."

"I assume you've checked for quirks in the sensor systems," remarked Simenon. "After all, we know only what they tell us."

"Checked and rechecked," the chief engineer replied. "They're working just fine."

"So we're sailing along at warp nine point nine five, and without even lifting a finger." Wesley shook his head, disbelieving.

"Curious," agreed the Gnalish.

"Apparently," Geordi told them, "we've gotten caught in some sort of subspace phenomenon. A *slipstream,* for lack of a more precise description. And it's carrying us ahead against our will." He paused, looking at the others. "I don't have to tell you what this means."

"We'll be at Daa'V in a matter of hours," said Simenon. "And out into uncharted space in a few days."

"That's exactly right," the chief engineer said. "And from what I understand, there could be problems if Morgen's late for the coronation ceremony—*big* problems. After all, not everyone on Daa'V is thrilled to see him succeed to the throne, and they'd love an excuse for denying it to him. Which is why we left ourselves plenty of time to get him there."

"Or so you thought," added the Gnalish.

"Or so we thought," Geordi echoed. "And even at warp factor nine point two—the maximum speed the *Enterprise* can sustain for any extended period of time— we're going to be able to return to Federation space only one-fourth as fast as we're leaving it. In other words, every day out is going to mean *four* days back. So if we're going to solve this problem, we'd better do it soon—before we find ourselves in the middle of a major interplanetary incident."

"Or worse," said Simenon. "We don't know very much about subspace phenomena, gentlemen—but the ones we've observed seem to be quite variable. That means we may continue this way for a while—but it is more likely we will suddenly be released. Or carried along even *faster.*" He looked at Geordi in particular, his serpentine eyes slitted. "And then, of course, there is a fourth possibility."

The chief engineer nodded. "The nature of the anomaly could change altogether. We could suddenly find ourselves in a subspace whirlpool—or something even *more* violent."

"The moral being to get the hell off this roller coaster," the Gnalish amplified. "Preferably, *before* it has a chance to do us in."

Wesley straightened. "You can count on me," he told Geordi.

La Forge smiled. "I know I can, Ensign."

Data had already pledged his best efforts. The chief engineer turned to Simenon. "And you, sir?"

The Gnalish's mouth quirked, "What do *you* think?"

For a brief moment, Geordi flashed back on a question the captain had asked of him up on the bridge, when nobody else was listening: *"Commander . . . is it possible that this was accomplished by an act of sabotage? That we were somehow maneuvered into this slipstream you speak of?"*

At the time, Geordi had said it was *not* possible. And he still believed that. No one—not even the best mind in the Federation—had a good enough grasp of subspace phenomena to use one in setting a trap.

But whoever the assassin was, that individual couldn't have been too upset about running into the slipstream. It was a distraction—a complication that could only work to his or her advantage.

And if the murderer was Simenon—a possibility the chief engineer had to consider, even if he found it unlikely—he would have every reason not to see their work proceed smoothly.

"I think," Geordi said at last, "that I'm glad to have you on my team."

The Gnalish smiled. "Naturally."

As the doors parted, Riker entered the apartment.

Morgen was standing in the center of the foreroom, looking a little too much like a caged beast for the first officer's taste. "I trust," said the Daa'Vit, "that you're not here just to check up on me. I could hardly have complied better with the captain's wishes—much to the detriment of my disposition."

"No," Riker assured him, "I'm not here to check up on you."

"What then?"

"We've got a problem. And since it may affect your arrival on Daa'V, Captain Picard felt you should know about it."

At the mention of his homeworld, Morgen's attention turned up a notch. "I'm listening," he said.

"The *Enterprise* has run into a subspace phenomenon," Riker explained. "Something we've never encountered before."

"Has it thrown us off course?" the Daa'Vit asked.

The first officer shook his head. "No. Our course is

unchanged. But the phenomenon has got us traveling at warp factor nine point nine five."

Morgen's forehead ridged over. "What?"

Riker nodded. "I know how it sounds, sir. But it's the truth."

The Daa'Vit gestured to one of the chairs. "Sit, Commander. Please."

The human conformed to the request. Morgen sat across from him on a rather queer-looking couch—a stone-and-moss affair which had come from ship's stores.

"Now," the Daa'Vit told him, "say that again."

Riker spread his hands. He went over the whole business, leaving nothing out. After all, it was Morgen's right to know—not only as the next ruler of his people, but as a captain in Starfleet. And his initial surprise notwithstanding, the Daa'Vit seemed to take it in stride.

"You know," he told Riker, "we had our share of close calls on the *Excalibur*. Maybe more than our share. Somehow, we always seemed to get out of them." He smiled as he remembered, the surliness brought on by his confinement forgotten. "After a while, you develop a belief that there's no problem you can't solve—no trap from which you can't devise an escape." He looked meaningfully at his guest. "Do you know what I mean?"

The first officer nodded. "Yes, sir. I do."

"Some might call that kind of confidence a trap in and of itself. And I suppose it could be. But more often, I think it's an asset. Because if you really believe you're going to upset the odds, you generally will." Morgen ran his palm over a clump of moss on the couch, studied it. "I really *believe* we're going to get out of this, Riker." He raised his head, fixing the human with his yellow eyes. "How about *you?*"

* * *

"And that," said Troi, "is our predicament as I understand it."

The rec cabin was empty but for the six of them—Troi herself, Ben Zoma, Cadwallader, Joseph, Greyhorse, and Asmund. The ship's counselor looked from face to face. "Questions?"

"I take it Simenon is already involved in solving the problem," said Greyhorse, his voice implying criticism of the idea—which was usually the case when he was talking about the Gnalish.

"That is correct," Troi told him. "He is working closely with Geordi La Forge."

The doctor added, "Much to Commander La Forge's delight, no doubt."

That drew a murmur of laughter; even the empath had to chuckle. Only Asmund, who sat in the back of the room apart from the others, seemed less than entertained by the remark.

"And Morgen?" asked Cadwallader.

"Commander Riker is discussing this with him separately. After all, there are political ramifications to his late arrival which will have to be dealt with."

"Is there anything the rest of us can do?" asked Asmund.

Troi shook her head, noting how the woman's professionalism had come to the fore as soon as she'd heard about the emergency. Otherwise, she would probably have resisted meeting with the others.

"Not at the present time," said the counselor. "But if the situation changes, you will, of course, be notified."

"Have you tried to contact any of our other ships?" asked Joseph. "The *Lexington,* for instance?"

The empath nodded. "We have sent out communications beacons. However, as long as we progress at this speed, no other ship can catch up to us—much less help us."

Ben Zoma, who was sitting next to Joseph, clapped his security chief on the shoulder. "Well," he said, "we all wanted to know what was out there. Maybe now we're about to find out." He looked at Troi, his dark eyes full of good cheer. "Don't worry, Counselor. We served on the *Stargazer*—we're used to blazing new territory."

Troi was grateful for his help in keeping his comrades' spirits up. And for Greyhorse's as well—though that had not necessarily been the doctor's purpose.

"If that's all," she said, "I should be getting back up to the bridge."

No one objected. But as she made her way to the exit, she found Ben Zoma walking beside her.

She had a feeling it was no accident, but they were in the corridor—out of earshot of the others—before he confirmed it. "Counselor," he said, looking straight ahead, "there's a problem—isn't there? I mean *beyond* this slipstream phenomenon."

"A problem?" she echoed.

He turned to her, as serious as she'd ever seen him. "I've been at this too long not to know when something's wrong. First of all, there's an excess of security officers around—even if they're trying their best not to be obvious about it. Second, Morgen's spent an awful lot of time in his quarters lately. And third, the holodecks are suddenly off limits. Now, I don't know what the others think, not having discussed this with them. But I'd be surprised if they weren't a little suspicious as well."

Troi looked him in the eye. "If you have a question," she suggested, "you should take it up with the captain." She smiled, hating the need to be evasive. "Even ship's counselors aren't privy to *everything,* you know."

Ben Zoma didn't quite buy her act; she could tell. But for now, he let the subject drop. "Very well, then," he said, a glimmer of humor creeping back into his voice. Or was it irony? "I'll let you go now. I'm sure you've got other duties to attend to."

"Thank you," she answered, and headed for the turbolift.

Picard glanced around the conference table at Geordi's four-member crisis team. "I'm afraid I don't understand," he said. "How will reversing engines allow us to escape this thing?"

"It won't," said Geordi. "But it might slow us down—buy some time."

The captain nodded. "And time is a factor here, isn't it?" He considered the strategy from all angles. "What about the stress it would place on the ship? Will the hull stand up under such circumstances?"

"There's no way of knowing for sure," said Simenon. "But my guess is that the stress will be within manageable limits."

"Plus, we can administer reverse thrust gradually," Wesley advised. "That way, if we see there's going to be a problem, we can back off."

Picard drummed his fingers on the table. "It's risky."

Data leaned forward slightly. "Captain, our present position is characterized by risk as well."

Picard looked at the android. "I suppose that is true, Commander." He turned to Geordi again, his decision made. "Very well, Mr. La Forge. We will give it a try."

Rising, he tugged down hard on his tunic and led the way out of the observation lounge. As he took his seat in the command center, he saw Data proceed to Ops and

Wesley to Conn, replacing the personnel who had been posted there. At the same time, Geordi took up his position at the engineering station.

Since the seats on either side of the captain's were unoccupied, Simenon took one of them—where Riker usually sat. "You don't mind, do you?" he asked Picard. "After all, I have to sit somewhere."

The captain almost smiled. "I thought you *hated* to be on the bridge."

"It wasn't such a novelty back then," explained the Gnalish, already intent on the viewscreen.

"Really," said Picard. It felt good to have Simenon beside him again—just like old times. Nor could the suspicion that had fallen on the Gnalish quite dampen the captain's confidence in him.

Putting such thoughts aside for the moment, Picard raised his head and spoke. "This is the captain speaking. Secure all decks. In a few seconds we will be attempting a maneuver which may toss us about a bit—but not to worry. The ship is well under control."

It sounded good. Now they would see how much *truth* there was to it.

Picard nodded to Wesley, who had turned around in his chair to wait for the captain's signal. Facing forward, the ensign made the necessary preparations.

"Warp factor one," said the captain. "Reverse thrust."

"Warp factor one," Wesley confirmed. "Reverse thrust."

"Engage," said Picard.

A shudder went through the ship, but only for a second. Then it stopped.

"No problems with hull integrity or ship's systems," reported Geordi. "But we haven't slowed down one iota."

The captain frowned. "Warp factor two, Mr. Crusher. Engage."

Wesley executed the order. Again, there was a brief vibration.

"Still nothing," Geordi said. "No cause for alarm, no change in speed."

Picard noticed that Simenon was staring at him. He turned to face his former chief engineer, and the Gnalish looked down at his hand on the armrest. Four of his scaly gray fingers were extended; his thumb was folded back. When he looked up again at the captain, his meaning was clear.

"Warp Factor Four," commanded Picard.

"Warp Factor Four," said Wesley, complying.

This time the ship's trembling was more pronounced, and it lasted longer. But when it was over, the streaks of starlight on the viewscreen were longer and a little less frantic.

"Progress," announced Geordi triumphantly. "We're down to warp nine point nine one."

"Which means we've cut our speed by a third," said Simenon. He looked at the captain. "Sorry. It's the professor in me."

"Quite all right," said Picard. If they had been alone, he would have clapped the Gnalish on the back—as he'd had occasion to do so many times on the *Stargazer*. "How is the ship holding up?" he asked.

"Considerable stress on hull integrity," Geordi told him. "But we can handle it."

"Should we try Warp Factor Five?" asked Wesley.

The captain glanced at Simenon's hand. There were still only four fingers extended.

"I wouldn't recommend it," called La Forge. "I think

138

we're on the edge now. And we've slowed down considerably—why take the risk?"

"Then we will remain at Warp Four," Picard decided. "And Mr. Crusher—do not anticipate."

The back of the ensign's neck turned red. "Acknowledged, sir."

"All right," said Geordi. "We've bought ourselves that time we wanted. Let's do something with it. Data, Crusher, Professor Simenon—you're with me."

The Gnalish gave the captain one last look as he swept past—a look that said his contribution was all in a day's work. Then he was on his way to the turbolift along with Wesley and the android, his tail switching back and forth over the carpeted deck.

Geordi was leaning on a bulkhead, his arms locked across his chest. He looked at Simenon, Data, and Wesley in turn.

Not the most upbeat bunch, he remarked to himself. But then, he wasn't feeling too upbeat himself just then. Of them all, only Data was still holding his head erect—and that was only because he wasn't human enough to know when he was licked.

"We've been at this for hours, and we've got nothing to show for it," Geordi said. "I'm opening the floor to any idea, no matter how wild. Hell, it doesn't even have to be an idea—just a half-baked notion."

The others looked at him. Simenon grunted.

"I mean it," Geordi said. *"Anything."*

Wesley straightened a little. "Okay. What if we separated the saucer section from the battle bridge?"

Simenon shook his head. "It wouldn't help. If we were moving strictly under engine power and you disconnected the saucer, it would drop out of warp. But since the warp field is being imposed on us externally, the saucer would continue to be dragged along with the battle bridge."

The android nodded. "That would be the most likely result."

"I agree," said Geordi. "All right—forget separation. How about the shuttles?"

"Same thing," responded the Gnalish. "They'd be stuck here just as we are."

"They might proceed more slowly," offered Data, "because of their lesser mass. Remember, we are not in normal space; Newtonian principles may not hold here."

"And what if they *did* proceed more slowly?" asked Simenon. "It would only be a stop-gap maneuver."

"Besides," said Wes, "none of them can travel faster than warp one—so whatever advantage we enjoyed on the way out we'd lose in spades on the way back."

Geordi nodded. "Even assuming there were enough of them to evacuate the ship—which there aren't, even including the lifeboat pods. Next."

"We launch a probe," said the Gnalish. "And then we blast it with photon torpedoes. Our shields should protect us from any damage, but the backlash—" Abruptly, he waved the idea away. "No. If we wanted to go backward more forcefully, all we'd have to do is go to warp five."

"That's right," said Geordi. "And we've already scotched that idea because of the safety factor."

Data's brow creased. "It may be that we are approaching the problem the wrong way."

"What do you mean?" asked Wes.

The android looked at him. "We seem to be focusing

on finding a way to slow down. Perhaps it would help us more to *speed up.*"

That *was* a fresh slant. "Go on," said Geordi.

"The slipstream is carrying us forward at warp nine point nine five. If we can exceed that speed, we might be able to outrun the phenomenon's frontal horizon—assuming it has one—and thereby free ourselves."

It was almost childlike in its conception. And yet, in a common-sense kind of way, it seemed as if it could work.

Of course, there was a rather large *practical* problem.

"You're talking about the ship traveling in excess of warp nine point nine five," Geordi pointed out. "We've never done that before."

"We've never *tried,*" said Wes.

"And if Mr. Data is right about there being a frontal horizon," added Simenon, "it might take only a fraction of a second to pierce it."

"Or it could take millennia," the chief engineer reminded him.

"Yes," the Gnalish conceded. "Or that. It depends on the magnitude of the phenomenon. And where we are in relation to its boundaries."

Geordi mulled it over. "I usually like to give the captain more than one option."

Silence from Data and Wesley. Simenon rolled his fiery red eyeballs at the notion. After all, it had taken so long to come up with *this* plan . . .

"But in this case," said La Forge, "I think I'll make an exception.

Standing in the corridor outside Morgen's door, Crusher was starting to become a little concerned. After all, she'd been there for more than a minute, waiting to give the Daa'Vit his routine follow-up exam, and there had been no response to her presence. Of course, Morgen could have been taking a nap—but it seemed unlikely with all that was going on.

Finally, she tapped her communicator. "Computer—where is Captain Morgen?"

The reply was nearly instantaneous. "Captain Morgen is in the forward lounge on deck seventeen."

"Thank you," the doctor said out loud. As she headed for the turbolift, she thumped herself on the head.

Dumb, Beverly. You should have checked out Morgen's whereabouts before you came all this way.

Nor could she just call him via the intercom system. If someone were with the Daa'Vit, they'd wonder why the ship's doctor wanted to see him. No, she would have to seek him out in person—and drag him back to his apartment only if he were alone.

The turbolift doors opened at Crusher's approach. She stepped inside.

"Deck seventeen," she instructed. "Forward lounge."

The lift's movement was imperceptible except for a subtle hum. And since she hadn't been more than a couple of decks away, she arrived in a matter of seconds.

As she exited, she made a left and followed the curve of the corridor. The lounge appeared on her right, its doors open—not uncommon, if there was nothing going on inside that would disturb others on the ship.

Voices. One was Morgen's—subdued yet resonant. The other was female, human. Not Troi's, or she would have recognized it. Nor Asmund's, unless things had changed drastically since dinner the other night.

Cadwallader's, she decided. And as she entered the lounge, she saw that she'd guessed correctly. Ben Zoma's

142

Number Two was sitting across a small table from the Daa'Vit, engaging him in a game of sharash'di.

At Crusher's arrival, they both looked up. Cadwallader smiled. "Greetings, Doctor. Fancy meeting you here."

Beverly smiled back. "I saw the doors open and I couldn't resist peeking inside." She indicated the game board. *"Sharash'di,* eh?"

Morgen nodded. "Commander Cadwallader thought it was high time I left that stuffy apartment you've given me—and spent some time in this stuffy lounge."

The doctor wondered about that. Had Cadwallader lured the Daa'Vit in here for something other than a simple diversion?

Certainly, the woman didn't look like the type to go around assassinating people. But the captain hadn't omitted anyone when he'd ordered his former officers watched—and he knew them better than she did.

Maybe I should stick around, she told herself. For a while anyway, just in case—

Abruptly, they heard Picard's voice addressing them over the intercom. All three of them looked up.

"As you know by now," said the captain, "we are caught in a subspace phenomenon. We will be attempting to escape that phenomenon in a few moments. Once again, I must ask that all decks be secured."

Well, Crusher mused, so much for whether I should stay or go. Picard's announcement had taken that decision out of her hands.

Cadwallader gestured to a chair. "Have a seat, Doctor. After I thrash Captain Morgen, you can have a whack."

Picard sat back in his command chair. In front of him, Wesley and Data had once more taken up their positions at the forward stations. And as before, Geordi was off to the side at the engineering console.

But with Riker and Troi on the bridge, Simenon was content to take the proverbial backseat. He now stood next to Worf at Tactical, no doubt scrutinizing the efficiency with which the Klingon did his job.

"Mr. Crusher," said the captain, "reverse engines."

Wesley carried out the order. Abruptly, the ship seemed to shoot forward again. The light streaks on the viewscreen resumed their earlier velocity.

"Engines reversed, sir," said the ensign. "We are now proceeding forward at warp four—or at least that's our engine speed." He glanced at another monitor. "Our actual speed is warp nine point nine five—just as it was before."

Picard nodded. "Thank you, Mr. Crusher. Go to warp nine point six."

"Aye, sir." Wesley touched the necessary controls.

It had absolutely no effect on their velocity. The captain knew that even before Data announced it.

"Warp nine point nine," Picard instructed.

Still no change—other than the fact that their warp drive was laboring as hard as it ever had before. At this speed, the engines would hold out for only a few minutes—then they'd simply turn themselves off.

And as they accelerated beyond warp nine point nine, their ability to maintain speed would no doubt diminish accordingly—perhaps to no more than a matter of seconds. Nonetheless, the captain was inclined to approach his goal by degrees. He refused to play Russian roulette with in excess of a thousand lives.

"Nine point nine three, Mr. Crusher."

"Nine point nine three, sir."

Geordi spoke up: "Estimate one minute and forty-five seconds until engine auto-shutdown."

Picard could feel the thrum of the engines through the deck. "Nine point nine five," he said.

"Nine point nine five, sir."

The vibration in the deck grew worse, joined by a high-pitched whine. Picard set his teeth against it.

They were moving as quickly as the slipstream now. Keeping pace with it, as remarkable as that seemed. He thought he could feel the g-force pressing him back into his seat. But of course, that was just his mind playing tricks on him—wasn't it? Or had the inertial dampers reached their limit?

"Estimate auto-shutdown in nine seconds," Geordi said over the whine. "It's now or never, sir!"

With an effort, the captain leaned forward. *Come on, Enterprise!*

"Nine point nine six, Mr. Crusher."

"Nine point nine six!" Wesley repeated, unable to keep the excitement out of his voice. Nor did Picard blame him—no Federation vessel had ever traveled even *this* fast under its own power.

The ensign made the necessary adjustments—and holding his breath, or so it appeared to Picard, pressed the "enter" key.

Suddenly, the bridge was caught in the grip of chaos. The viewscreen seemed to burst with blinding light, while the whine became the worst kind of spine-shivering squeal. Worst of all, the captain felt himself thrust back as if by a giant hand, crushed into his command chair.

Then, as abruptly as it began, it was over. No whine, no vibration, no intrusion of g-forces. The viewscreen was blank, the ship's visual sensors having apparently overloaded. Picard took a deep breath, let it out.

He looked around. "Is everyone all right?"

Everyone was, though some of the bridge officers seemed to have lost their footing in that last violent moment. Geordi was one of them.

"Mr. Crusher," said Picard, rising and approaching the Conn station. En route, he gave his tunic a short, effective tug. "What is our situation?"

When Wesley turned around, he looked disappointed. "The warp engines are down, sir. And we're still moving at warp nine point nine five."

A bitter thing to swallow. But the captain accepted it with equanimity. "I see" was all he said.

"Life-support nodes have switched to impulse power," Data reported. "However, lighting and ventilation systems are experiencing widespread failures, though none that suggests imminent danger to the crew."

Picard nodded. "Thank you, Mr. Data." It occurred to him to pose another question. Turning to Geordi, he asked: "Did we achieve warp nine point nine six, Commander?"

La Forge shook his head. "I'm not sure, sir. We had some instrument malfunctions."

Picard accepted that too. "See what data you can collect," he advised. "Perhaps we can learn something from this."

"Aye, sir," said the chief engineer. "Just as soon as I get the engines up and running again."

The captain turned back to the viewscreen. Despite its emptiness, he could see imagined stars streaming by all too quickly.

Picard sighed. They had given it their best shot—and failed.

* * *

In the lounge on deck seventeen, the only illumination was supplied by the starlight that came through the observation port—and that wasn't much at all. However, Crusher's eyes were adjusting to the darkness. She could now discern her companions from the shadowy silhouettes of the furniture.

"Whatever our captain did," said Cadwallader, "it destroyed more than a few circuits. Even the emergency lighting's not working."

"Other parts of the ship may be in better shape," Morgen offered. "We should try to reach them."

"Seems like a good idea," said the doctor.

"The doorway is over *there,*" the Daa'Vit announced. Beverly felt him take her by the arm and usher her toward the exit.

"Careful of that chair." That came from Cadwallader, apparently guided by Morgen as well.

"I see it," said the Daa'Vit. "Thanks."

And a moment later they emerged into the corridor. Windowless, it was even blacker than the lounge. Crusher pointed to the left—a pretty useless gesture, she realized. If *she* couldn't see her hand, how could her companions?

"Turn to the left," she told them. "There's a turbolift a few meters from here. On the right—just past the curve."

"It's a good thing you're with us," said Cadwallader, "or we'd have a devil of a time trying to—"

Suddenly, the darkness ahead of them exploded in a burst of fiery red light. Instinctively, the doctor brought her arm up to protect her eyes—but before she could do even that much, she was wrenched off her feet by a pair of hands and sent flying backward.

A second blast followed the first; this time there was no doubt. *Someone was firing a phaser at them.* And judging from the odor of burning duranium in the air, that someone was out for blood.

Morgen cried out, then Cadwallader. Through the prism of her hot, burning tears, Crusher tried to see who it was that had attacked them, and where he was aiming his weapon.

But it was no use. There was too much happening and it was happening too quickly; all she could do was press herself against the bulkhead and call for help, and hope that the intercom was working better than the lighting system.

A third blast—a shriek and a curse, and the muffled thump of a body hitting the deck. Putting aside her fear, the doctor crawled in the direction of the sound, bracing herself for what she might find.

After all, the beam had pierced the bulkhead. There was no limit to the havoc it could have worked on a human body—or a Daa'Vit, for that matter.

But if she got there in time, she might be able to help. To stabilize the victim's condition until he or she could be transported to sickbay.

Never mind the fact that she might be a victim *herself* by then. She was a doctor, damn it!

Zzt—

She dropped flat against the deck as another ruby bolt sliced across the corridor—not more than a foot above her head. By its light, she saw the shape of the fallen figure before her.

Cadwallader.

Crusher couldn't tell how badly the woman was hurt, but the way she just lay there wasn't encouraging. As the darkness closed down again, the doctor snaked forward —far enough to close her fingers around Cadwallader's shoulder.

Suddenly, the corridor echoed with distant voices. Faraway lights cast grotesque shadows, and Crusher had an all-too-vague impression of the killer as he—or she—disappeared around the curve.

Morgen—visible also now—took off in pursuit, as the Starfleet captain in him gave way to the Daa'Vit hunter. She called after him, to remind him that the killer was still armed and had the advantage over him. He seemed not to hear.

Turning her attention back to her patient, the doctor noted gratefully that Cadwallader was still breathing. Her face was a mask of pain and the entire right side of her tunic was already crimson, but there was still hope for her.

She tapped her communicator. "This is Dr. Crusher. I need a trauma team on deck seventeen—*now.*"

Stripping off her lab coat, she tucked it under Cadwallader and up around her shoulder. Then she pressed down hard, in an attempt to staunch the flow of blood. The phaser emission had stabbed right through the woman, and the hole in her back was worse than the entry wound—but with any luck the weapon had been set on narrow aperture. Cadwallader moaned, her eyelids fluttering.

Come on, Crusher exhorted inwardly, as the security team bounded past her after Morgen and the assassin. *Come on, before she bleeds to death . . .*

CHAPTER 10

As the captain strode into the specially blocked off critical care area, Crusher and Morgen were there waiting for him. Cadwallader, he noted with some relief, was well enough to turn her head a bit in recognition of his approach.

The doctor looked worn out herself, but she managed a smile. The message was clear: in time, Cadwallader would be all right.

Picard nodded gratefully to her. Then he looked down at his former communications officer. She was pale—terribly pale—but her eyes were as warm and vibrant as ever. Her hand lay on top of the thermal blanket; he took it, squeezed it. Cadwallader squeezed back, surprising him.

"She's tougher than she looks," Morgen observed.

The captain grunted his assent, replacing the woman's hand on the blanket, then looked up at the Daa'Vit. "What happened?" he asked, the cold, flat calmness of his voice belying the anger that raged inside him.

"We were assaulted in a corridor during the power outage," Morgen explained. "A single assailant with a phaser. Adjusted to setting six, if the holes in the bulkhead are any indication."

"Setting six?" repeated Picard. "But—"

"I know," said the Daa'Vit. "Our killer must have disabled the communications module in the phaser so it couldn't talk with the ship's computer."

"The phaser didn't know it was on the ship," Beverly expanded. "So it didn't restrict itself to setting five."

"Then you recovered the weapon?"

"Unfortunately, no," the doctor said. "At least, not yet. Worf is looking for it now; I'm just speculating."

The captain frowned. "And you couldn't tell who it was? Not at all?"

Morgen shook his head. "It was too dark, and we were blinded by the phaserlight. After the security team scared him—or her—off, I tried to follow. But as I said, it was dark. And our assailant knew how to go quietly."

Picard gazed at Cadwallader again. "You say Mr. Worf is investigating?"

Crusher nodded. "He mentioned something about blocking off the area—so he could keep what happened from becoming common knowledge."

"I see," the captain said. "In that case, I'll be on deck seventeen if you need me." He looked down at Cadwallader again, managing a smile. "You do everything the doctor tells you," he advised. "I want you up and about in time for the ceremony on Daa'V."

Cadwallader's eyes smiled back at him.

When the call for Picard came up from sickbay, a chill played along Riker's spine. And when Dr. Crusher subtly declined to discuss the matter in public, the first officer's fears were pretty much confirmed.

There had been another attempt on Morgen's life.

And as before, someone had gotten hurt. But who? Had the assassin been injured in the course of being apprehended? Or was there another victim—maybe even a fatality?

Of course, Deanna was as much in the dark as he was. She wasn't a mindreader—not as a full-blooded Betazoid would have been. She could only gauge emotions—and neither the captain's nor Crusher's were telling her anything instructive.

On the other hand, someone had to look after the ship. So he and Deanna remained on the bridge, striving to remain calm—trying not to exchange too many worried glances.

In the past, when they were in trouble, Riker had been able to take solace in the celestial beauty captured on the viewscreen. But now, with the starpaths stretched as taut as tightropes—reminders of the slipstream that was propelling them toward who-knew-what—even that option was closed to him. He almost wished that Geordi's engineering team hadn't gotten the damned thing working again.

It seemed like years before they heard from Picard. And though his voice was well under control, the nature of his request only aggravated their misgivings: "Commander Riker. Counselor Troi. Avail yourselves of my ready room, please. I would like to have a word with you."

Getting up from the captain's chair, the first officer escorted the empath to the captain's private office. Since Picard wasn't actually inside, there was no need to wait until their presence was acknowledged. Instead, they walked right in.

Riker looked up at the intercom grid. "We're in your ready room, sir. What's happening down there?"

"Nothing good, Will. There's been another attack, as you probably guessed. A *phaser* attack. Cadwallader's been hurt."

Riker felt his throat constrict. "How badly, sir?"

"She'll recover completely, Dr. Crusher tells me— though it'll be a few days before she's ready to leave sickbay. And a couple more than that before her tissues have fully regenerated." A pause. "She was hit with a phaser beam at setting-six intensity."

The first officer gritted his teeth. At setting six, a phaser beam could punch a hole in duranium. Cadwallader was lucky she was even alive.

"Where and when was she attacked?" Deanna Troi asked.

"Deck seventeen," Picard answered. "She was with Morgen and Dr. Crusher, in one of the lounges, when we tried to outrun the slipstream. The killer took advantage of the power blackout to try again. Morgen and Dr. Crusher escaped without injury, but Cadwallader was not so fortunate."

Riker bit back his anger. "Did they get a look at the assassin?"

The captain's sigh was audible. "They did not. However, Mr. Worf is engaged in an analysis of the scene now. Perhaps he will turn up some clues as to the killer's identity. In fact, that is where I am headed once our discussion is over."

"Is there anything we can do?" the first officer asked.

"Not right now, Number One—you are needed on the bridge. I just thought you should know what happened."

"Thank you, sir," Riker said.

Picard didn't reply. Apparently, he had already started out for deck seventeen. In the silence, the first officer turned to the ship's counselor.

"Rotten news," she commented.

He nodded. Right about then he should have said something clever and optimistic—"silver linings" kind of stuff. That would have been characteristic of him.

But somehow, he didn't feel like it. All he could think about was Cadwallader, and how she might have died without ever knowing why he'd canceled their dinner. It was sort of maudlin—but hell, it was the way he *felt*.

He desperately wanted to see her. To sit down at her bedside and explain. But he couldn't. The captain had left specific instructions that he was to remain on the bridge.

"Will?"

Abruptly, he remembered that Deanna was standing in front of him. He'd been staring right past her.

"Sorry," he said. "I've got a lot on my mind."

She smiled—half sadly, he thought. "You care for her, don't you?"

He started to ask to whom she was referring—and then stopped himself. Denying something to Deanna was like denying it to himself.

"Yes," he told her. "I guess I do."

There was a time when he would have felt funny admitting that to her—a time when their own relationship was too fresh in their minds for them to talk about other lovers. But things had changed between them—for the better, as far as he was concerned.

"Now I understand," she said.

"Understand what?"

"The feelings I have been sensing in you lately. The conflicts. As long as Cadwallader was a suspect, you had to submerge your feelings for the sake of the investigation."

He said, "I had to break a date with her. It was one of the hardest things I've ever done—believe it or not."

"I believe it," she told him.

Riker looked at the empath. "Deanna, be careful out there, all right? If this could happen to Cadwallader . . ."

She put a hand on his shoulder—a gesture of reassurance. "I am a big girl," she told him, grinning. "But thanks all the same."

And gently but firmly she steered him toward the door.

Worf turned as the turbolift doors opened, cursing inwardly. He had programmed the lift to bypass this floor until their investigation was over.

Then he saw the captain come out into the corridor, and he realized that his order had been overridden by one of the few individuals on the ship capable of doing so. Nor did he have any problem with that—the bypass would be back in place as soon as the doors closed behind Picard.

He squared his shoulders as the captain approached, making his way through the crowd of security personnel carefully analyzing the assault from all angles. "Sir," said Worf.

Picard gazed with distaste at the phaser burns on the bulkheads—samples of which were being taken by Burke and Resnick. Then he turned his attention to the Klingon. "At ease, Lieutenant." He took a deep breath, let it out through his nostrils. "Anything to report— beyond the obvious, that is?"

The security chief extracted the phaser from his belt and handed it over. Picard's eyes narrowed as he accepted it.

"The weapon used in the assault," Worf explained, though it was all but unnecessary. "As we suspected, its communications module has been disabled." He paused. "We found it in a refuse bin about twenty meters forward of here. Apparently, the assassin did not want to take a chance that it would turn up in a room search— but was in too much of a hurry to decompose it."

The captain examined the phaser for a moment. Slowly, his eyes widened. "Lieutenant—this phaser—"

Worf nodded. "It is one of ours. Stolen from the security section."

Picard regarded him. "How could that have happened?"

The Klingon looked past him, trying to contain his shame. "Loyosha—the officer on duty—was found unconscious shortly after the attack. He was drugged— something in his food, I believe. It appears he was eating his dinner when he passed out. Of course, it is only a theory. We have secured the remainder of the food so it can be tested."

The captain frowned and returned the phaser. Worf replaced it on his belt. "Where did Loyosha's meal come from? The food service unit outside Security?"

"That is the most likely possibility," the Klingon confirmed. "We have secured the unit as well."

Picard nodded. "Good." He started to walk along the corridor, away from the main focus of activity, in the direction from which the attack had come. He would, of course, have been able to tell that from the phaser scars on the bulkheads. Worf walked along with him, silent at first.

Finally, the security chief swallowed. "Sir?"

"Yes, Worf." The captain wasn't looking at him. He was looking back and forth from one end of the corridor to the other, apparently trying to satisfy himself as to some aspect of the attack.

"Sir," said the Klingon, "if the food service unit was tampered with, it is my fault. I insist on taking full responsibility for the incident."

The captain turned to him. He had a strange look in his eyes—as if Worf's comment had struck some kind of chord.

"Lieutenant," the older man said finally, "we are dealing with someone who has an extraordinary grasp of this ship's systems. Considering the unit's proximity to Security, I am certain the assassin did not reprogram it in person. And if he—" He paused. "Or *she* reprogrammed it from afar, I am certain even Mr. La Forge would be hard pressed to say *how.*"

Worf scowled. "Nonetheless—"

Picard dismissed the idea with a wave of his hand. "Nonetheless *nothing.* You have more important things to do than waste time on self-recrimination. Do I make myself clear?"

The Klingon straightened, feeling appropriately chastised. "Aye, sir," he said.

"Now take me through this assault as you've reconstructed it. And don't leave out any details."

Worf nodded. "As you wish."

The critical-care area was off limits to all nonmedical personnel, with the exception of Picard, Riker, and Worf. Those were the orders Crusher had left when she'd gone to her office, in order to more closely analyze the vital-sign readings she'd taken from Cadwallader.

Simple. In retrospect, *too* simple.

She'd forgotten that Carter Greyhorse was a medical officer, and that none of her doctors and nurses—

who knew only half Cadwallader's story themselves—
would have a reason to keep the high-ranking visitor
out.

So when Crusher returned to critical care, satisfied
that the patient was safe from any serious complications,
there was her former colleague—hovering massively
over Cadwallader's unconscious form, one huge hand
brushing a stray lock of hair off her forehead. Before she
could say anything—after all, what *could* she say?—
Greyhorse had sensed her presence and turned around.

She had never seen him display much emotion. But
she saw it now. His eyes blazed beneath lowered brows.

"Damn it," he said. "Why didn't you *tell* me about
this, Beverly?"

Crusher shrugged. "It happened just a few minutes
ago. And we don't normally bring in visitors to help with
patient care."

He struck the biobed—hard. "When it comes to
Cadwallader, I am *not* just a visitor. I've put a lot of
effort into this woman over the years. When she's hurt, I
want to know about it."

"I'll take that under advisement," Crusher told him,
stiffening under his barrage. Then she remembered the
circumstances, and she forced herself to take a gentler
approach. "I know how you feel, Carter. She's your
friend—"

"She's *more* than my friend," Greyhorse said. He
glanced back at Cadwallader. "At Maxia, we had taken
some direct hits. Sickbay was a mess—fires all over. And
debris—I was pinned under some of it. It was nearly
impossible for me to get out—or for anyone else to get
in." A pause. "*She* refused to leave—at least until she
knew if I was alive or dead. Cadwallader and Picard and
a few others stayed behind while the shuttles were taking

off. Finally, she found me—cut me free of the wreckage just before sickbay became a bloody inferno. And with some help hauled me onto the last shuttle. By then I'd lost consciousness—too much smoke inhalation." He turned back to Crusher. "If not for Cadwallader, I would have died a pretty grisly death."

"I didn't know," said Crusher.

Greyhorse cleared his throat, a little embarrassed. "Now you do." He tilted his head to indicate the patient. "*Phaser* burns? Where in God's name did she get *those?*"

Crusher cursed inwardly. Too late, she looked up at the monitor above the bed, which had a full display of Cadwallader's tissue damage. Any doctor worth his salt could tell the molecular disruption patterns had been caused by a phaser beam.

There was no point in lying. Greyhorse was good; he would see through any explanation she could make up.

"Come on back into my office," she told him. "It's a long story."

Geordi shook his head. "This is crazy. Absolutely crazy. As if the slipstream wasn't trouble *enough!*"

Picard's intercom voice was ominous: "Keep an eye out in your section, Commander. If this killer of ours is as enterprising as he seems, and as adept at engineering . . ."

"I get the picture, Captain."

"Good. Picard out."

Geordi regarded Data, who was sitting on the other side of the chief engineer's desk. He took a deep breath, let it out. "It's getting scary," he told the android.

Data looked apologetic. "Intellectually," he said, "I recognize the concept. However, as I am myself incapable of fear, I cannot share the feeling."

Geordi grunted. "No need to be sorry about that. Right now it's important we keep our heads. No matter *who's* getting shot at—or sabotaged in the holodecks."

He regarded Wesley and Simenon though the transparent wall of his office. They looked as tired as he felt—particularly the Gnalish. With his snappy sense of humor and his alien appearance, it was easy to forget that he was verging on elderly. But a few days' worth of theoretical headbanging had made him start to look his age.

One thing he knew, at least, was that Simenon hadn't been responsible for the phaser attack. The Gnalish had been with him during the power dip and every moment thereafter.

Unless he had an accomplice . . .

"Should we not join the others?" Data prompted. "They will be wondering what is keeping us."

"I was just thinking," Geordi told him. If there was *more* than one person involved in the murder attempts . . . a *conspiracy* . . .

Simenon could have arranged the holodeck incident —and left the phaser attack to someone else. Maybe the Gnalish was able to get a signal to his co-conspirator that a blackout was in the offing, and that it would be a good time to take another shot at Morgen. Maybe—

"Nah," he said out loud. Why look for a complicated solution when it was most likely a solo operation? It was hard enough to believe *one* person was nutty enough to want to kill Morgen—much less *two.*

"Nah?" echoed the android.

Geordi smiled. "Just discarding a theory, Data. Nothing to be concerned about." He got up. "Come on. Maybe we can finish those subspace field calculations before I conk out completely."

Data looked at him in that puzzled sort of way. He was doing that less and less these days—but the engineering chief must have hit on a colloquialism with which the android wasn't yet familiar.

"Conk out," La Forge repeated. "As in stop due to lack of sleep."

As understanding registered on his face, Data rose too and followed Geordi out of his office.

Picard had never been more greatful for his ready room. Right now he needed time. Time to think. Time to absorb the sights of Cadwallader stretched out on a biobed and the corridors of deck seventeen blackened with phaser fire.

Time to put aside Worf's insistence on claiming responsibility—which had sounded so much like Pug's comments twenty years before, after another, equally horrible occurrence. . . .

In a little while he would return to his command chair. He would exude confidence. He would inspire others.

But not just now. For a moment at least he would lean back and close his eyes and try to obtain some perspective on the whole bloody mess.

Obviously, Cadwallader was no longer a suspect. The captain had read enough Dixon Hill stories to know that a murderer might injure himself to avoid suspicion—but Cad had been hurt too badly for him to believe that. And besides, the phaser had been in someone else's hands; both Beverly and Morgen had sworn to it.

Picard chewed the inside of his cheek. He couldn't help but feel that he was overlooking something. That there was a clue huddling in some dark corner of his brain, waiting only for him to shed some light on it.

I should know who is doing this, he told himself. *I was*

their captain, for godsakes. I should have some insight into them.

Indeed, how could he ask Worf or Will to find the killer when *he* couldn't? Who knew Idun and Pug and the others better than Jean-Luc Picard?

The answer welled up unbidden. *Jack.* Jack Crusher knew them better than their captain—better even than their own mothers, in some cases.

Yes. Jack would have known who was trying to kill Morgen. People had trusted him with secrets they entrusted to no one else. After all, how could anyone with that earnest, well-scrubbed farmboy face be capable of betrayal?

And in a uncomfortable way, the captain had been jealous of that quality in his friend—hadn't he? Picard shook his head. He hadn't thought of that for a long time—his envy of Jack Crusher.

It had never gotten in the way of their friendship, certainly. Nor had Jack ever known about it. But there was something in the young Jean-Luc Picard—the one who had taken command of the *Stargazer* with somewhat less assurance than he'd let on—that yearned to be loved the way Jack Crusher was loved. Not just respected or admired, but *loved.*

In time, of course, he had gotten over that. And it was precisely then that he realized he *was* loved—though in a slightly different way. People seemed to have an affection for Jack the first time they met him. In the captain's case, love was something earned over the course of days and months and years.

And who was to say which kind of love was better? Certainly not Jean-Luc Picard, for whom affairs of the heart were still more dark and terrifying in some respects than the farthest reaches of the unknown.

The captain gazed at the empty chair opposite him. *Ah, Jack . . .*

For a moment Picard imagined his friend sitting on the other side of the ready room desk, his long body folded up into the most businesslike posture he could manage.

"A problem, Jean-Luc?"

The captain nodded. "A big one," he confirmed.

"Anything I can help with?"

Picard sighed. "There is a killer on board, Jack. One of our friends—and he or she is after Morgen."

Jack's features took on a more serious aspect. "Trying to accomplish what Gerda couldn't."

"Exactly. And I haven't a clue as to which of them it is."

His friend nodded grimly. "When you have problems, you don't fool around."

"There's an answer, Jack. I know there is. I just wish I knew where to find it."

Jack appeared to want to say something—as if he had the answer to the riddle. As if he knew who the killer was. But in the end, he couldn't get it out. All he could do was shrug.

"It's all right," Picard said.

"I'm sorry," Jack whispered at last.

"No." The captain regarded his friend, missing him more than ever. "Really. It's all right."

Suddenly, the chair was empty again, though Picard wished mightily it were otherwise.

CHAPTER 11

Riker had wanted to come before this, but he couldn't exactly leave the bridge in the middle of his shift to pursue personal matters. As he entered sickbay, he caught sight of Dr. Crusher.

She was just emerging from behind the critical-care barrier—the one that separated Cadwallader's biobed from the rest of the facility. Noting his presence, Crusher regarded him. "Something I can do for you, Commander?"

"Yes," Riker said, "there is." He indicated the barrier. "I was hoping to visit with our guest."

The doctor frowned slightly. "She's sleeping now. She really shouldn't be disturbed."

His first impulse was to protest—but he subdued it, knowing it wouldn't do him any good. Beverly Crusher could be pretty stubborn when it came to protecting her patient's interests.

Besides, if Cadwallader needed her sleep, who was he to deprive her of it? His explanation of what had happened the other night could wait.

"If you need to know anything about what happened," Crusher told him, "you can ask me."

It took him a second or two to figure out what she was talking about. He shook his head. "No. Nothing like that. I just wanted to see how she was."

Crusher looked at him for a moment—and she seemed to understand. "Oh," she said. "In that case, why don't you come back a little later?"

He nodded. "I'll do that." A second thought. "Would it be okay if I just peeked in on her?"

The doctor thought about it. "I suppose that I can allow that," she decided finally. There was a twinkle in her eye as she said it.

The first officer smiled. "Thank you." And under Crusher's scrutiny, he advanced to the barrier.

Sticking his head around the side of it, he peered inside. As the doctor had informed him, Cadwallader was asleep. But her face was turned in his direction.

Riker sighed. To tell the truth, he had expected worse. But it was still something of a shock to see her lying there wan and weak-looking, when she had been spinning around a horizontal bar not so long ago.

"Commander . . . ?"

He turned and saw Crusher standing behind him. "I know, Doctor. I know." Reluctantly, he retreated from the barrier.

"Perhaps," she suggested, "I could let her know you were asking for her."

"I'd appreciate that," he told her.

As they walked back toward the center of sickbay, Crusher looked up at the first officer. "There's no need for worry," she said. "Actually, our patient is doing quite well."

He nodded. "That's good to hear, Doctor."

But he would continue to worry—and not just about Cadwallader.

There were the rest of the *Stargazer* survivors to consider as well. . . .

Data sat in engineering, going over computation after computation in his positronic brain. He had been engaged in this activity ever since Geordi had sent everyone on the crisis team to bed.

"No sense in killing ourselves," the chief engineer had said. "We'll be able to think a little straighter in the morning."

Simenon had agreed. Wesley too, though reluctantly.

But Data needed no sleep. So when Geordi and the others left for their quarters, he remained. And hours later he was still there.

Unfortunately, he hadn't gotten very far. There were too many variables in his equations, too many unknowns. If only he had a better understanding of subspace dynamics . . .

"Pardon me."

The android turned at the sound and saw Dr. Greyhorse standing behind him. The man shrugged his large shoulders.

"I guess everybody's called it quits for the evening."

"On the contrary," Data responded, swiveling around in his seat. "*I* am still here. Therefore, not *everybody* has called it quits."

Greyhorse's eyes crinkled slightly at the corners. "Right you are, Commander. Your logic is impeccable." He looked around. "But everyone *else* has called it quits—yes?"

"That is true," Data replied.

The doctor pulled up a chair and sat down heavily. "Too bad. I was hoping to lend a hand."

"In what way?" the android asked, curious now.

Greyhorse shrugged again. "You know. With this damned slipstream problem we've run into. I come from a long line of engineers, and I've had some training in the field myself. I just thought that I might be of service."

"I see," Data said. "I apologize. I did not know of your engineering background."

"It's all right. No one does, really."

"Are you familiar with the problem?" the android asked.

"Not exactly." Greyhorse chuckled dryly. "Or to be more blunt about it, hardly at all. I just know that we're caught up in a subspace phenomenon that's affecting our velocity."

Data nodded. "Allow me to give you a more detailed picture."

And for the next half hour, that's just what he did. For the doctor's part, he listened intently, interrupting only once or twice when he needed something explained in greater detail. Toward the end of the briefing, he didn't interrupt at all—a fact which Data took as a token of Greyhorse's increasing understanding. As it turned out, he was right.

As soon as Data was finished, the man began to rattle off suggestions. Good ones too. But they had all been suggested—and rejected—already. And of course, Data was forced to say so. After a while Greyhorse's enthusiasm began to wind down; he began to run dry of ideas.

"Lord," he said, "I guess I was right to go into

medicine after all. I wouldn't have made a very good engineer."

"On the contrary," the android told him, "your suggestions were quite good. The fact that they were made already is a tribute to your ability, not a condemnation of it." He saw Greyhorse's expression take on new life. "Remember, Doctor, three of the finest engineering minds in the Federation could not do any better."

The man looked at him. "Three? Who are you excluding, Data—not yourself, I trust?"

"I do not consider myself highly skilled in the area of engineering," the android explained. "A good engineer, as I have been told time and again, is one part knowledge and two parts intuition. I certainly qualify in terms of knowledge, but intuition is one of my weak points."

Greyhorse shook his head. "You know, Data, there's intuition and there's intuition. My relatives would fit your great-engineer model to a T. They're intuitive as hell—when it comes to machines, at least. But put them in a room with other humans and they have as much intuition as the furniture. Same with me, I'm afraid. I never wanted to be like them, but . . . well, you know the saying. The apple doesn't fall far from the tree. I'm a whiz when it comes to dealing with people's bodies. But when it comes to dealing with their minds—dealing with them as people—I'm a zero. A *robot.*" He smiled. "You, on the other hand, appear to be a machine. You *believe* yourself to be a machine. But trust me on this, Data. You're more human—more intuitive in many respects—than the entire Greyhorse clan put together."

The android found that hard to believe. He said so.

"You haven't met the Greyhorse clan," the doctor pointed out.

"No," Data agreed. "But I have met *you*. And you do not seem to be lacking in positive human qualities."

The doctor peered at him from beneath the ridge of his brow. "Appearances can be deceiving, Commander. Deep down I am a very uncaring person. You need an example?"

The android didn't quite know what to say.

"I'll give you one anyway," Greyhorse offered. He leaned closer. "I know about the attack on Tricia Cadwallader. I walked into sickbay and saw her lying there, and your Dr. Crusher told me the whole story."

Data was surprised, given the captain's orders to keep the assassination attempts secret. However, he didn't interrupt. He merely filed the information away for future consideration.

"I know," the doctor continued, "and yet I cannot really say I feel for Commander Cadwallader. Oh, I am concerned on a professional level—I have as much pride in my work as the next surgeon, and I hate to see it marred or mucked up. But as far as my feelings for Cadwallader the individual—the person with whom I worked closely for years and years—I find I have none. The fact of her injuries leaves me cold as clay."

Data cocked his head as he so often did when comprehension eluded him. "But what about your efforts regarding the slipstream?" he asked. "Did you not say you came to help?"

Greyhorse waved the suggestion away with his large, meaty hand. "Self-preservation, my friend. Nothing more, nothing less. If the ship is lost or destroyed, so am I. And I prefer to survive—to return to Starfleet Medical, where I can go on with my charade: the humane and dedicated healer."

He got up. Data watched him, trying to make sense of what the doctor had said.

"Sorry I couldn't be of more help, Commander. If anything comes to me, I'll let you know." He paused. "Oh, and . . . I'd appreciate it if you didn't mention my visit to Professor Simenon. He'd only mock me. You know, for overstepping my professional bounds."

"I understand," the android assured him.

"You see?" Greyhorse said. "You really *are* more human."

Then he left.

The captain was still sitting in his ready room, still thinking, when the sound of chimes interrupted his reverie. Someone out on the bridge wanted to see him. Picard looked to the room's only entrance, wondered briefly who might be out there. Then, reluctantly, he straightened in preparation for *whoever* it was.

"Come," said the captain.

The doors opened.

It was Ben Zoma. And he did not look very happy.

"Have a seat," said Picard.

His former first officer sat down on the opposite side of the captain's desk. It was a familiar position for both of them; they'd conversed this way on the *Stargazer* hundreds of times.

But this is not the Stargazer, the captain had to remind himself. And Ben Zoma was no longer his exec. What had his life been like for the past decade? Could he have changed enough to become a killer?

"Jean-Luc," began the olive-skinned man, no longer

his usual jovial self. "I want some answers. And I want them now."

Picard met his gaze. "What sort of answers, Gilaad?"

Ben Zoma leaned back in his chair. "Where is Cadwallader? And don't tell me you don't know. She doesn't answer my intercom calls. And when I went to her quarters, there was no answer there either."

The captain decided to be truthful—if only up to a point.

"She is in sickbay," he said. He watched for his friend's reaction, hoping to discern something that would give away Ben Zoma's guilt. And at the same time, hoping even more fiercely *not* to.

"Sickbay," echoed the other man, suddenly concerned. And as far as Picard could tell, the concern was quite genuine. "Is she all right? What happened?"

Here came the lie. It didn't exactly emerge trippingly from his lips.

"During the engine shutdown, emergency life support short-circuited on deck seventeen, causing an explosion in the ventilator shaft. An air vent blew out; Cadwallader was in the wrong place at the wrong time."

It *could* have happened that way. In fact, Geordi swore he'd actually *seen* an accident just like it—years ago, back on the *Hood.*

Ben Zoma nodded, taking it in. "And Cadwallader?"

"She's fine," said Picard. "Some minor surgery, that's all. She could probably be up and about tomorrow, though Dr. Crusher will no doubt want to keep an eye on her a little longer."

Ben Zoma nodded again. The skin between his brows crinkled.

"You know," he said, "when you serve under a man for almost twenty years, you come to know him pretty well. You know when he's tired, or frustrated, or saddened. Even a man like *you,* Jean-Luc—one who hides his feelings well." He leaned forward, not so much angry as hurt. "And you know when he's lying through his teeth. You, my friend, are lying through your teeth."

"Indeed."

"That's right. As I told your Counselor Troi, there's something happening on the *Enterprise*—something you're not telling us about. The beefed-up security, the holodecks being out of order . . . and Morgen's sudden inclination toward solitude. And now Cadwallader." He shook his head. "You can't tell me that you're not hiding something."

The situation dictated that Picard carry on the charade—that he continue to suspect Ben Zoma along with the others. But his instincts told him otherwise. And a starship captain, he had learned early on in his career, had to ultimately follow his instincts.

He took a deep breath. "You are quite correct," he told his friend. "I am lying. In fact, Cadwallader was wounded by a phaser blast. And Morgen has become a hermit at my request—after he nearly lost his life in a sabotaged holodeck."

Ben Zoma was silent for a second. Then he said: "Details. Please."

Picard sketched out the situation for him. By the time he was done, the man's eyes had narrowed to slits.

"So you see," the captain said, "someone is trying to kill Morgen. And more than likely, the assassin is one of *us.*"

Ben Zoma frowned. "I wish I could disagree with you." A pause. "Do you think it was Idun?"

"Personally," said Picard, "no. It's too obvious—especially after the way she has alienated herself from the group. Though I am sure the assassin would like us to *believe* Idun is guilty."

"Obvious or not, she's the only one with a clear motive," Ben Zoma pointed out. "Revenge for her sister's death."

"Commander Riker came up with another one—the completion of Gerda's mission."

Muscles rippled beneath the other man's graying temples. "I hadn't thought of that—but he's right."

Picard shook his head. "No. I still think Idun is innocent."

"A hunch?" asked Ben Zoma.

"If you like."

"You can't operate on hunches, Jean-Luc. Not in a matter like this one."

The captain smiled grimly. "It was a hunch, Gilaad, that led me to trust *you.*"

Ben Zoma smiled back. "Good point," he said.

Picard recalled something else from the meeting in the observation lounge. "Tell me about your mission to Daa'V. You were with Pug and Cadwallader, delivering medicines, as I understand it?"

The dark man looked surprised at the seeming non sequitur. "Yes. Decacyclene. The Daa'Vit were hit hard by Marionis syndrome, a virus that originated on Marionis Six—" He stopped as he saw what Picard was getting at. "You want to know if we came in contact with anyone opposed to Morgen's return. And if they could have influenced one of us."

"Exactly."

Ben Zoma shrugged, his eyes glazing over as he gave the proposition some thought. "There were those who asked after Morgen—but no one who actually came out for or against him. Not in my presence, anyway. And as far as influencing the others . . ." He shook his head. "I couldn't vouch for all the medical personnel—you'd have to ask my chief medical officer about that. But Cadwallader and Pug hardly left my side while we were down there. I doubt anyone could have tampered with them in any way."

The captain looked at him. "In Pug's case, it might not take much tampering at all." He chose his words carefully. "Gilaad . . . you see him on a daily basis. Has his resentment gone so far that it would make him want to kill?"

Ben Zoma answered without even thinking. "He's resentful, all right. And in some ways—small ways—it has affected his performance. Certainly, his drinking doesn't help in that regard either. You've seen how he puts away the synthehol."

Picard nodded.

"But I would bet my life that Pug has nothing to do with these murder attempts. Down deep, he's a gentle man. He always *was* a gentle man."

The captain sighed. "All true. But *someone* has designs on Morgen's life. And if it's not you or Cad or Pug . . ."

"I know," Ben Zoma said. "It's hard to imagine Simenon or Greyhorse practicing violence. And if Idun is innocent, as you say, that doesn't leave a huge number of suspects, does it?"

Picard looked at him. "No. It doesn't."

Ben Zoma spread his hands. "I wish I could be of more help, Jean-Luc. I really do."

For a fleeting moment he resembled Picard's vision of Jack Crusher. The captain blinked.

"That's all right," the captain assured him—just as he had assured Jack. "Eventually, I suppose, we will find the person we're looking for. I just hope Morgen survives until then." He squared his shoulders. "In the meantime, Gilaad, not a word of this to anyone. Not even Morgen or Cadwallader."

"You've got my word," said Ben Zoma. He stood. "And thank you."

Picard was genuninely confused. "For what?"

"For having enough trust in me to confide all this."

The captain nodded. "Just do me one favor."

"What's that?" asked Ben Zoma.

"Don't turn out to be the murderer."

His friend nodded. "It's a deal," he said.

Just then Beverly Crusher's voice came over the intercom. "Captain Picard?"

"Here, Doctor. One moment, please." He looked at Ben Zoma meaningfully.

"You want me to leave?" asked the other man.

"I do."

"But I already know what's going on. And it might be news about Cad."

"If it is," the captain assured him, "I'll let you know."

Ben Zoma frowned. "All right," he said finally. "It's your ship. I suppose you can conduct your investigations any way you like."

Reluctantly, the former first officer of the *Stargazer* got up and left. The ready room doors closed silently behind him.

Looking up, Picard addressed the intercom grid. "Sorry, Doctor. I had some company."

"I understand. In fact, I had some myself a few moments ago."

"Really."

"Yes. Greyhorse." She took a deep breath—so deep it was audible over the intercom system. "Captain, I told him what was going on. He barged into sickbay and saw Cadwallader and—and it was pretty obvious what had happened to her. At that point it made more sense for him to know than to have him asking a lot of questions all over the ship."

Picard cursed inwardly. If he'd been aware of this, he'd never have—

"Sir?"

"Doctor . . . our friend Greyhorse is not the *only* one who knows. I just let Ben Zoma in on the details myself."

For a second or two, Crusher was silent. "Well," she said, "it seems our secret is no longer as secret as we would like."

"That much is certain. I think it's time we had another meeting. I'll see you in the conference lounge in ten minutes."

"Aye, sir."

The captain stood. He could feel matters getting out of hand.

It was time to rein them in.

CHAPTER 12

Picard looked around the table—at Riker, Troi, Worf, and Crusher. "And so," he said, "I take full responsibility for my decision to confide in Captain Ben Zoma—just as Dr. Crusher takes responsibility for confiding in Carter Greyhorse. But I do not want anyone else let in on this—not under any circumstances."

"It's going to get harder and harder to keep it under wraps," Riker pointed out. "If Ben Zoma noticed, others will too."

Troi nodded. "Ben Zoma said as much."

"Nonetheless," the captain insisted, "we will do everything we can to maintain security. Any questions?"

There were none.

"Very well, then. Let us turn to our investigation. Counselor Troi?"

"Unfortunately," the empath said, "I have nothing of substance to report. A couple of our visitors—specifically Asmund and Joseph—have problems. But none I could point to as a prerequisite for murder."

Picard turned to Worf. "Lieutenant—your findings."

Worf scowled. "We analyzed the meal eaten by

179

Loyosha just prior to his losing consciousness. As we suspected, it was laced with a narcotic that induces sleep. The source of the meal was the food service unit near Security—which was programmed to include this narcotic in three of Loyosha's favorite dishes." He looked at Picard. "The unit showed no signs of tampering, sir. So it must have been reprogrammed from another location—just as you suggested."

"Reprogrammed from another location?" Riker whistled softly. "Our assassin's grasp of technology gets more impressive all the time."

Picard grunted. "What about the rest of your inquiry?" he asked Worf.

The Klingon's scowl deepened. "I personally traced the whereabouts of each visitor at the time of the blackout. Morgen and Cadwallader, as we know, were with Dr. Crusher. Professor Simenon was in engineering with Commanders Data and La Forge. Captain Ben Zoma, Dr. Greyhorse, Commander Asmund, and Chief Joseph were in their quarters. At least, that is the information recorded by the computer, based on the locations of the suspects' communicators."

"But," Riker reminded them, "it's a simple matter to remove one's communicator. Then one need not worry about being located—either at the moment of the crime or later on."

The captain nodded. "But thank you, Lieutenant. It was worth a try." He regarded the others. "Suggestions?"

No one seemed to have any.

"Are we beaten that easily?" he asked. "Perhaps we should just concede defeat now and get it over with."

That seemed to shake them up a bit.

Picard stood. "I do not care what it takes," he insisted.

"I want this would-be assassin found. Before he becomes an assassin in *fact.*"

He scanned the faces at the table. For a moment he could have sworn Jack Crusher's was among them. Then he looked again, and Jack was gone.

Steadying himself, the captain said: "This meeting is adjourned."

The holodeck doors opened on a majestic scarlet forest shot through with long shafts of golden sunlight. Wesley took a step inside, applying his weight to the seemingly mosslike substance that covered the open spaces between the trees. It was springy underfoot—so springy, in fact, that it was difficult to keep his balance. But after a few more steps, he found the way to negotiate it was to bounce along instead of trying to resist it.

The Gnalish wasn't immediately visible, but there seemed to be a path full of the springy stuff that cut the forest in two. Half walking and half bouncing, Wesley followed it, shading his eyes when the sunbeams got in them.

It was still along the path, windless and empty of animal life. No doubt, his presence had sent all the earthbound creatures scurrying into the bushes.

But it hadn't done anything to hamper the activity above him. Small flying things darted from branch to branch, looking carefree and idyllic. They weren't a whole lot different from the birds Wesley remembered from his childhood on Earth—though no Terran bird ever made those deep-throated sounds, or shed so many feathers as it flew.

Smiling, the ensign watched the flight of one feather as it descended directly in front of him. It glistened in the sun, dark purple around its stem and green at its fringes.

Intrigued, Wesley knelt to pick it up—and drew his hand back quickly as he felt the prick of something sharp. Examining his finger, he saw a bead of blood at the tip.

"If we were really on Gnala," said a voice, "you would have about twenty seconds to make peace with your gods."

Wesley jumped at the sound. He'd been so intent on the feather, he'd forgotten that he wasn't alone in the holodeck. Turning, he saw the Gnalish sitting with his back against a tree trunk, his scarlet robes exactly the same color as the foliage.

"I didn't mean to scare you," Simenon said, getting to his feet. "It just occurred to me that you might find a little background information interesting. Including what's poisonous and what's not."

The ensign looked at the feather in a fresh light. "It's so pretty. It's hard to believe it's harmful."

"Appearances can be decieving." The Gnalish smoothed out his robe. "There's an antidote, of course —but you would have to have taken it in advance. Once you've been pricked, it's too late." He shaded his eyes and pointed to the flying things among the branches overhead. "That's how they secure their sustenance. They wait until an animal brushes against a feather and is incapacitated by the poison. Then they descend and pick it apart. Quick workers too. Usually, they can clean a carcass before the poison shuts down the victim's brain."

It wasn't a pretty image. Wesley shuddered involuntarily, imagining a path full of tiny four-legged skeletons.

"Of course," Simenon went on, "the poison doesn't affect the *colunnu*—the flyers. They have a natural immunity to it."

Wesley let go of the feather. He watched it waft to the mossy ground. "I'm glad," he said, "that you decided to leave a few details out of your program."

The Gnalish grunted. "So am I. Back on Gnala, I used to have to wear thick boots to go for a walk in the woods." He picked up the hem of his robe. "Here, I can go au naturel."

Wesley looked at Simenon's feet. For the first time, he realized that the Gnalish was barefoot.

"So, young man, have you followed me in here for a reason? Or just to chat?"

Wesley smiled, a little embarrassed. "Geordi—I mean Commander La Forge—wanted me to make sure you were all right. You didn't show up in engineering this morning."

"If I was all right?" Now it was Simenon's turn to smile. "He could have found that out over the intercom. Commander La Forge just wonders what I'm doing in this holodeck when we have a problem to solve."

The ensign nodded. "I guess that's another way of putting it."

"And to solve a problem," the Gnalish went on, "we must stand around the master situations monitor, looking ominously at one another."

Wesley winced. "I don't think that's *exactly—*"

Simenon dismissed the notion with a wave of his hand. "It's all right. You need not defend your Commander La Forge. At his age, I would probably have approached it the same way." He regarded the ensign. "However, I am older and wiser now. And I know that the best way to approach a problem, sometimes, is to forget about it entirely." He indicated the scarlet forest with a sweeping gesture. "To play a little hooky, as your Earth expression goes."

183

He began to walk down the path. Wesley just watched him, not knowing exactly what to do. Should he continue to badger the Gnalish? Or consider his mission completed and return to engineering?

Suddenly, Simenon turned around. "Well?" he asked. "Are you coming or not?"

The ensign hesitated for a moment. "Me?" he repeated lamely.

The professor snorted. "I don't see anyone else standing there."

What the hell, thought Wesley. It wouldn't hurt to take a break—just a short one.

He started after Simenon.

"That's better," said the Gnalish.

"Where are we going?" asked Wes.

"Down to the lake. Where else?"

It wasn't very far. A couple of twists in the path, and they were there, the water reflecting the splendor of the trees that towered all around it.

Simenon stopped in the vicinity of a small pile of stones—one which he had gathered some time before, apparently, or else simply programmed into the scene. Abruptly, without a word to his companion, he knelt, his ruby eyes darting around until they fixed on something a meter or so away. Using his tail to sweep the ground, he brought his find closer to him—and when it was close enough, picked it up with his fingers.

Another stone. The Gnalish examined it. But after a second or two, he tossed it away. Watching the whole strange scenario, Wesley couldn't help but chuckle. It seemed so funny for an Academy professor to be squatting barefoot and scavenging for rocks.

"What are you laughing at?" asked Simenon, abruptly

indignant. "It takes time to select the right specimens." Holding yet another one up at eye level, he turned it around, inspecting it from various angles.

"The right specimens?" the ensign echoed. "Right for *what?*"

The Gnalish put the stone down in the pile and began to scrutinize another.

"For skimming, of course."

Wesley looked at him. "What's *skimming?*"

That got the Gnalish's attention; he looked up. "You mean you don't know?"

The ensign shrugged. "Should I?"

Simenon looked at him as if he'd just eaten one of the rocks. "*Should* you? Of course you should. Weren't there any lakes where you grew up?"

Wesley thought about it. "I . . . I guess so. But that was when I was really young. I've spent a lot of time on starships since my mom joined Starfleet."

The Gnalish looked a little sad—or was that the ensign's imagination? "You mean," he said, "you've never skimmed a rock? That's absurd! Every youngster skims rocks." He shook his serpentine head. "Well, we'll have to rectify that gap in your education right now."

He picked up one of the rocks he'd put in the pile—a small round one with one flat side. Aligning one of its edges with the inside of his scaly forefinger, Simenon took a couple of steps down to the edge of the lake, stopping only when the water was lapping gently at his bare feet. Then he leaned his upper body at a funny, almost awkward kind of angle—and sent the rock flying with a flick of his wrist.

The rock sailed over the water, hopping high into the

air three times before it finally sank some twenty meters away. The Gnalish turned back to Wesley, looking quite satisfied with himself.

"That," he instructed, "is how one skims a rock." He returned to the pile, bent, and picked up a replacement. Then, straightening again, he offered it to Wesley. "Care to try it?"

The ensign took the rock and tried to fit it into the curl of his forefinger as Simenon had done. The edge cut painfully into his skin.

"No," said the Gnalish. "You're holding it too tight. Let it rest on the side of your middle finger." And manipulating Wesley's hand, he showed him what he meant.

The ensign nodded. That felt better. Trying to lean as Simenon had, he looked at the Gnalish. "Now I just throw it?"

Simenon shook his head. "You don't *just* throw it. There's a knack to it." He pantomimed the procedure with his own empty hand. "You see? The bottom of the rock must be held parallel to the surface of the lake. And when you release it, you put a backspin on it—so that it remains stable when it hits the water."

Wesley went through the motion a couple of times until he felt he'd gotten the hang of it. Then he turned toward the lake, drew the stone back, and flipped it out over the water.

It turned sideways as it flew, made a loud *plunk* when it hit the lake, and sank like a—well, like a stone. The ensign frowned.

Simenon sighed. "I can see we've got some work ahead of us."

Riker had expected to see Beverly Crusher presiding over sickbay. It was only after he walked in and saw Dr.

Selar standing there giving orders that he realized Crusher had gone off duty. A few minutes ago, he calculated— the same time his own shift had ended.

Usually, he was on top of little things like that. But right now he was a little preoccupied.

He waited patiently for Selar to finish her other business. When she finally saw him standing there, she didn't seem the least bit surprised. "Commander," she said, inclining her head slightly by way of a greeting. "I was told you might be coming by."

That caught him a little off his guard. "Really?"

"Yes. Dr. Crusher mentioned it."

"Oh," he said. "Right." Boy, he really *was* preoccupied, wasn't he?

The Vulcan indicated the barrier behind which Cadwallader's biobed was situated. "You wish to see our patient?"

He nodded. "If it's not a bad time."

"Actually," Selar told him, "it is not a bad time at all." And without further ado, she led him back to the critical-care area, where they stopped as she leaned around the barrier. "Commander?"

"Mmm?"

"A visitor for you."

A rustling of the bedcovers. "By all means," the patient said, "let him in."

Riker smiled. Cadwallader's voice was stronger than he had expected it would be.

But Selar didn't allow him to go right away. "Please be brief," she advised. "Her progress is exemplary, but she looks better than she feels. We must help her conserve her strength."

"Don't worry," he said. "I won't wear her out."

The Vulcan gave him a wary look before departing to attend to her duties. Riker watched her go.

Then he came around the barrier and found Cadwallader looking up at him. She was propped on a pillow, her arms entwined across her chest.

She wasn't as pale as when he saw her last. But he remembered what Selar had said about that appearance being deceiving.

"You look rather comfortable," he told her.

She shrugged. "I suppose—considering I took a phaser beam not so long ago. Isn't modern medicine wonderful?"

He looked into her eyes. They had that old sparkle.

"Listen," he said, "I promised Dr. Selar that I'd stay only a min—"

Cadwallader frowned. "Bugger Dr. Selar," she told him. "I'm in much better shape than she thinks. Stay as long as you like."

His eyes narrowed in mock-reproach. "I think Dr. Selar deserves a little more respect."

Cadwallader grunted. "Dr. Selar deserves a good pinch." She considered him. "And for that matter, so do you."

He gave her his best apologetic look. "I know. I'm sorry."

"That was a lousy thing you did, Will Riker."

He nodded. "Just try to see it from my point of view. At the time, you were a murder suspect."

She looked at him questioningly. "You didn't really think that, did you?"

Riker shook his head. "No. But I couldn't take the chance that I was wrong. And even if you weren't the murderer, I couldn't just come out and tell you about the investigation. You might've given it away without realizing it—a nervous look at the wrong time, a slip of the tongue . . ." He let his voice trail off. He shrugged.

Suddenly, Cadwallader grinned. "You look pretty foolish when you're trying to apologize—you know that?"

He feigned injury. "Thanks a lot."

"Especially," she added, "when there's no need. I've had a little time here to think, you know. And it didn't take me long to understand why you did what you did." She put out her hand; he took it. "So don't get all maudlin on me. You're forgiven, as far as that goes."

Riker squeezed her hand. "I'm grateful."

"Besides," she said, "you'll have plenty of opportunity to make it up to me. That is, after we catch the murderer and give this subspace phenomenon the slip. And dodge whatever other perils pop up in the meantime."

He chuckled. "You sound pretty confident."

"I am," Cadwallader replied. "But then, I've looked death in the eye and lived to tell of it."

Riker rolled his eyes. She laughed softly—just as he intended.

"You know," he told her, "you're pretty remarkable, Tricia Cadwallader."

"Yes," she said. "I know."

Someone cleared her throat behind him. Even before the first officer turned around, he knew it was Selar standing there. She looked at him, one eyebrow arched meaningfully, not needing to say a word to make her message clear.

He turned back to Cadwallader. "Time to go. I'll see you soon," he said.

She nodded. "Soon," she echoed—showing just the least bit of doubt, and thereby giving the lie to all her brave talk.

It was with that unsettling impression lingering in his mind that he headed for the exit.

Beverly Crusher flopped down on her bed, bone tired. Not so much from tending to Cadwallader, though seeing to the woman's care had kept her in sickbay for quite a long time. After all, that was her job; she was prepared for it.

What had *really* worn her out was the *wondering.* The suspicion. And the knowledge that no place on the ship was really safe.

If the assassin could make the holodeck a deathtrap, why not sickbay? Or engineering? Or the bridge?

The killer had known the blackout was coming. Had been able to find Morgen at just the right time, under just the right circumstances. The attempt's failure might have come down to the only unlooked-for element—the doctor's presence. By being there, Crusher had given the murderer three targets instead of two. And that might have meant the difference between a timely rescue and a bloodbath.

If she hadn't thought to go looking for the Daa'Vit, or if she hadn't arrived before the blackout . . . the assassin might have succeeded. And Daa'V might have found itself without a monarch.

She couldn't avoid the thought: *it still might.* They had no more idea who the murderer was now than they'd had after the first incident.

He could even get me *here,* she mused. *Even here in my own quarters.* At any moment she might turn around and see those phaser beams stabbing at her again. Or maybe something else—something equally deadly.

No. The murderer is after Morgen, she assured herself. That's what all the evidence suggests. Alone, you're safe.

Before she knew it, she'd taken out the box of tapes. And a moment later she was rummaging through Jack's recorded messages again. Seeking security in the sound of his voice? Maybe. And why not? She had never felt so safe with anyone as she had with her husband.

She selected a tape at random—just as she had before. And as before, as she read the stardate, she recalled her circumstances at the time.

It was the hardest part of her stay in San Francisco. Still plugging through med school. Still pre-Wes, though many of her friends at the time were either pregnant or raising young children. And still waiting for that first shore leave, missing Jack terribly.

Maybe not the most riotous time in the life of Beverly Crusher. But that didn't mean Jack's tape would be gloomy as well. It always seemed his most upbeat messages came when she needed them the most—as if he'd had a sixth sense about her that transcended the thousands of light-years separating them.

What the hell. Without giving it another thought, she popped the tape into the player.

"Hi, Bev. I hope things are as exciting for you as they are for me."

Crusher closed her eyes and smiled. *Just what the doctor ordered.*

"We've just gotten back from Coryb, the fourth planet in the Gamma Shaltair system, where we were surveying the Coryb'thu civilization as a precursor to formal first contact. Up until now, the only surveys I'd been on were the flora-and-fauna kind—never anything that involved a living, breathing civilization. You can't imagine what it was like walking through their cities, brushing against them, exchanging smiles with them—and none of them ever suspecting that you weren't one of them. Kind of eerie and exhiliarating at the same time. And whenever it got more eerie than exhiliarating, there was Ben Zoma or Pug or Idun nearby to haul me back to reality.

"The funniest part was having to wear these prosthetics that Greyhorse designed for us. The Coryb'thu are basically humanoid, but the middle part of their faces extend forward into kind of a snout. The prosthetics created the same effect. And they weren't even all that uncomfortable. The only problem is they take a while to remove, which is why I'm still wearing mine as I speak. We cut a deck of cards to determine the order in which we'd have our faces restored to us—and I picked the two of diamonds. Oh, well. You know what they say—lucky in love, unlucky in prosthesis removal. And speaking of love—either that relationship of Greyhorse's ended as soon as it began, or I really *was* seeing things. I'll keep you posted on that."

Greyhorse's relationship? Beverly shook her head. There could hardly have been two subjects farther apart in her mind than romance and the former medical officer of the *Stargazer*. She wondered who the lucky girl might have been—assuming, of course, that it hadn't just been Jack's imagination getting the best of him. She'd have to ask Carter about it.

"Got to go now. As you know, we get only so much time in these subspace packets. Love you. Miss you like crazy. And study hard, damn it—someday, I want to be able to turn around and see you standing there next to me."

End of tape. Crusher sighed. Hearing Jack's voice

had had the desired effect. She felt better—much better.

Almost safe, in fact.

"There," said Simenon. "That's more like it."

Wesley frowned, visualizing the flight of his last toss before it sank beneath the surface of the lake. Two hops—not bad, but not great. The Gnalish had gotten as many as four without even trying.

"Don't stop to think about it," Simenon advised. "Thinking has nothing to do with it. After all, you're only throwing rocks—your ancestors did that with brains a good deal less developed than yours."

The ensign chuckled and picked up another stone. Positioning it the way the Gnalish had taught him—the procedure having become second nature by now—he pulled back and let it fly.

One hop, two.

Three.

And it wasn't done yet. With one last burst of energy, the stone leapt in a high fluid arc—the rock-skimming equivalent of a grace note.

Four. The ensign turned to Simenon. "Well?" he asked.

The Gnalish puckered up his face and grunted approvingly. "Much better," he said, studying Wesley intently. Something changed in his eyes, softened.

Wesley hesitated, then decided to say what was on his mind. It didn't look like he'd get a better opportunity. "Professor? You said you'd tell me more about my father—about how he died."

Simenon nodded, cleared his throat. "I did, didn't I? Very well, then." The Gnalish switched his scaly, gray tail back and forth over the forest floor, as if gathering himself. Then he began. "You're familiar, I assume, with the problem we encountered?"

"The Nensi phenomenon," Wes told him. "A ball of matter and energy thought to have its origin in a special category of supernova. Very rare, but very destructive—and almost impossible to distinguish from a rogue comet except at close range."

"Exactly. Of course, back then we had no idea as to its origin—and neither did Nensi—considering it was the first time anyone had ever encountered the bloody thing. In any case, it all but stripped the *Stargazer* of her ability to defend herself. Shields went down. Sensors went down. Weapons went down. And we started to record an overload in the starboard warp field generator. Shutting down the warp drive stabilized the situation, but there was still a lot of energy cycling through the nacelle. We were afraid that the generator would just blow up—and whether it would take the rest of the ship with it was anybody's guess. Remember, we had no shields with which to protect ourselves.

"Unfortunately, we couldn't just separate into two parts as the *Enterprise* can. But we had to disassociate ourselves from the starboard nacelle, and as quickly as possible. We batted the problem around until we were ready to chew one another's heads off. Any moment, we knew, we might be obliterated in midsentence. Finally, your father came up with a solution. Someone had to get outside the ship and sever the nacelle from the rest of the *Stargazer*."

Wesley had gone over this part in his head a thousand times. Going outside, cutting away the nacelle with phaser rifles, had been the only way. The *Stargazer* wasn't set up to fire on itself, even if ship's phasers had been working at the time. And to approach the project

through the power transfer tunnels was unthinkable—
they were too full of energy seepage from the warp field
generators.

"Naturally," Simenon said, "your father volunteered
—it was his plan. Others came forward also—Ben
Zoma, Morgen, Asmund, Vigo. Even Greyhorse. The
captain didn't like the risk involved. Hated it, to tell the
truth. But in the end, he chose a team of two: your father
and Pug Joseph. Both of them had had experience in hull
repairs. Both of them knew how to negotiate the ship's
skin. And since the transporters had been damaged
along with nearly everything else, that was pretty
important—to be able to get to the nacelles and back
again.

"They set out from the airlock nearest their
destination—a tiny one, used only in drydock to check
the torpedo-launch mechanism. For us, it served a
different purpose. The worst part was our inability to
track your father and Pug on our sensors. We could talk
to them through their helmet communicators, but that
was about it. And once they got going, there wasn't a
great deal of conversation—as little as possible, in fact.
Just a remark now and then to let us know everything
was all right."

The Gnalish snorted. "Anyway, they reached the
nacelle assembly pretty quickly. But it took forever to
cut through it. The *Stargazer*'s transfer tunnels weren't
as wide as what you've got here on the *Enterprise*—but
they weren't pipe cleaners either. And as you know,
phaser rifles can't sustain a beam indefinitely. They've
got to be given time to cool down. So while we waited on
the bridge, strung tight as Vulcan harpstrings, your
father and Pug hacked away until their limbs were
trembling with the strain.

"The tricky part was when they got into the transfer tunnel. With all the energy in there already, the phaser beam could have stirred it up even more—or had no effect at all. Most likely, we knew, it was going to be something in between—which is why Pug and your father had been cautioned to approach that juncture carefully.

"For a long time after they began that stage of the work, we heard nothing from them. The captain was as worried as the rest of us. He was about to call for a progress report, when your father's voice was heard over the intercom: 'We're in,' he said. 'And no problems to speak of. Just a lot of fireworks.' We thought the worst was all behind us.

"A couple of moments later, their communicators went dead. Nothing to worry about, necessarily. In fact, I'd predicted it would happen, what with all that energy running out of the assembly. But it was an ominous thing, that silence. Someone began to pace—I forget who. Ben Zoma, maybe.

"It went on like that for quite a while. The waiting, the pacing. The faces that looked like they'd been stretched too tight. Finally, there was no denying it—they'd been out there too long. Something had happened—something bad. Picard said as much. He said that someone had to go out and bring them back.

"As before, there were volunteers. But the captain wouldn't listen. He was determined to keep the body count down, he said; he was already thinking in those terms. Ben Zoma argued with him, but to no avail. Pulling on a suit, he went after your father and Pug.

"The explosion came sometime later. I don't remember exactly when. It felt as if we'd been pummeled by a giant fist. And when it was finished, we all stood there, afraid to move—because moving was a step toward facing the reality of what had happened.

"The worst possible event hadn't occurred—we hadn't been destroyed, the ship was still intact. The instruments showed us why. It wasn't the generator that had blown; it was just a pocket of accumulated energy. And the nacelle was floating free, which was what we'd wanted all along.

"But three of our friends were still out there. At last, Ben Zoma got up from his seat and headed for the turbolift. I followed. So did Greyhorse, though he was barking orders to his trauma team the whole time. The others had to stay at their posts.

"We got to the airlock about the same time as Greyhorse's people. There were also a couple of security guards, handpicked by Pug beforehand. They started to put on containment suits—but before they could get out of the lock, they saw Picard coming in. And he had Pug with him—alive.

"The captain had found him drifting alongside the hull, unconscious. There was no way he could have brought both Pug and your father in at once—he had to make a choice, and Pug was closer. As it was, he barely managed to get them around the curve of the ship before the explosion. If he'd gone after your father instead, all three of them would have died."

He looked at Wesley. "The captain went back for your father, of course, but we all knew it was too late to help him. Afterward, Pug explained that the energy build-up had been too much for them, that they blacked out—first your father, then Pug himself."

He grunted. "With the nacelle assembly ripped away,

we were able to stagger away on impulse. So in the end, your father and Pug accomplished everything they set out to do. The only problem was one of them didn't live to see it."

Wesley found he had an ache in the back of his throat. He tried to swallow it away, found that he couldn't.

The Gnalish's eyes narrowed. "Are you all right, Ensign?"

Wes nodded. "Yes," he said finally, his voice huskier than he would have liked. "I'm fine. Really." He bent for another rock, trying to take his mind off his feelings. "Let me see if I can repeat that last performance."

After a moment, he heard Simenon grunt. "Of course." A pause. "The trick is to be consistent. There, that's a good one—the one to your—"

Abruptly, a voice came out of nowhere.

"Wesley?"

The ensign looked up at the holodeck's intercom grid, hidden in the illusion of scarlet treetops. *Oh, no.* How long had he been here? It seemed like only a few minutes, but Geordi's tone suggested it had been much longer.

Wesley steeled himself. "Yes, Commander?"

"What the devil is going on up there? When I sent you after Professor Simenon, I didn't expect the *two* of you to disappear."

The Gnalish snorted derisively and shook his head. Wesley tried to ignore him. "Sorry, sir. I guess I, um . . . just lost track of time."

"Lost track of—damn it, Wes! Did you forget what kind of mess we're all in? Maybe Professor Simenon has the option of fiddling while Rome burns—but you don't, not as long as you're wearing that uniform. Understood?"

The ensign grimaced. Out of the corner of his eye he saw Simenon pick up another rock. "Aye, Commander."

"Then get down here on the double. You can tell me in person what you found so enthralling that you—"

Geordi was interrupted by a high-pitched yelp that made Wesley whirl in alarm. His first thought was that the Gnalish had fallen into the water and was drowning. Of course, that was unlikely given his reptilian anatomy —but that didn't come to mind until moments later.

In any case, Simenon wasn't in any trouble, aquatic or otherwise. He was just standing there with a strange expression on his face. A wide-eyed, open-mouthed sort of expression.

"Wes? Is everything all right?" Geordi asked.

The ensign looked at Simenon. "I think so," he replied. He tilted his head to get the Gnalish's attention. "It is all right—isn't it, Professor?"

Suddenly, Simenon's features broadened into a smile. "You're damned *right* it's all right," he said. He looked up. "Mr. La Forge—make some tea. We'll be there in a minute."

Wesley regarded him. "Make some tea?" he echoed.

"I *like* tea," said the Gnalish. "Who do you think introduced your captain to Earl Grey?" He hurried past the ensign on his way to the holodeck exit.

Wesley fell in after him. "But—that *sound* you made—"

Simenon dismissed it. "I always make that sound," he shot back over his shoulder, "when I'm about to save the ship."

As Riker entered the turbolift, leaving sickbay behind, he knew that the place where Cadwallader had been attacked would yield no physical evidence of what had taken place there. The curving stretch of corridor had already been restored, the phaser-scarred sections of bulkhead replaced, and the bloodstains leeched from the floor covering.

But he still wanted to see it again for himself. He had the feeling that if he stood there long enough, if he gave sufficient thought to the details imparted by Morgen and Dr. Crusher, he would find an angle that Worf's security teams had overlooked.

At worst, he would feel as if he were making a contribution. The idea that there was a killer aboard had certainly concerned him before—but Cadwallader's close call brought the problem closer to home. Now it was *personal*.

"Deck seventeen," he said. Though he couldn't feel it, the turbolift started to move.

A moment or two later the doors opened. He stepped out.

And saw Ben Zoma kneeling in the middle of the corridor, eyes narrowed, intent on something in the distance.

The captain of the *Lexington* looked up as Riker exited the lift. He seemed surprised—but just a little. And he made no effort at all to cover up his interest in the place.

For a second or two they just stared at each other. Then Ben Zoma cracked a smile. "Fancy meeting you here, Commander."

The first officer refrained from smiling back. "Mind if I ask what you're doing, sir?"

The older man stood, winced, and massaged the back of his neck. "Damn," he said. "There's that tightness again. The old body's not what it used to be—though I'll deny it if you tell anyone I said that."

"You haven't answered my question," Riker reminded him.

"True," Ben Zoma said. "That was rude of me. On the other hand, I think you know why I'm here. I imagine it's the same reason *you're* here—to go over the scene of the crime. To see if there might not be something the others overlooked."

Riker nodded. "How long have you been here?" he asked.

"Just a few minutes."

"And?"

Ben Zoma shook his head. "No brilliant insights—unfortunately." He gazed past Riker. "The killer came from that direction—more than likely was already waiting for Cad and the others when they came groping for the lift in the dark." His nostrils flared. "I wish he were here now. And I wish I had a phaser too."

Riker regarded him. "Not exactly the kind of talk Starfleet encourages in its captains."

"No," agreed Ben Zoma, "it's not." He turned back to the first officer. "But then, there's no one around to hear it but the two of us." He cocked his head. "And if it were Dr. Crusher who'd gotten hurt, or Counselor Troi, wouldn't you feel the same way?"

Riker hesitated.

"Come now—be honest."

The first officer decided to be as honest as the dark man had been. "Maybe. But wanting and doing are two different things."

"No argument there," Ben Zoma told him. "Many's the time I wanted to take someone's head off—and didn't."

"I'm glad to hear it," Riker remarked.

"Well," said the *Lexington*'s captain, "I should be

going. Cadwallader could probably use some company. Though I'm sure Dr. Crusher will be as suspicious of my intentions as you are—*still.*"

The younger man shrugged. "The fact that the captain chose to trust you is a mark in your favor. But it doesn't *necessarily* mean you're not the killer."

"Absolutely right," Ben Zoma said, the corners of his eyes crinkling. "Now I know why Picard described you the way he did."

While Riker tried to decipher that last remark, the captain's friend walked past him into the empty turbolift. Just before the doors closed, he heard Ben Zoma utter a single word: "Sickbay."

Once inside the lift, Ben Zoma shook his head appreciatively. Some officer, that Riker. Jean-Luc's instincts had been right five years earlier, when he'd offered the man the first officer's position on the *Enterprise.*

He still recalled vividly their conversation on Starbase 52, where the *Lexington* had put in for repairs. Ben Zoma had been pleasantly surprised to find his former captain there, awaiting transportation to his new assignment, and Picard had insisted on standing him to a few drinks.

"I tell you, Gilaad, I never thought I would find an exec like you again. But I think lightning has managed to strike twice."

"Who is he?"

"His name is Riker. Will Riker. He's with DeSoto on the Hood."

"Yes. I think I've heard of him. His father's a civilian strategist, isn't he? Specializing in the frontier regions?"

"That's correct. He's one of the top men in his field.

And for my money, his son is even better." Picard leaned forward. *"You know DeSoto—he never says a good word about anyone unless he absolutely has to. And he sings young Riker's praises like a nightingale. Of course, DeSoto is not happy about the man leaving—he hates like hell to lose such a fine first officer. But he says Riker has earned the right to choose his own destiny."*

"Very impressive, Jean-Luc." Ben Zoma shook his head. *"A Galaxy-class vessel and a first-rate exec. What lucky star were you born under?"*

"You know, my friend, I ask that question of myself sometimes."

It was a moment before Ben Zoma realized that the turbolift had come to a stop. And another moment before he could wipe the nostalgic grin off his face, so whoever entered wouldn't think he was some sort of imbecile.

Then he saw who was standing there, and he smiled anyway.

"A pleasant surprise," he said. "I meant to come see you."

"Oh?" said the newcomer as the lift doors closed again.

"Yes. I thought we should—"

Suddenly, there was a flash of something metallic. Too late, Ben Zoma realized what it was. Before he could prevent it, the knife had slipped between his ribs and out again.

Lord, he thought, *I've found the killer. But not the way I had in mind.*

As a second strike headed for his face, he ducked— and the blade hit the turbolift wall instead. Carried forward by the momentum of the attack, his adversary fell against him and they grappled. Ben Zoma somehow found the hand that held the knife and managed to keep it at bay.

But he didn't have much time and he knew it. Already, his side was a fiery, gut-wrenching agony as his nerves woke to the damage inflicted on them. Nor did he dare look down to see how much blood he had lost—no doubt, it was considerable. Putting all his ebbing strength into a single uppercut, he managed to stagger the knife's owner backward. And at the same time to bellow at the intercom grid for security.

Unfortunately, his adversary recovered sooner than Ben Zoma had expected. This time he couldn't avoid the knife altogether—and it cut deep into his shoulder. Gritting his teeth against the pain, he slumped against the wall of the lift and kicked desperately at his attacker's knee.

By then, however, he was too cold and numb to know if his blow did any damage. The last thing he saw was the knife descending yet again. The last thing he felt was it plunging into his chest.

Worf estimated that four minutes had gone by. Four minutes from the time he heard the request for help until he reached the turbolift on deck thirty-three. It would have been faster for him to override the last occupant command and bring the damned thing up to the bridge —but for some reason the lift doors wouldn't shut.

Half a corridor away, he'd seen why. There was an arm stretched out across the threshold—to prevent just the sort of quick attention the Klingon had had in mind. Cursing out loud, he'd noted the blood on the bare hand.

And now, as he knelt beside the body, he cursed again. It was Ben Zoma.

The man had been stabbed a half-dozen times—at least twice in the chest. Nor could Worf ignore the fact, even in his eagerness to do his job and preserve Ben Zoma's life, that he had seen this kind of wound before.

Very *definitely,* he had seen it before.

Removing his honor sash and stripping off the top of his uniform, Worf wrapped Ben Zoma tightly in the fabric of the shirt. It would help to keep the man warm—an important measure, since he'd already gone into shock. Also, it might slow down the loss of blood—which had already been excessive, judging by the pool of gore on the floor of the turbolift.

Placing his forefinger against Ben Zoma's neck, the Klingon felt for a pulse. There was movement there—terribly weak, but discernible nonetheless.

"My God!" said a voice.

Worf looked back over his shoulder and saw the two women in civilian garb, grimacing at the sight of Ben Zoma. He couldn't recall their names, but he knew they were in one of the science sections. A moment later two other civilians approached from the other direction, immediately as stricken by horror as the first two.

"What's happened?" cried a man.

"Keep back," the Klingon growled. "The situation is under control."

It was only another moment before Dr. Crusher arrived with a medical team in tow. Making their way through the swelling throng of onlookers, they lifted Ben Zoma onto a gurney and moved him into the turbolift.

"Sickbay," Crusher said. At the same time, she was taking readings with her tricorder. "Give him twenty cc's of cordrizene. That ought to keep him going until we can stabilize his condition." Her voice betrayed none of the emotion she must have been feeling.

But when she looked up at Worf, her anger was hard not to miss. "How long," she asked in a subdued tone, "is this going to go on?"

"It is finished," he rumbled.

Her brows came together. "What do you mean? Did you get a look at the killer?"

He shook his head. "No. But I *know* who it is."

CHAPTER 13

As Riker followed Picard out of the turbolift, the younger man had to hustle to catch up. He had never seen the captain so intense—so driven.

It had to be hard on him, the first officer thought. He could only imagine how hard.

If it were anyone else, he would have suggested that they stay on the sidelines, commanding officer or not. In cases like this one, personal involvement usually led to trouble.

But Picard wasn't just anyone. Riker had never once seen him lose his composure, not in the four years and more that he'd served under the man. He could only trust that the captain would not make this instance the exception.

Down the corridor, the trio of armed security personnel was doing exactly what they'd been told—remaining silent and well back from the door monitor, so that they wouldn't alert anyone inside to their presence. They'd been instructed not to make any move on their own unless the killer tried to leave.

As Riker and Picard approached from one direction, Worf approached from the other. Momentarily, the first officer wondered why the Klingon was naked from the waist up—and then he remembered Worf's account of his discovery of Ben Zoma. He swallowed as he recalled the bloody details.

Quickly, wasting no time, the captain pointed to Worf and to Burke, who'd been in charge up until now. Then he indicated either side of the door, showing them where he wanted them to position themselves.

Even as he drew out his phaser, the Klingon looked none too happy about the idea. "Captain," he whispered, "you cannot go in first—"

But Picard cut him short with a simple raising of his hand. "I can," he whispered back, "and I will." He turned to the door, gathering himself. "This is my responsibility. I should have discharged it some time ago."

It was a clear admission that he'd been wrong about the assassin's identity—and that Riker had been right. But the first officer derived no satisfaction from the fact. There were no winners in this situation, only losers. And, unfortunately, Ben Zoma had been the biggest loser of all.

While the captain and Worf were engaged in their exchange, Burke had been working to override the door's programming with a security-level code. Finished now, he nodded to Picard.

"Ready, sir," he breathed, taking out his phaser. Holding it close to him, he pointed it at the ceiling.

Without hesitation, the captain walked forward, confident that there would be no beeping inside the apartment to serve as a warning of his approach. Stripped of any programming instructions to the contrary, the doors opened to admit him.

As luck would have it, the apartment's occupant was sitting at a table in the center of the reception room. She barely turned her head as Picard entered with Riker close behind.

Idun Asmund looked from one to the other of them, remarkably calm—though she had to know that they were on to her. Captains and first officers didn't just march into their guests' quarters unannounced. "To what do I owe the honor?" she asked, half smiling.

"You are charged," Picard responded, his voice flat and mechanical, "with the attempted murder of your fellow officers. On three separate occasions—including one just moments ago, when you savagely attacked Gilaad Ben Zoma with a *Klingon ceremonial knife.*"

The woman's brow creased. "What are you talking about? I haven't touched my knives since I came aboard. If this is a joke—"

"It's no joke," said Riker.

Asmund stood. She darted a glance out into the corridor, where she must have caught sight of Worf and his security team—because the crease in her brow deepened. She turned back to the captain, "Sir, if Ben Zoma's been hurt, I had nothing to do with it. You must believe that."

Picard's nostrils flared. "I wish I could, Idun. I truly do. But both Worf and Dr. Crusher agree—only a Klingon ceremonial knife could have inflicted wounds such as Ben Zoma sustained. *You* carried such weapons onto the *Enterprise.* And outside of Worf, you are the only one here practiced in their use." A pause. "What's more, you have no alibi—other than the computer record of your having been in your quarters at the time. But the computer only records the presence of your *communicator.*" He scowled—a sincere expression of his pain and regret. "I have no choice but to place you under arrest."

She shook her head. "You're making a mistake, Captain. If you'll tell me what's going on, I can—"

"You'll be notified of the charges in detail," said Picard, "once you're in the brig." He looked to Riker. "See to it, Number One. And don't forget to check her for poisons."

The first officer nodded. "Aye, sir." Worf had told him how Klingons imprisoned by their enemies often chose suicide as an honorable alternative to captivity.

"Thank you," Picard said.

It might not have been plain to anyone else, but Riker knew how this was tearing the captain up inside. Asmund had been part of his crew—just as he and Troi and Worf were now. No, more than his crew—his *family.*

It wasn't easy to confront the fact that a member of one's family was a murderer. Not under *any* circumstances.

As Picard turned to leave, Asmund appealed to him. "Captain—this is insane. I would never do anything to hurt Ben Zoma or anyone else. If anyone knows that, it's you."

Picard headed for the doorway, appearing not to hear her. And after he was gone, Worf filled the opening, glancing meaningfully at Riker. The first officer nodded.

He turned to Asmund. She stared back at him, hard. As if she were fighting to keep her grip on emotions so powerful they might rip her apart.

Momentarily, Riker's heart went out to her. It was a

terrible thing to see one who had been Klingon-bred fighting to maintain her dignity.

Then he remembered what had been done to Ben Zoma. And to Cadwallader. And his sympathy for the woman melted away.

"If you please," he told her, indicating the exit.

With a visible effort, Asmund collected herself. Then, without another word, she gave herself up to the security officers waiting outside in the corridor.

"Let me get this straight," the engineering chief said. "You think we can *skim* the *Enterprise* out of the slipstream?"

"In a word," Simenon answered, "yes."

They were gathered again around the master situations monitor in engineering—Geordi, the Gnalish, Data, and Wesley. And the ensign was finding it increasingly difficult to keep quiet.

It was Simenon's theory, Simenon's plan. So it only made sense for Simenon to explain it. But Wes was so sure it was going to work that he could feel himself bubbling inside with excitement.

"You see," said the professor, "I was teaching Wesley how to skim stones. You know—flat rocks?"

Data looked puzzled. "I am not familiar with the activity."

"That's all right," said Wesley. "You don't really have to be."

The android took the ensign's word for it. "Very well," he said. "Please proceed, Professor."

"Anyway," Simenon went on, "in all my years on Gnala and elsewhere, I've skimmed hundreds—maybe even thousands—of stones. But I never gave much of a thought to the principles of physics that govern it. After all, they are so basic, so simple, as to be taken for granted. The stone's surface and the water's surface collide; the resulting exchange of energy between the two objects impels the stone upward as well as forward. In short, it *skips.* Its momentum has been diminished some, thanks to things like friction and gravity and the energy absorbed by the water in the collision—but not by much, as long as two conditions are satisfied: the angle of collision must be fairly oblique and the stone must be relatively flat."

As the Gnalish paused for effect, Geordi leaned forward over the monitor to look at him. "Professor, this is all very enlightening. But what's it got to do with—"

Simenon stopped him with a raising of his scaly hand. "All in good time, Commander. All in good time." He frowned. "Where was I?"

"Fairly oblique and relatively flat," Wesley reminded him.

"Oh, yes." He punched up a schematic of the *Enterprise* on the monitor screen. "Let's say this ship is such a stone. It has left our hand, and is hurtling along parallel to and just above the slipstream."

"Excuse me," said Data, "but we are *in* the slipstream —not on it."

Simenon snorted. "Commander, you would never make it as an engineer—or a Gnalish, for that matter. There are very few precise analogies in this life— particularly when we're talking about something as esoteric as a warpspace phenomenon."

Geordi nodded, placing a reassuring hand on Data's shoulder. "It's all right, Professor. We'll bear with you."

"My gratitude," the Gnalish muttered, "is boundless.

In any case, the *Enterprise* is hurtling along, basically parallel to the surface—perhaps skipping every now and then without knowing it, because so little energy is lost in each collision. However, the collisions are what serve to keep us on the right path. Now, if we could somehow change the angle at which we strike the surface, we might go shooting off in a different direction entirely. If we approach it edge-down, for instance, we might go *under* the surface—which would put us in a completely different medium. A slower medium—just as regular space is a slower medium than subspace. Still with me?"

"Still with you," Geordi replied. "Of course—"

"Of course," the Gnalish interrupted, "we *can't* change our position. The slipstream won't let us—because we're dealing with not one surface, but many. In fact, they're all about us, surrounding us—bouncing us back on course with every little collision, channeling us forward. A good assumption?"

"It would appear so," Data replied.

"Fine. That leaves us only one other option—to change the shape of the rock. Or, rather, in this case, the *Enterprise.*"

The android looked more puzzled than ever. "Professor, are you suggesting we separate the saucer from the battle section—as was suggested earlier?"

Simenon shook his head. "Not at all. Because it's not really the ship that presents a surface to the slipstream."

Geordi snapped his fingers. "That's right. It's the *shields!*"

"Exactly." The Gnalish punched some additional information into the situation monitor, and the schematic began to move. "All we need to do is change the shape of our force shields—"

Finally, Wesley couldn't stand it any longer. "And in effect," he continued, "we'll be changing the shape of the rock. Instead of a streamlined object designed for maximum efficiency in flight, the slipstream will be confronted with an angled surface front and back."

"Which," Simenon resumed, seemingly without breaking stride, "should skim us out of the slipstream. No muss, no fuss. All we have to do is present opposition to the flow—at precisely the right angle. One that's obtuse enough to substantially change the force vector situation, but not so obtuse as to place intolerable stresses on the *Enterprise.*" He looked around, with particular attention to Geordi. "So? What do you think?"

The engineering chief frowned as he considered the idea. "It might work," he said, "and it might not. Even if the theory is sound, we're going to have to find the correct angle at which to pitch the shields—or we could be so much subspace debris."

"Isn't the what computer models are for?" Wesley asked.

For a moment Geordi thought about it some more. Then his frown dissipated. "All right," he decided, starting to input instructions to the situation monitor. "Let's see what we can come up with."

Picard frowned as he stood in Beverly Crusher's office, staring at the opaque barrier that separated critical care from the rest of the medical facility. The doctor sat across her desk from him, holding a cup of coffee in both hands. She looked terrible—worn out.

"Jean-Luc?"

He turned to face her.

"Are you all right?" she asked.

He nodded. "I am fine." Then: "What are his chances?"

Crusher took a deep breath, let it out. "Hard to say. We've transfused him, stabilized him—done everything we could. But . . ." She shook her head. "He suffered massive trauma. Lost a lot of blood." She looked down at her coffee. "He was in excellent health when it happened—that's a mark in his favor. But I can't tell you what the outcome will be."

He had never felt so helpless—so frustrated. *He is one of my oldest friends. And all I can do is wait. And hope.*

But not here. He had other business to attend to.

"Excuse me," he told Beverly.

"Of course," she said, managing a smile. "Don't worry. I'll hold down the fort."

As the captain left her and made his way through sickbay, he could see Riker waiting for him at the entrance—just as he had requested. The first officer straightened as he noted Picard's approach.

His eyes searched the captain's face as he wheeled out into the corridor. A moment later Riker used his long strides to fall into step beside him. "Not good," he concluded without even having to ask.

"Not good," Picard confirmed. Then, since there was nothing more that could really be said on that subject, he turned to another. "It appears we were mistaken, Number One—about Morgen being the only target, I mean. Gilaad Ben Zoma was alone when he was attacked. And in retrospect, one must wonder if Cadwallader's shooting was as unintentional as we first believed."

As the turbolift came up on their right, they turned and headed in. The doors opened as soon as the mechanism's sensor recorded their presence and closed after they were inside.

"Bridge," Picard instructed. Silently and without even a hint of motion, the lift began to carry them upward.

"Revenge," the younger man concluded, as if he had come to the end of an internalized dialogue. He turned to the captain. Judging by Riker's expression, the word had left a bad taste in his mouth. "Revenge on everyone who had anything to do with her sister's apprehension—and imprisonment." He paused thoughtfully. "But talk about a warped sense of justice. Gerda did what she did of her own volition; no one on the *Stargazer* twisted her arm. And once you knew about it . . . what else could you do but try to stop her?"

Picard frowned. "There was no other choice. You and I know that. But to Commander Asmund . . . who can say? It is not easy to accept the death of a loved one, much less a twin. Tragedy can do strange things to people's judgment—make them see villains where there are none."

Riker shook his head. "And not just tragedy."

The captain looked at him.

"Sometimes," the first officer explained, "the desire to protect will do that too. Look at us." He smiled ruefully. "I was seeing assassins everywhere I turned."

Just then the doors opened and the bridge was revealed to them. Though the command seat was empty, all seemed to be in order, so they proceeded to the observation lounge.

Once again a set of doors opened for them. They walked in and saw that everyone who was supposed to be there *was* there. With one exception.

The captain turned to Counselor Troi, who had chosen to wait for them by the door. "Simenon?" he asked.

"He's in engineering—a can't-wait kind of meeting,

apparently. Geordi says that they may be on to something." She paused. "Under the circumstances, I thought I would speak to the professor later—on my own."

Picard nodded. "I agree, Counselor. You were correct to let them be." He turned then to those positioned about the conference table. Morgen, standing by an observation port and frowning, his arms crossed over his chest. Pug, sitting at the table already, drumming fingers and looking more than a little leery. Greyhorse, waiting stoically with his hands locked behind his back.

"Ah," the doctor said. "At last. Now, perhaps, we can find out what's going on."

"Indeed," the captain assured him. "Please—all of you—sit down."

They sat. Picard and Riker were the last to push their chairs in.

The captain gazed at the expectant faces of his former officers. And at Pug Joseph's in particular.

"Before I go any further, Pug, I must tell you that the others here have an advantage over you—at least *some* knowledge of what has transpired. It was not by my choice that this became the case; it was dictated by circumstances."

Joseph shifted in his seat. He seemed more curious than resentful.

"Nonetheless," Picard went on, "I regret that it was not possible to let you in on the secret as well. I trust that you will understand—as a security officer and as a friend."

He turned to the others. "I have bad news. Gilaad Ben Zoma was assaulted just a little while ago in a turbolift on deck seventeen. He is in sickbay now—in critical condition."

Morgen cursed elaborately.

"My God," Greyhorse whispered. "*How* critical?"

The captain regarded him. "Dr. Crusher says there's no way of knowing at this point."

Pug just sat and stared. He seemed lost, unable to connect with what he was hearing.

"On the other hand," Picard added, "we have found the assassin. She is in the brig, under guard."

To Morgen and Greyhorse it was fairly obvious to whom he was referring. Besides Cadwallader, Asmund was the only female in the Daa'Vit's escort.

To Pug, however, it was not quite so obvious. The captain spelled it out: "Idun is the one who tried to kill Ben Zoma, Pug. Just as she tried to kill Morgen and Cadwallader earlier."

The security officer leaned back heavily in his chair. Finally, he uttered his first word since Picard had entered the room: "Why?" He looked around for help from his *Stargazer* shipmates. "What the hell would she want to do that for?"

Picard told him—about the attacks, the suspicions, everything. By the time he was finished, Joseph's complexion had darkened to an angry red.

"But now it is over," the captain announced. "It hurts me that Commander Asmund could have come to this. And it hurts me even more that Captain Ben Zoma is in such straits. But at least it is over."

Greyhorse sat up a little straighter. "Captain, if there's anything I can do . . ."

Picard shook his head. "Nothing at the moment. But I will relay your offer to Dr. Crusher."

The Daa'Vit trained his feral yellow eyes on the captain's.

I know, Picard responded silently. *We need to talk.*

* * *

O'Brien scanned Ten-Forward from his vantage point near one of the observation ports. The place was buzzing like crazy.

"News spreads fast around here," Eisenberg noted.

The transporter chief nodded, regarding the young man across the table from him. He'd met Eisenberg only a couple of weeks before, when the medical technician expressed an interest in joining O'Brien's notorious poker enclave. Of course, O'Brien had had to explain about the length of the waiting list, which was longer than ten *Enterprise*s put together.

But at the same time, he'd taken a liking to the fellow. In fact, in some ways, Eisenberg reminded O'Brien of himself at the outset of his first starship assignment. Eager but unseasoned, and a little daunted by the danger—which was considerable at the moment, the transporter chief had to admit.

That's why O'Brien had made it his personal mission to lighten the younger man's load. To help him forget his worries, if only for a little while. And Ten-Forward had seemed like the best place to do it—until the crowd began to pour in, all a-flutter with accounts of Ben Zoma's discovery and Asmund's subsequent arrest.

"Fast?" O'Brien gave out with a short, sharp laugh. "That's an understatement if I ever heard one." He used his glass to indicate the entirety of the lounge. "On a good day, you can start a rumor on the bridge at 0800 hours—and it'll reach the last table in Ten-Forward before you have a chance to close your mouth."

Eisenberg looked at him a little skeptically. "Really."

The transporter chief shrugged. "Well, maybe I'm exaggerating just a bit. I don't get up to the bridge that often, y'know. But I think you get the idea."

The med tech took a drink, then put his glass down. "I

guess everyone's just relieved. Can't say I blame them, either." He shook his head. "Can you imagine? A murderer on board—shooting phasers, plunging knives into people . . ."

"Tampering with holodecks," O'Brien added, thinking it sounded a little more benign—as long as one left out the details.

"That too. It gives me the willies just thinking about it. And for the murderer to turn out to be one of the captain's guests . . . damn. I thought they served with him a while back. I thought they were his *friends.*"

"They are," the transporter chief explained. "A bad apple doesn't make a bad bunch."

Eisenberg didn't seem to have heard him. "You know what they say. With friends like those, who needs the Romulans?" He sighed. "You should have seen that poor Ben Zoma fellow. I've never seen so much blood." The younger man's gaze grew distant.

O'Brien eyed him mock-seriously. "Y'know, Davey, you're starting to depress me. And that's not easy."

The med tech leaned back in his chair, genuinely repentant. "Sorry."

"Why don't you take a peek at the bright side? The woman's been caught. She's in the brig, where she can't hurt anybody else."

"I suppose so," Eisenberg told him. For a brief moment he seemed content. Then he started to think again. "But that's not our only problem, is it?" He glanced out the port, where the stars continued to streak by at an ungodly speed. "What about *that?* I heard that this phenomenon can suddenly change shape—become something else. And tear us apart like old-fashioned tissue paper."

O'Brien could see he had his work cut out for him.

"You *could* look at it that way—doom and gloom and all that stuff. Or you could tell yourself that Commander La Forge and his helpers will get us out of this—like they always do. And in the meantime, we have ringside seats for the greatest show in the galaxy."

O'Brien swung his chair around to face the observation port and the flat lines of light beyond it. Raising his glass in a toast, he said: "To warp nine point nine five. May she always be so beautiful."

Then, without looking to see Eisenberg's reaction too quickly, he took a sip of his synthenol and savored it. "Ah," he commented with a bravado he didn't quite feel. "What life's all about."

Finally, he gave his companion a sidelong glance. The younger man was staring at him.

"Join me?" O'Brien asked.

Gradually, Eisenberg lifted his glass. And smiled—if only faintly. "When you put it that way," he said, "how can I refuse?"

After everyone else left, it was just the two of them. Morgen paced the length of the observation lounge, looking for all the world like a caged beast. And the captain watched, leaning back against the edge of the conference table, his arms folded over his chest.

"Damn her," the Daa'Vit growled. "No—damn *me*. How could I have brought her aboard? *How?*"

"There was no way of predicting this," Picard told him.

"You're wrong," Morgen insisted. "I knew I was inviting trouble—in my heart, I knew. But I wanted to show her that I could put the past behind me. I wanted to be forgiving. Benevolent. All the things my years in Starfleet taught me to be." He shook his head. "And look where my benevolence has gotten me. Your security officer is endangered. Cadwallader gets a hole burned through her. And Ben Zoma—brave, goodhearted Ben Zoma—"

Suddenly, Morgen seemed to erupt—to go mad. He growled hideously at the top of his lungs and pounded his fists on the table. Picard's instinct was to retreat from the spectacle, but he stood his ground—reminding himself that the tortured creature before him was his friend. That he had nothing to fear from him.

Still, it was not easy. He had never seen such an explosion of Daa'Vit fury before—and he had no wish to see it ever again.

In the end, Morgen's fit lasted just a few seconds. But even when it was finished, his chest still heaved. "I am sorry you had to see that," he said.

"It is all right," the captain told him. "We are friends. Old friends."

"No," the Daa'Vit insisted in a deep slow voice. "It was . . . inappropriate." He massaged the fingers of his left hand. "But even so, I was right. I should have listened to my head, not my heart. I should have known better."

Picard could see no good coming of further self-recrimination. He decided to change the subject. "Will it hurt your ability to ascend to the throne?" he asked.

The Daa'Vit looked at him. "What?"

"Being without Ben Zoma and Asmund. Will it hurt you politically?"

If Morgen saw what the captain was doing, he didn't object. He thought for a moment, then shook his head. "It shouldn't. True, it will make people wonder when I show up with a smaller escort than that which was announced. But there will still be four of you—yourself,

Pug, Cad, and Greyhorse. And four is the minimum required by law." He cleared his throat, which must have been scoured raw by his outburst. "Blazes—anyone who hasn't got four friends in the whole universe isn't *fit* to rule."

The Daa'Vit began to pace again. But he seemed under control, contemplative. Almost calculating, in contrast to the fit of unbridled emotion Picard had just witnessed. Preferring this Morgen to the other—at least for now—the captain didn't interrupt.

"Of course," the Daa'Vit said after a little while, "the size of my escort is one thing—and the circumstances in which it was diminished is another. If the true story gets out on Daa'V, it could be embarrassing. *Most* embarrassing."

The captain shrugged. "Then no one on Daa'V need *know* the circumstances."

Morgen nodded. "Good." His eyes narrowed. "Now all we have to do is get there. What about this idea that Simenon's had?"

Picard shook his head. "I don't know anything about it—except that Commander La Forge seemed to think it was promising."

"Perhaps we should find out, then." A hint of irony had crept back into his voice. Of amusement, almost.

The captain saw it as a good sign. "Perhaps we should," he agreed.

CHAPTER 14

As Worf negotiated the corridor that led to the brig, he asked himself exactly why he'd come.

Initially, he had decided it made sense for the chief of security to check up on a prisoner like Asmund—one who had proved both so brutal and so resourceful. But by the time he was descending in the turbolift, he had been honest enough to admit—if only to himself—that there was more to it than that.

He was curious about this female—and had been since the beginning. After all, she had been raised on the Klingon homeworld. She had been exposed early on to the customs and traditions *he* had missed—that is, until he sought them out as a teenager.

But he was also repelled by her. She was an anomaly —neither human nor Klingon, but a strange admixture of the two. Just as Worf himself was—and that was what made him so uncomfortable.

Up until now, his repulsion had dominated his curiosity. He hadn't exactly avoided her—he was too busy avoiding Morgen—but he had managed to keep busy enough with his duties to prevent any chance meetings.

Then there had been the incident in the holodeck, and he had had a more compelling reason for shunning the woman. As long as she was a suspect in the murder attempts, he could not afford to have his vision clouded with emotion. What if he came to respect her? To like or even admire her? It could only have been an encumbrance in the discharge of his duty.

And of course, once he realized it was she who had made the attempts on Morgen and the others, personal contact had been out of the question. She had become an adversary, and a deadly one.

But now, with Asmund sequestered in the brig, his curiosity had come to the forefront.

Why? Because she had committed a violent crime—more than one, in fact. And because of the possibility that her Klingon upbringing, in some way—twisted or otherwise—had had something to do with it.

Hadn't there been a fear deep inside him, since the day he arrived at the Academy, that the Klingon in him would rise up at the wrong time—with grisly results? That a superior would confront him in the heat of an armed conflict and pay the price? Or that a crewmate would simply surprise him in the gym—and regret it for days afterward?

Gradually, on a purely rational level, he'd discovered that his fear was unfounded. He'd learned that he was sufficiently in control to subdue his instincts, dysfunctional as they sometimes were in the context of accepted Starfleet behavior.

That had driven his anxiety into a dark corner of his psyche. But it hadn't kept it from gnawing at him.

Now he could see the product of his fear—given flesh and substance. Given reality. What was the expression? *There but for fortune . . .*

It was the *real* reason he was coming to see Asmund. Because he had to determine for himself if her immersion in Klingon ways had had any bearing on the murders she'd attempted. He had to know to what extent Asmund herself was responsible—and to what extent it was the fire in her blood.

One final turn of the corridor and the brig came into view. In accordance with Worf's orders, there were two gold-shirted security officers—Burke and Nevins—standing guard outside. *Despite* the fact that the facility's force field had been activated.

After all, Asmund had already proven her ingenuity in using shipboard technologies to her advantage. She might have had the foresight to tamper with the brig—just as she tampered with the holodeck and the food service system. It was a long shot, given the highly secure nature of the detention area—but why take chances?

The security officers straightened at his approach. He acknowledged them with a nod. "At ease," he said. Then, turning to Burke, who was the senior of the two, he asked: "Problems?"

"None, Lieutenant. Commander Asmund hasn't said a word for hours." He paused. "Any luck with the other knife, sir?"

Inside the detention cell, Asmund was sitting by herself, watching the conversation on the other side of the transparent energy barrier. She was looking at the Klingon in particular. Worf met her gaze for a moment, then turned back to Burke.

"No," he told the man. "No luck. At least, not yet."

"I guess it would be easier if were made of *shrogh,* or some other distinctly Klingon material."

"Yes," Worf agreed. "That would have made our search a good deal easier."

But by the end of the sentence, he was no longer looking at Burke. Once again he was regarding the prisoner—who had stood up and was approaching the threshold of her cell.

"Careful, Commander," Burke warned her—not out of compassion, but because it was his duty. "That barrier has a kick to it."

"I know," said Asmund, addressing the human. "I am familiar with starship security facilities, thank you." She turned her gaze on Worf. "Lieutenant, I would like to have a word with you." Her eyes were hooded, her chin held high. All in all, a very Klingonlike posture.

"I am listening," he responded.

She shook her head. "Alone."

It came out sounding more like a demand than a request. If he hadn't been so curious about her to begin with, he wouldn't have given it a second thought.

But the idea of gaining insight into her motives was an alluring one. Too alluring for him to pass up.

"Sir," Burke said as if he could read his superior's thoughts, "the commander isn't your typical prisoner. I wouldn't advise it."

Asmund's mouth twisted up at the corners. Worf read the scorn in the gesture, calculated to sting his Klingon pride.

"Are you so frightened of me," the blond woman asked, "that you dare not face me even across an energy barrier? Is that what it's come to—Lieutenant?"

He knew what she was up to. He knew that she was taunting him for a reason. But try as he might, he couldn't believe she was in a position to harm him. Even if she somehow managed to remove the barrier, she was unarmed—and he had his phaser.

"Leave us," Worf told his security people, never taking his eyes from Asmund's.

"But Lieutenant—" began Burke.

"*Leave* us," repeated the security chief—this time a little more forcefully.

Burke and Nevins had no choice but to comply. With obvious reluctance, they withdrew down the corridor until they disappeared around the bend.

"All right," Worf told the prisoner. "We are alone."

Asmund nodded. "Thank you." Her gaze seemed to soften a bit. "You didn't have to do this."

It caught him off guard. Up until then, her attitude had been haughty—dancing on the edge of arrogance. Suddenly, there was a touch of weakness in her. A sense of vulnerability no true Klingon would have permitted himself. Was it an attempt to lull his suspicions? If so, he resolved, it wouldn't work.

"Agreed," he told her. "I did not have to do it. Now, what is it you wished to speak about?"

She took a half-step toward him. It brought her dangerously close to the energy field. "You were the one who identified the knife wounds," she said. "It could only have been you. Correct?"

"Correct."

"And it was your duty to report what you found."

"Correct again."

Asmund nodded. "Then you believe I am guilty."

Something shifted uncomfortably in Worf's gut—as if he'd eaten too many serpent worms. "That is for others to judge."

"Of course it is. But what do *you* believe?"

He shrugged. "I must believe the evidence."

"But there *is* no evidence," she insisted, her voice

229

rising an octave. With a visible effort she took hold of herself again. "Or, rather, what there is is circumstantial."

"I leave the shades of legality to the advocate general's office," he told her. "My job is to see that the ship and her crew are safe."

"Then do your job. But look beyond the evidence—if you want to call it that. Follow your instincts." A pause. "What do they tell you? That a Klingon would have tampered with a holodeck? Or opened fire on three unarmed and unsuspecting victims? Or tarnished a ceremonial knife with an enemy's blood?" She struck her chest suddenly and viciously. "*I* am a Klingon, Lieutenant. I would not have dishonored my family with such behavior—even if I *were* inclined to kill someone." The woman's eyes blazed with a cold fire. "My sister tried to kill Morgen—a fact it seems I will never live down. But she wasn't a coward. She didn't do it with sabotage or attacks in the dark; your files will confirm that. Misguided as she was, Gerda's attempt on Morgen's life was in keeping with the Klingon tradition of assassination. I say it again: she did *not* act like a coward."

The thing in Worf's gut began to writhe. He had to admit it—Asmund's words had the ring of truth to them.

"You know I'm telling the truth, Lieutenant. And you know also the importance of one's name—one's honor."

The Klingon flinched inwardly. Did she know of his discommendation? Apparently she did. But then, it was hardly a secret in the Empire. And if Asmund maintained any contact at all with the family that raised her . . .

"Yes," he said with as much dignity as possible. "I know of that."

"I must clear my name, Worf." She had dropped the Starfleet title and was using his given name; the significance of that choice was not lost on him. Asmund was calling upon him as a Klingon might call on another Klingon—as a warrior might call on another warrior. "I must find the assassin and bring him to justice. And I can't do that while I'm sitting in the brig."

The security chief's eyes narrowed. "What would you have me do? *Free* you?"

She regarded him. "Talk to Captain Picard. Make him see—he'll listen to you." Her hands became fists. "I'm not your killer, Worf. I am *not* the one you're after."

He looked at her—looked deep into those strange, blue-shadow eyes—and found he believed her.

"Please," the blond woman said—not like a warrior this time, but like a human. "There is no one else on this ship who might understand. You are my only hope."

Worf took a breath, let it out. "I will consider what you've said. Beyond that, I make no promises."

"Tell him I can help in the investigation." She came closer, her face only inches from his now. "Tell him I can be of use to you." Asmund reached out to him. "I *can* be of use, you kn—"

She must have reached out just a little bit too far— because there was a savage burst of light and the woman was flung back into her cell.

Worf resisted the impulse to go in and help her. The energy barrier worked in both directions; he would have suffered the same fate.

So he could only watch as Asmund shook off the effects of the force field and pulled herself to her feet. Watch—and gain a measure of respect for her stamina.

Humans weren't supposed to be able to get up so quickly after being jolted like that.

She looked at him. "That was stupid."

He agreed. He said so. Then he added: *"Maj doch SID ghos nagh."*

It was a Klingon saying—in essence, "Good things come to those who wait."

Asmund must have wondered exactly what he meant. But she nodded. *"Tuv nagh."* I will be patient.

A moment later Worf called for Burke and headed back to the turbolift. There were no computer stations in the corridors of deck thirty-eight—for security reasons —and he wanted to learn more about Gerda Asmund's approach to the murder of Ensign Morgen.

"Come in," Morgen told him.

The doors to the Daa'Vit's apartment opened and the Klingon walked in. Their eyes met and locked, their instincts taking over for just a moment before they remembered who they were and the experience they had shared.

"Sorry to bother you," Worf said.

"Don't be," Morgen assured him. He indicated a seat. "Please."

The security chief acknowledged the kindness with a slight inclination of his head. He sat.

"What can I do for you?" the Daa'Vit asked.

Worf frowned. "I need to know about that first attempt on your life. The one that Gerda Asmund staged twenty years ago."

Morgen looked at him. "Any particular reason?"

"Yes," the Klingon told him. "But for now I would prefer it remain my own."

The Daa'Vit considered the response. "All right," he

said finally. "I will respect that. But couldn't you have found what you seek in the ship's computer?"

"No. I tried that, and all I could get was a reference to the crime. No details."

"What sort of details were you looking for?"

"Everything," Worf said. "As much as you can remember."

Morgen considered it. "Let me see, then." He leaned back on his couch—a strange rock-and-moss affair. "I was an ensign at the time. One of my duties was to periodically check the shuttle bay operation consoles—in essence, to run the self-diagnostic sequences. It was something the regular shuttle deck personnel could have done easily enough, but Captain Picard insisted I learn everything there was to know about a Federation Starship. In retrospect, not a bad idea." His bright yellow eyes lost their focus as he reentered the past. "That particular day, a crewman named McDonnell was in charge of the shuttle deck. A slow-moving, slow-talking sort of fellow, but one you could always rely on. When I arrived, he was nowhere to be seen. The deck was empty."

"There was only *one* crewman on duty?" Worf asked.

"That is correct. The *Stargazer* was a deep-space explorer, remember. Constellation class. We didn't carry the same kind of crew that the *Enterprise* does. We didn't need to."

The Klingon nodded. "Of course. Please proceed."

"I called for McDonnell, but there was no answer. What I should have done at that point was alert Pug Joseph. But I was young and cocky—and besides, I didn't expect that there was really anything very wrong. So I took a look around.

"Finally, I found McDonnell. He was stretched out

233

behind one of the shuttles, either dead or unconscious. Later, I found out he had only been knocked out. But at the time I wasn't sure, so I rushed to his side. And as I bent down to see him, Gerda leapt down on me from her perch on top of the shuttle.

"She must have hit me pretty hard. The next thing I knew, there was the taste of blood in my mouth. My vision was blurred and my ears were ringing too loudly for me to think. I didn't know it was Gerda attacking me. I wasn't even certain I'd been attacked. I just knew that something bad had happened, and that I should try to keep it from happening again.

"As I tried to get my bearings, I caught a glimpse of something swinging toward me—something long and heavy-looking. Just in time, I rolled away; it missed me. There was another blow, which I also managed to elude. Gradually, I came to realize that my life was in jeopardy —and that it was Gerda who was jeopardizing it, though I couldn't understand why.

"By the time Gerda came at me again, I had made a further connection with reality: I recognized the weapon she held in her hands. It was a *rikajsha* stalk. What the Federation science manuals refer to as Klingon ironroot."

The reference prodded Worf's curiosity. *"Rikajsha?"* he repeated. Ironroot grew only on the Klingon homeworld. "Where did she get it?"

"From the ship's botanical garden," Morgen explained. "Gerda brought it aboard when she signed on with the *Stargazer*. Apparently, she was planning my assassination even then—arranging to have a weapon at hand that need not arouse anyone's suspicion. After all, it was only a long, skinny garden plant—even if it was capable of breaking someone's skull when placed in the right hands."

"Actually," Worf told him, "Klingon legend is full of references to the *rikajsha* being used as a weapon. I assure you," he said, "I would allow no such plants in the botanical gardens of the *Enterprise.*"

Morgen nodded. "I know. I checked." A pause. "At any rate, I couldn't avoid Gerda's attacks forever. That first blow had been a telling one, and it put me at a severe disadvantage. Before she was done, she'd broken one of my arms in two places and cracked a couple of ribs. But I was able to reel and stagger around long enough to avoid being killed before help could arrive. And arrive it did—compliments of dumb luck.

"It seems a crewman named Stroman, a geologist with a bent toward charcoal sketching, had been doing studies of some of the specimens in the botanical garden. Noticing that the *rikajsha* was missing—had been violently uprooted, in fact—this crewman notified Pug Joseph on the bridge. Picard and Ben Zoma overheard and wondered about it, and they contacted Gerda. Seeing it was she who had brought the plant there in the first place, they thought she might know something about it.

"Unfortunately—for Gerda, not for me—their call went unanswered. Gerda had left her communicator in her sleeping quarters so as not to be traced to the shuttle deck. She had no idea that anyone was trying to reach her—nor, I suspect, would she have cared very much at that particular moment.

"Concerned, Picard queried the computer about her whereabouts. It told him that she was in her room— even though she was supposed to be on her way to engineering, to help calibrate a new navigation system.

"Even more concerned now, the captain had Pug Joseph dispatch a security team to Gerda's quarters. At the same time, Ben Zoma ordered Cadwallader to conduct an internal sensor search for Gerda—just to confirm that she was truly in her room. We'd had instances of people forgetting their communicators, and he didn't want the security team wasting time on a wild chase of—what is the expression?" He looked to Worf for help.

"Goose," the Klingon offered. "A wild goose chase."

"Right. Thank you. After a little while—internal sensor searches being the slow things they are—Cadwallader determined that Gerda was not in her quarters at all. She was on the shuttle deck—where neither McDonnell nor myself were responding to Cad's intercom calls. Moments later the captain, Ben Zoma, and Pug burst in and rescued me—just as Gerda's blows were starting to connect again."

Morgen smiled humorlessly. "You see what I mean? Dumb luck. Except for anticipating Stroman's desire to sketch the *rikajsha,* Gerda did everything right. She picked a time and a place when I would be relatively isolated from other crewpeople. McDonnell was the only one who would be around—and he was someone she could easily deal with. What's more, there was little chance of anyone finding my body before she made good her escape." He stopped himself. "Do you know about that? The escape, I mean?"

The security chief shook his head. "Not very much. As I said, the computer was far from helpful."

"It was masterful—in theory, anyway. The *Tagh'rat*—the Klingon splinter group's ship—was awaiting Gerda's signal. When she finished with me, she needed only to contact her allies and open a hole in the shields—using the shuttle deck's instrumentation. By the time the hole was recognized and closed by bridge personnel, the *Tagh'rat* would have gotten close enough to snare Gerda in its transporter beam and take off."

Worf had to agree. It was a good plan. If Gerda had been successful in her assassination attempt, it would probably have worked.

"I wish," the Daa'Vit said, "That I could have made Stroman part of my escort. I didn't have that option, though. He died at Maxia Zeta."

"Too bad," the Klingon remarked.

"Yes. It is."

Worf let a moment go by before he resumed his questioning. "Tell me . . . did Gerda try to take her life after she was apprehended?"

Morgen looked at him. "I believe she did."

The security chief nodded once. "Thank you. You have been most helpful."

CHAPTER 15

Picard sat in Geordi's office and scrutinized the readouts on Geordi's desk monitor. "Insufficient data," he read.

"That's right," said the chief engineer. "We can't construct a really dependable model for the professor's theory—we simply don't know enough about subspace physics." He sat back in his chair. "Of course, we've been able to come up with some *relatively* dependable models. But to do that, we had to make some rather large assumptions." Touching a space on his keypad, he brought up one of the models to which he was referring. "This is an example. If all our assumptions are correct, we ought to be home free at twenty-six degrees. But if we're off a bit here or there, we could need as much as *thirty*-six degrees."

The captain looked at him. "However, you still think the basic theory is sound."

Geordi nodded.

"And the warp engines are capable of bearing that kind of burden again?"

He nodded again.

Picard gauged his officer's confidence level. It was about as high as he'd ever seen it—despite the trouble with computer modeling.

"All right, then," he told La Forge. "Let's give it a chance."

Geordi leaned forward again. "You've got it, sir. I'll just need a few minutes down here to finalize things."

The captain stood. "Take as much time as you need. I will be up on the bridge." He paused, gazing in the direction of the master situations monitor, where Simenon, Data, and Wesley were fiddling with yet another set of variables. "Commander . . . how did the professor take the news?"

Geordi shrugged. "Right in stride. But then, that's more or less what I expected of him. He's not one to let his feelings show—is he?"

Picard shook his head. "No. He's not." Another pause. "I just wondered."

As the captain and the chief engineer exited La Forge's office, the crisis team looked up. They waited for a sign.

Geordi gave it to them. Thumbs-up.

"It's about time," the Gnalish commented. Wesley probably though the same thing, but he kept his sentiments to himself—and wisely so. He had a lot of dues to pay before he could get away with Simenon's brand of antics. Only Data seemed to take the go-ahead in stride.

Without a comment, Picard left engineering and headed for the nearest turbolift. Stepping inside, he said: "Bridge."

In the silence that followed, he had a moment to ponder his decision. To wonder if he was doing the right thing.

He was still wondering when he emerged from the lift—only to be confronted by his Klingon security chief. Judging by the expression on Worf's face, there was a matter of more than routine concern on his mind. And with all that had occurred on the *Enterprise* lately, Picard was not eager to anticipate what it might be.

"You wish to see me," Picard said. It wasn't a question.

The Klingon nodded his massive head. "Aye, sir." He indicated the ready room with his eyes. "In private, if you don't mind."

"Of course," the captain responded, and led the way inside. As the doors closed behind them, he took a seat behind his desk. Worf sat down as well. "All right," Picard said, leaning back. "I take it this is a security matter."

The Klingon hesitated. "Yes," he replied at last. "But perhaps not in the way you mean."

The captain found his curiosity piqued, but he decided to let Worf proceed at his own pace. "I am listening," he said simply.

His chief of security frowned as he searched for the right words. "Sir," he began at last, "I don't believe Commander Asmund is the killer."

The statement caught Picard off guard. "*Not* the killer," he echoed, giving himself time to recover. He leaned forward. "Lieutenant, you yourself presented the evidence that damned her. Are you now saying that you were *wrong?*"

"Not about the knife wounds," Worf explained. "They were made by a ceremonial blade—I would stake my life on the fact." He licked his lips. "But I no longer believe that Commander Asmund was the one who wielded the knife."

Picard regarded him. "And what has occurred to change your mind?"

Worf's brow lowered—a sign of sincerity, of earnestness, Picard had learned over the years. "Captain, I had occasion to speak with Commander Asmund. She claimed that she was innocent—no surprise under the circumstances. But in the process of defending herself, she made some points that rang true. About honor—*Klingon* honor."

Picard was interested enough to hear more. "Go on," he said.

"In essence, Commander Asmund told me that the murderer's approaches weren't worthy of a Klingon—which she considers herself to be. In this, I had to agree. None of the attempts fit in with the Klingon tradition of assassination."

"But we know that some of your people take that tradition less seriously than others," the captain pointed out. He had firsthand knowledge of that fact, having been the intended victim of a *dis*honorable attempt back on the Klingon homeworld.

"True," Worf conceded. "That is why Commander Asmund referred me to the details of her sister's crime. You recall those details?"

"I do." Picard saw the scene again, just as it had been presented to him when he and Ben Zoma rushed onto the shuttle deck: Gerda swinging the deadly ironroot. Morgen lurching to avoid the blow, and only barely succeeding. And McDonnell lying prone in the foreground. "They are not easy to forget."

"You recall, then, that Gerda Asmund did not kill the one called McDonnell—though it would have been well within her power, and even advisable. A loose end is a loose end, yet Gerda chose to avoid unnecessary death."

The captain nodded. "That is correct."

"What is more, Gerda used a simple weapon—as

prescribed by Klingon tradition. Usually a knife is the weapon of choice, but certainly an ironroot is not out of the question."

"The point being that she probably could have gotten her hands on a phaser—but chose not to."

"Exactly." Worf paused to let the significance of that sink in. Then he went on. "Note also that the assassination attempt was carried out by a single individual—one on one. And finally, that the first blow was not a killing one—giving the intended victim an opportunity to view the face of his killer, so he would know whom to curse in the afterlife." His voice grew weightier. "Finally, there is the matter of the poison."

The captain couldn't help but wince at the memory. No one had expected Gerda to have a *ku'thei* nodule under her armpit—not even Idun, who had shaken off her shock long enough to warn them about a suicide attempt. Fortunately, Greyhorse had gotten to Gerda in time.

"Again," Worf finished, "all in accordance with Klingon custom. All honorable."

Indeed. And the crimes committed on the *Enterprise* had been anything *but* honorable—just as Idun had pointed out. Picard measured one set of facts against the other. "What you are saying, then," he told Worf, "is that since Gerda Asmund acted according to your code, Idun—as her identical twin—would have done the same. And because the murder attempts were conducted dishonorably, by Klingon standards, they could not have been the work of Idun. Eh?"

Worf scowled. "Is it not a logical conclusion?"

"Perhaps," the captain conceded. "And if less were at stake here, I might be inclined to accept it. But we are dealing with life and death; we cannot take the chance that our logic is flawed." He leaned back again. "It is no secret that I have been one of Idun Asmund's staunchest supporters. Even when some of your fellow officers were ready to condemn her, I refused to believe them—to judge her on the basis of her sister's actions. But now . . ." Picard shook his head. "I cannot release her. I cannot risk another murder. You may log your observations for the judge advocate general's office, Lieutenant —but the matter is really out of my hands. I am sorry."

The Klingon lifted his chin. "I understand," he said. Though his disappointment must have been keen after all the trouble he had gone to—after what he had deemed the truth was proven to have no practical value—he still held his duty above all. And his sense of duty dictated that he accept the captain's decision. "Nonetheless, I have increased security to the point at which it stood before Commander Asmund's arrest."

"Naturally," Picard agreed.

Having received the captain's blessing, the Klingon rose.

On the other side of his desk, Picard got up as well. But one matter was still unresolved. "A question, Worf."

The Klingon, who had just started to turn away from him, looked back. "Captain?"

"Where did you get all this information? It is not available in the ship's computer files. I know—it was by my order that the details were left out."

Of course, they were still on file at Starfleet Headquarters. But he had not wanted the material to be available to curiosity seekers—especially since it might have hampered Idun in her career.

"I spoke with Captain Morgen," the Klingon answered.

Picard swallowed his surprise. What had happened to that fabled hostility between Klingons and Daa'Vit?

"I see," he said. "Carry on, Lieutenant."

Worf inclined his head slightly. "Aye, sir."

A moment later the chief of security had departed, leaving Picard with even more to ponder than when he arrived on the bridge.

Good God, he mused. *Is it possible that a murderer is still loose on my ship?*

Guinan stood behind the bar, looked around, and smiled.

Ten-Forward was quiet again. Not *really* quiet, of course; there were murmured conversations and the tinkling of glasses and the sound of chairs clattering against tables. But it was placid in comparison to the rush of the last several hours.

Commander Asmund's arrest had raised quite a stir. And understandably so. Asmund wasn't some hostile life-form who'd invaded the *Enterprise* with her phasers blazing; she was a Starfleet officer who had walked beside them, even sat down to dinner with them—all the while plotting to commit murder in their midst.

For once, even Guinan had been caught off guard. Usually, there was very little that occurred on the ship that got past her. But neither she nor Troi nor anyone else had managed to catch on to the killer—not until Worf identified her by her handiwork. It was disconcerting, to say the least.

As the doors opened, Guinan glanced in their direction. It was a reflex by now, part of the routine of running Ten-Forward. She felt more comfortable knowing who was coming in and who was leaving. And people liked the idea that she took note of them; it made them feel special.

Then she saw who had just entered her domain. *Well,* she mused, *maybe "special" isn't quite the right word in this case. "Hunted" or "persecuted," but definitely not "special."*

It was Pug Joseph. And he'd been drinking again. She could see it in the dark, puffy rings under his eyes and in the waxy pallor of his skin.

For a moment, Pug didn't seem to notice her—maybe because there were a couple of waiters obscuring his view. She watched him scan the area out by the observation ports, eyes narrowed. Looking for his nemesis, she thought: *me.* Failing to find her, he smiled and took a couple of steps toward the nearest concentration of tables.

Apparently, Pug had gotten tired of drinking in his room. And despite his earlier failures, he still thought he had a shot at taking his binge to Ten-Forward.

Then the waiters moved away, and Guinan was revealed to him. As their eyes met and locked, his expression changed—became tense, almost hateful.

Stifling his fury, he turned and walked out of the lounge.

Beverly lay stretched out on her bed, staring at the ceiling, trying to face the prospect that Ben Zoma was beyond her help. It wasn't easy. She had done her best, brought to bear all the medical technology at her disposal—and he still had less than a fifty-fifty chance.

That irked her. It wasn't as if she had never lost a patient—every doctor in Starfleet had to deal with occasional failure. But Ben Zoma had been her husband's friend, his comrade. He had joked with him, shared sorrows and triumphs with him. In a way, she felt that losing Gilaad Ben Zoma would be letting Jack down. And she desperately didn't want to do that.

Jack. The thought of him made her turn to the box of tapes resting on her commode. She wanted—needed—to hear his voice.

Opening the box again, Beverly peered inside. She longed to hear something upbeat, optimistic, like the last one—but after a moment she realized that she didn't remember the content of any individual tape very well. In fact, they were pretty much a blur to her.

It took her a few minutes, but she eventually found a tape that seemed to fit the bill. In fact, she realized with a little pang of delight, it was one of the first subspace messages Jack had ever sent her. She even remembered the messenger who had brought it—a stocky young woman who took her duties quite seriously. She used to check and double-check Beverly's signature against her records before releasing a tape, no matter how many she brought—at least until they replaced her with someone less memorable.

And it was summer, wasn't it? Beverly remembered that too, because she couldn't understand how it could be summer and be so cold. Of course, she'd never lived in San Francisco before. She'd never even lived on *Earth* before.

But Starfleet's medical college was in San Francisco, and it was the best in the Federation. And when she'd actually gotten *accepted* there, she could hardly justify staying on Arvada Three, as much as she loved the colony.

So, shortly after her marriage to Jack, they'd moved to a second-floor apartment in the shadow of Starfleet headquarters—which seemed a little oppressive at first.

Later, however, she came to appreciate it; it had made her feel closer to her husband and his work. And it enabled her to get subspace messages that much more quickly.

Shaking her head, she inserted the tape into the player. It took a second or two before Jack's message came up.

"Hi, sweetheart. Life on the *Stargazer* is . . . how can I put it? Eventful. For the last couple of weeks we've been charting a couple of gas giants on a collision course in the Beta Expledar system. The theory was that if two of these gas giants come together with enough force, the resulting body will be heavy enough for its own gravity to instigate fusion—in other words, for the thing to become a star in its own right.

"Well, it's no longer a theory. I wish you could have seen it. You can't imagine the outpouring of light . . . the sheer magnitude of the spectacle . . . I know I'm not very good with words, but I think you get the idea. It was magnificent.

"On a more mundane note, I've made friends with my first Pandrilite—a fellow named Vigo, who's in charge of the weapons around here. Don't worry—he hasn't had any chance to use them yet, and he probably never will. In any case, he's trying to teach some of us this game called *sharash'di*. I've never heard of it, but it looks interesting, and Vigo says I've got quite an aptitude for it. I think he means for a *human*—but I just might surprise him one day.

"Fortunately, we've got a good group on the *Stargazer*. When you're working in close quarters, that's pretty important. You've been hearing about Jean-Luc for a long time, of course, but my respect for him grows each day. There can't be a man alive better suited to head up a deep-space exploration. Ben Zoma's another born leader

—though he's got a much more low-key approach. Sometimes I think he'd rather hear a good joke than eat. And then there's—"

Jack's voice was drowned out by that of Jean-Luc Picard, coming over the *Enterprise's* intercom system: "This is the captain. Once more we will be attempting to free ourselves from the subspace anomaly. The maneuver may take some time and involve a fair amount of turbulence; please take all necessary precautions."

Reluctantly, Beverly switched off the tape mechanism and got to her feet. She would resume, she promised herself, once this "maneuver" was over.

Off duty or not, she wasn't about to let sickbay get bounced around without being there to pick up the pieces.

As Worf approached the brig, the two security officers faced him and straightened. He set them at ease with a nod and came to stand before the force barrier.

Asmund had been sitting on her bunk. She looked up—and saw immediately that he had nothing in the way of good news for her.

"I am sorry," he said. "I spoke with the captain on your behalf—"

The woman finished the sentence for him: "But he won't take the chance."

He eyed her. "That is correct."

She nodded. "I suppose I'm not surprised. As one who was raised a Klingon, I hate the idea of sitting here, caged, while the one who arranged it runs loose." Her eyes blazed with dark fire. "The very idea," she began, her voice trembling, "the very idea consumes me."

It took her a few moments to achieve control again. "But as a Starfleet officer," she said, "I can't blame the captain. I would probably have made the same decision myself."

"If you are innocent, it will come out in a court-martial." He did not expect that to be of much comfort to her now—but what else could he say?

Asmund grunted. *"Tuv nagh?"* Wait for weeks, months, while someone else decides my fate? And I remain an object of scorn and loathing? I am not *that* patient, Lieutenant. But then, that is not your concern. You have done all you could; I am grateful."

Turning away from him then, she went back to her bunk and sat down. He stood there for a moment, watching her. Wondering what he would do, how he would feel, if he were in her place.

Then he turned and, with a brief acknowledgment of the officers on guard, made his way back to the bridge.

CHAPTER 16

Standing at his engineering console, Geordi scanned the bridge. Every one of his fellow officers was in his or her place—not to mention Morgen and Simenon, who had gotten the captain's permission to witness the maneuver from a position near the aft stations.

Getting up from his command chair, Picard turned to look at the chief engineer. "You may proceed, Commander."

"Aye, sir," Geordi answered. Focusing his attention on his monitor, where the shields were depicted as a series of blue lines surrounding the ship, he took a last look at such items as environmental resistance, energy consumption, and field integrity. Satisfied, he tapped in the first set of alterations. Immediately, the blue-line configuration began to writhe and change.

"Forward shields flattening," Data reported. "Forming a surface perpendicular to the axis of our passage."

For Geordi, the information was redundant. His monitor showed him the effect in some detail.

"Obverse stress increasing," Wesley announced.

The ship quivered momentarily—just as it had when they'd tried reversing engines. It was a good sign, La Forge told himself.

Unable to keep the excitement out of his voice, Wesley said: "We're slowing down, Captain. Warp nine point nine four five . . . warp nine point nine four zero." He leaned back. "Stabilizing at nine point nine four zero."

"Hull integrity?" Picard snapped.

"Stresses are well within acceptable limits," Worf replied from Tactical.

A *very* good sign, Geordi noted.

Simenon had been right—shield structure had an effect on their progress through the slipstream. But would it have enough of an effect to dump them out of it?

There was only one way to find out. A second time, his fingers skipped nimbly over the console.

"Rear shields flattening," Data informed them.

A shiver ran through the deck, through the bulkheads. It was more strident, more noticeable than the one before it.

"Obverse stress *de*creasing," Wesley declared. "Accelerating . . ." He shook his head. "Back up to warp nine point nine five now."

Worf raised his gaze from his monitor board. "Stress has intensified considerably, sir. It is as if we were being sandwiched between two forces."

Picard looked over his shoulder at his security chief. "Any danger, Lieutenant?"

"No *immediate* danger," the Klingon advised him.

In his seat at the captain's side, Riker consulted the readouts built into his armrest and frowned. "So far, so good."

Yes, Geordi mused. *So far, so good.* But the easy part

was over. From here on in, the going would get a lot rougher.

With careful precision, he instructed the computer to tilt both shield surfaces—forward and rear. Not a lot—just ten degrees.

This time, the deck didn't just shudder—it jerked. So badly, in fact, that La Forge had to grab on to the edges of his console to keep from falling.

Through it all, Data's voice was as calm and matter-of-fact as ever. "Shield surfaces pitched ten degrees," he said.

Picard let go of his chair, which he'd used to steady himself. Straightening to his full height, he looked around. "Mister Worf?"

The Klingon's answer was a second or two in coming. "Minimal damage, sir." Another pause. "No serious injuries."

The captain nodded. "Good." He turned to Wesley. "Velocity? Bearing?"

"No change," the ensign told him.

Picard cast a glance in Geordi's direction. The chief engineer looked back, and a wordless communication passed between them.

Continue?

Continue.

Adjusting the blue lines on his monitor another ten degrees, LaForge input the change. And hung on.

It didn't help. The ship bucked so badly that he found himself on the floor anyway. And it didn't stop bucking —not completely—though the echoes weren't nearly as vicious as the original jolt.

"Shield surfaces—" Data began.

But Worf's cry drowned him out. "Structural damage

to decks twenty-two and twenty-three. Evacuating affected areas and sealing off!"

Could have been worse, Geordi mused, lifting himself up off the carpet. Twenty-two and twenty-three were engineering decks which were less than crucial at the moment. And since they were sparsely populated, it would only take a few moments to clear them.

"Same speed and heading, sir!" Wesley called out.

More importantly, Geordi noted, the shields were maintaining their shape, despite the forces imposed on them. The drain on the engines was tremendous, but they were doing their job—and doing it well.

Behind Worf, Morgen was helping Simenon to his feet. The Gnalish had hit his head on something; he was bleeding. But he refused to leave the bridge.

La Forge didn't blame him. Under the circumstances, he wouldn't have left either.

As he got another grip on his console, Geordi exchanged looks with the captain again. Picard looked a little rumpled; he must have fallen as well. But he seemed no less resolute than before.

"Decks twenty-two and twenty-three evacuated," Worf growled.

The captain nodded. Geordi nodded back.

Turning to his monitor, the chief engineer manipulated the shields. *Ten degrees more. That's thirty altogether—pretty much an average of what the models said it would take.* On the screen, it looked like a lot. But would it be enough to free them?

Or just enough to tear them apart?

He called out: "Hang on, folks." Then, bracing himself, he pressed "enter."

Idun Asmund hadn't said a word to the two security officers outside her cell since they started their shift an hour or so ago. Nor had she spoken to any of the guards on the shifts before that.

A cool customer. That's how one of them had put it, thinking she hadn't heard. Well, she'd heard all right. And though she hadn't corrected the woman, she was anything but *cool.*

She was hot. She was *seething.* Just as any Klingon would have seethed, penned in like an animal.

Of course, this time it was more than her breeding that made her crave freedom so intensely. She had a *job* to do—a job that couldn't wait. And she couldn't do it from the brig. It ate at her, that while she sat, helpless, blood-justice went unsatisfied.

But she had long ago learned to contain her Klingon-bred tendencies to vent emotion. So well, in fact, that those on the Stargazer and elsewhere had seen her as some sort of iron maiden—highly disciplined, highly controlled. *A cool customer indeed.* She savored the bitter irony of it.

When the captain's announcement came over the intercom, the goldshirts exchanged brief remarks. But she remained silent—even though she had an idea of the risks they had to be incurring. The last set of maneuvers had blacked out parts of the ship—and they hadn't accomplished a thing. She didn't know much about warpspace engineering, but she knew this—any serious attempt to escape the slipstream would place an even greater strain on the Enterprise. A strain that would put them all in jeopardy.

If her guards hadn't fully appreciated that fact, the first jolt gave them an inkling of what was to come. She noted the look of alarm that crossed both their faces.

"Huh," one of them muttered—a big man whose hair was as pale as hers. His first name was John—she'd overheard that. "The captain wasn't kidding."

His companion was smaller, dark and bearded; name unknown. "That's all right," he said. "Let's just hope it does the trick."

The second shock was worse. The blond man was thrown to the floor. The dark one managed to keep his feet by clutching at the bulkhead behind him.

And even then, it wasn't over. There were aftershocks that made the ship tremble unnervingly.

"Damn." John picked himself up, despite the continuing disturbances. "What's going *on* up there?"

The other man just shook his head. He was looking at the light that indicated the barrier was still in effect.

Though Asmund couldn't see it from her bunk, or indeed from anywhere in her cell, she gathered that the light was still on. Otherwise, her guards would have reacted to the fact. But the dark one was still scrutinizing it.

"What's the matter?" asked the blond man, noting the direction in which his colleague was staring.

"I thought I saw the light flicker."

John considered it himself. "It's not flickering now," he said.

"No. It's not." He shrugged. "My imagination, maybe." He turned to his companion. "I guess that was it. My imagination."

That's when the third jolt came. Actually, it was more of an upheaval.

The floor of her cell came crashing up at her, and the world went black.

Lifting himself off the deck, Geordi straightened his VISOR. In the grinding, shifting moment of chaos that followed his implementation of the last shield-shape alteration, it had fallen askew. *Along with half my vertebrae,* the engineering chief remarked inwardly, noting the pain that was only now emerging in his lower back. And both his knees. And his left wrist.

He winced as the VISOR clicked softly into place. *Must have hit my head too,* he decided. *Damn. What a mess.*

Then, as his unique variety of vision was restored to him, he realized just why he was so sore. He was no longer at the engineering console—he was no longer anywhere *near* the engineering console. Their effort to escape the slipstream had flung him clear over to the food dispenser—a good thirty feet!

As he looked around he saw that other members of the bridge contingent had been similarly strewn about. The captain, Riker, and Troi, for instance, had all been pitched forward and to the right, so that they were now dusting themselves off near the emergency turbolift. Worf was in front of the command area instead of in back of it, and Wesley had been plastered against the forward viewscreen—which had gone blank somewhere along the line.

Neither Morgen nor Simenon was immediately visible—not until they poked their heads up from behind the Tactical station. The Gnalish muttered a curse.

Only Data had somehow managed to remain in his seat—though now that Geordi looked more closely, he could see that it had been at the expense of his control board. The thing was flipped up and mangled at one end—no doubt, where the android had gripped it to anchor himself.

This kind of stuff wasn't supposed to happen on a ship

like the *Enterprise,* Geordi noted. Not with all the damping and stabilizing features built into her. But then, no spacegoing vessel was designed to do what they had done.

"Is everyone all right?" Picard asked.

There were some groans, but no seriously negative replies. The captain nodded. "Good. Now let's see where we stand."

By then La Forge was already making his way back to the aft stations. He was pleasantly surprised to see that his monitor had fared better than the viewscreen: it still showed the blue-lined diagram that he'd been using to set up each maneuver. Unfortunately, most of the blue lines were gone.

"Damage?" Picard demanded, having resumed his place in the command center.

By then Worf too had returned to his original position. "Reports coming in from all decks, sir. Damage to ship and systems is considerable." He looked up. "Nothing, however, that cannot be corrected by repair teams."

"Warp drive is disabled again," Geordi chimed in. "But we pretty much expected that. What shields we've got left are running on impulse power."

"Injuries?" the captain asked.

The Klingon consulted his board again. "Widespread. But so far, none appears to be life-threatening."

Picard's forehead wrinkled. "I would say we were lucky, under the circumstances." He turned to Wesley. "The question is *how* lucky. Mister Crusher?"

The ensign hunched over his monitor and frowned. He shook his head. "I wish I could tell you, sir. But astrogation is down." He swiveled in his chair to face the captain. "I don't know if the maneuver worked or not."

Picard grunted, unable to quite conceal his disappointment. "I see."

"There's a way to find out, though," Geordi reminded them. "All we have to do is find an observation port."

"Good idea," Simenon said. And without waiting for anyone else to agree, he headed for the observation lounge.

A half-dozen others moved to follow him—Morgen, Picard, Riker and Troi. And finally, Geordi himself.

The lounge doors parted, revealing the cabin and its conference table. And beyond it, a generous helping of starlit space.

La Forge smiled. Past those who had entered before him, he could see that the stars were standing still—no longer streaks of light, but mere points.

They were out of the slipstream, back in normal space. And though it wasn't clear yet exactly *where* in normal space, it felt pretty good to be there.

Simenon was standing in the front of the group. As Geordi watched, he turned his serpentine head and looked back at him. And winked. As if to say *we did it!*

Though nobody saw it—not even Simenon—La Forge winked back.

When Asmund regained her senses there was a nauseating, dull ache in the vicinity of one of her temples. She touched the area gingerly, winced at the pain even that light contact provoked, and inspected her fingertips. Blood—and not a little of it.

But her guards had come through even worse. The bearded man was out cold, one of his legs twisted in such a way that it had to have been broken. And the one called John, while conscious, was gripping his side and grimacing in anguish. For the moment, he seemed to have forgotten about his phaser; it was lying on the deck a couple of feet from where he lay propped against the bulkhead.

She saw all this in darkness, aided only by the strobe of a naked, fizzling circuit—though she couldn't at first pinpoint its location. Then it dawned on her. It was the one just to the side of her cell—the one that controlled the energy field.

Rising from the floor, she approached the place where the barrier should have been. Carefully, ever so carefully, she reached out.

And watched her hand pass over the threshold, unscathed. No flash of light, no energy charge to make her regret her trespass. No barrier.

No barrier.

Then she looked down and saw that John was watching her. That he had realized the barrier was down as well.

Without a word, he launched himself in the direction of his phaser. Ignoring the pounding in her head, Asmund dived for the weapon too. Unfortunately for her, he got to it first, managed to raise it and fire.

Twisting in mid-air, Asmund somehow eluded the narrow beam of red light. And before the blond man could take aim again, she grabbed hold of his wrist with both hands.

Knowing what she knew about pressure points, it wasn't difficult to make him scream out and drop the phaser. But all her faculties focused on the task, she never saw the blow from his free hand. It hit her in the back of the neck, stunning her, intensifying the spike of pain in her temple.

Still, she found the strength to lash out backhanded—
to hit her adversary across the face hard enough to knock
him out. As he slumped beside her, she laid claim to the
weapon and got to her feet.

The other guard was still unconscious, his breathing
shallow but regular. She passed up the temptation to
look for his phaser as well, deciding a second one would
be of only marginal value—and she had no time to
waste. At any moment, they might realize she was free
and send a security team after her.

Phaser in hand, she took off down the corridor.

Like everyone else on the bridge, Wesley was still
shaking his head over the success of Professor Simenon's
idea. The ensign grinned as he watched the Gnalish
regale Picard with the third retelling of his stone-
skimming exploits in the holodeck. With Riker and Troi
having departed to oversee repair and relocation efforts,
and Morgen gone along with them, the captain and
Simenon had the command center all to themselves.

Suddenly, the professor pointed to Wesley, and the
others turned his way as well. The ensign felt himself
blush as Picard smiled appreciatively and nodded; he
could just imagine what Simenon was telling him.
*Wonderful boy you've got there. Couldn't have done it
without him. So how is it he never skimmed stones before?
Who's responsible for his education anyway?*

Swiveling away before his blush became permanent,
Wesley returned his attention to his board. Much to his
surprise, the astrogation function had been returned to
it; that section of the display was outlined again in green
light.

Touching the appropriate keys, he called up their

position. Instantly, the coordinates appeared on the screen.

He froze as he realized the significance of what he saw. No, he told himself. *Please* say this isn't right. With an effort, he forced his fingers to run the system through a diagnostic check.

There was nothing wrong with it. It was functioning perfectly. Swallowing, Wesley turned again toward the captain.

And drew Picard's attention. Abruptly, the captain stopped smiling—and came striding down to the Conn station.

"What is it, Mister Crusher? You look positively green."

Then Picard looked past him and saw the coordinates. As Wesley watched, the muscles in the man's jaw rippled.

"Commander La Forge," the captain called, hardly raising his voice. His eyes remained fixed on the astrogation readout.

"Aye, sir?" Geordi came down the ramp from the aft stations. "Something wrong?"

Picard nodded. "Apparently."

"What is it?" Simenon asked, rising from his seat in the command center.

"Come see for yourself, Phigus."

By that time, Geordi had arrived and was beginning to appreciate the situation. He whistled soft and low.

Wesley knew that *someone* had to come out and say it. But he waited dutifully for the Gnalish to arrive and curse beneath his breath before he fit words to the problem.

"We're in Romulan space," he announced—a bit

262

more loudly than he'd intended. It attracted some stares from around the bridge.

"Indeed," Picard said. Then, a little more softly: "The question is, what are we going to do about it?"

As if sensing that the question was directed toward him, Geordi looked up. "Captain, the engines are in bad shape. And even if we *had* warp speed, I don't think I'd want to risk using it."

Picard's eyes narrowed. "Because we might get ourselves stuck in the slipstream all over again?"

"That's right, sir." La Forge bit his lip. "To be safe, we've got to put some distance between ourselves and the phenomenon. And even at full impulse, that's going to take some time. Hours, anyway."

"At least," Simenon chimed in.

Picard frowned at La Forge. "We don't *have* time, Commander. There could be a Romulan ship on our tail at any moment." His frown deepened. "How quickly do you think you can give me warp one?"

La Forge shrugged. "I don't know. A day, a few hours—it's hard to say, sir."

"Three hours," Picard told him. It wasn't a request and it wasn't an order. It was just a statement of what they needed.

Geordi sighed. "You'd better excuse me," he said, and headed for the forward turbolift. Without waiting to be asked, Simenon fell in right behind him.

Picard turned to Wesley. "How far are we from the Neutral Zone at full impulse?"

Wesley quickly performed the necessary calculations. "Sixteen hours, thirty-two minutes," he said, though the captain had moved close enough to the Conn to see the computations on-screen himself.

Picard nodded. "Lay in a course, Mister Crusher. When the use of our warp drive is restored to us, we'll be that much closer to salvation."

Sixteen hours, Wesley thought. *There's no way we can go unnoticed for that long.*

Behind him, he heard Lieutenant Worf grunt—as if in agreement with the ensign's unarticulated analysis. Then the Klingon spoke.

"We have another problem, sir," he said evenly.

Picard turned away from the newly restored viewscreen to face his security chief. "Yes, Lieutenant?"

Worf's expression was grim. "Commander Asmund has escaped."

CHAPTER 17

Picard's eyes narrowed as he absorbed the information. "I see," he said, his voice level and controlled. "And her guards?"

"Injured, but not badly." The Klingon added: "The brig's security systems were damaged in the escape from the slipstream."

"Is she armed?"

"She has a phaser, sir."

He nodded. "And potential victims all over the ship." The captain frowned. "Go after her, Worf. *Find* her." His tone was decisive, authoritative—but his eyes were full of regret. "And give her no quarter. Commander Asmund is a most resourceful individual."

Worf nodded, already starting to move toward the turbolift. "On my way, sir."

"Lieutenant . . ."

The Klingon stopped.

Picard opened his mouth to say something—but thought better of it. He shook his head. "Nothing. Just keep me posted."

"Aye, sir," said the security chief. But he knew what the captain had been about to say—something about not allowing personal feelings and beliefs to keep one from doing one's duty. It would have been an unnecessary instruction; he was glad that Picard had kept it to himself.

As the captain turned back to the viewscreen, Worf entered the turbolift. "Computer," he asked, "what is the location of Commander Idun Asmund?"

The response was quick and concise. "Commander Asmund is in a lift compartment in the vicinity of deck eight, primary hull."

Worf straightened as if he'd been slapped in the face. The battle bridge was located on deck eight of the *secondary* hull. It would be a simple maneuver for Asmund to move from one hull to the next—and if she could rig the holodeck and the food processor, she could probably gain access to the battle bridge as well.

And she could control the entire ship from there.

She was clever. She had fooled him once, with her protestations of innocence. She would not fool him again.

"Deck eight," he said, his teeth clenching as he prepared himself for the inevitable confrontation.

Had Morgen been more familiar with the layout of a Galaxy-class vessel, he might have had some prior idea of which cabin he was entering. As it was, he was almost as surprised to see the roomful of young children as they were to see him.

There were about a dozen of them, peering up at him with eyes fresh from crying. A couple still had trails of tears on their faces.

266

A woman who was kneeling among them—their teacher, apparently—looked up at Morgen. "Hello," she said, unable to conceal the trepidation in her voice.

It wasn't the first time he'd evoked that kind of reaction since he'd set foot on the *Enterprise*. Nor was it difficult to understand, given the imposing Daa'Vit physique and the fact that so few of his people were seen on Federation starships.

A moment later, noticing the pips on the Daa'Vit's collar, the woman said, "Oh. You must be one of Captain Picard's guests."

"Yes," he told her. "I'm Captain Morgen. Is everyone all right in here?"

She nodded. "We're fine." She scanned the faces of the children. "A little frightened, but fine."

Just as she said that, a little girl began sobbing. And before the woman could comfort the child, a little boy followed suit.

Smiling, Morgen lowered himself onto his haunches. "Come on, now," he said, glancing from the girl to the boy and back again. "If you cry, it's going to make *me* start crying too. And when I start crying, I can't stop."

Then, before he lost their attention, the Daa'Vit opened his tear ducts and let the clear serum inside them flow copiously down his cheeks.

As he'd intended, it got the children's attention. So fascinated were they by the sight of his tears, they forgot their own problems. A couple of them even started giggling.

Morgen mugged an expression of sadness, and they giggled some more. More mugging, more giggling. Before they knew it, they were laughing out loud.

The woman shot him a look of gratitude. He nodded a

little and went on with his act—one that had become a favorite of the children on his own ship over the years.

One little boy even came over and put his arm around the Daa'Vit. "It's all right," he said. "There's nothing to be scared of."

Morgen turned to him, still releasing great globby tears. "Are you sure?" he asked.

"Uh huh," the child assured him. "Captain Picard will take care of us. That's what my mom always says."

As if on cue, the Daa'Vit's communicator beeped. Tapping it out of reflex, he opened the communications channel on his end. "Morgen here."

"This is Picard," the captain told him. "We've got a problem—or more accurately, *another* problem. Are you alone?"

"One second, please." Standing, the Daa'Vit winked at the children. Then he retreated to the other side of the cabin. "All right. You can go on now."

The captain didn't waste any time. "Asmund has escaped her cell. She's at large and she's got a phaser."

Morgen digested the information. "Acknowledged."

"I want you to return to your quarters."

The Daa'Vit made a sound of disgust. "I've spent enough time in my quarters," he complained. "More than enough time. Your people need my help."

"My people," Picard said, "will survive better without you." The level of authority in his voice went up a notch. "You are a *target,* Morgen. And as such, you are a danger to everyone around you."

The Daa'Vit looked back at the children.

"Report to your quarters, my friend. Or I will have a security team escort you there."

The Daa'Vit forced himself to be objective—to see

the wisdom in his former captain's words. "As you wish," he answered finally. "Morgen out."

He lingered only another second or two—just long enough to consider the little ones and the woman in their midst. None of them had any idea what kind of dangers they faced—both from within and without. And that was probably just as well.

"Do you have to go?" a little girl asked.

He nodded. "I'm afraid so. But thanks. I feel a lot better now that you've cheered me all up."

Then, before he could entertain any rebellious second thoughts, he took his leave of them.

The Klingon in Worf urged him to face Commander Asmund alone—but the security chief in him recognized he had a greater chance of success if he called in backups. In the end, the security chief won out.

As he reached deck eight, however, none of his backups had arrived. And the situation didn't allow for delay. Drawing his phaser, Worf pressed his back against the bulkhead, and quickly but silently made his way along its curving surface.

At any moment, he knew, he might come face to face with the fugitive—though given the head start she had, it was far more likely she'd already gotten into the battle bridge. And that was the reason for his haste.

When he slid within view of the bridge doors, he noticed that they were closed. Nor did they show any signs of having been forced.

A neat job indeed. He'd hardly completed the thought when reinforcements arrived in the forms of Nevins and Loyosha.

"Is she in there, sir?" asked Nevins.

Worf was about to answer in the affirmative when he realized he was only going on a supposition. Turning his face upward, he queried the computer as he had earlier: "Computer—what is Commander Asmund's location?"

Again, the answer was immediate. "Commander Asmund is in a turbolift on deck eighteen."

Worf looked at his security officers. They looked back.

"Deck eighteen?" Loyosha echoed.

What was she doing? Trying to forestall the inevitable?

Worf didn't believe it. Asmund was too smart to believe she would elude them for long this way.

Putting himself in her place, the Klingon conceded he might throw a single curve at his pursuers—and the battle bridge would have served him well in that regard.

But deck eighteen? What was on deck eighteen except living quarters and—

He cursed. If he could locate Asmund, then Asmund could locate *Morgen.* Why didn't he think of that before?

"Computer," he barked, "where is Captain Morgen?"

"Captain Morgen," the computer replied, "is in the educational facility on deck eighteen."

Worf hurtled down the corridor, with Loyosha and Nevins in close pursuit.

"Commander?"

La Forge looked up from his workstation, where he'd been working feverishly to get the warp drive back online. On the other side of engineering, the Gnalish was standing at an identical workstation, complementing his efforts.

"Progress?" Geordi asked hopefully.

Simenon shook his lizardlike head, never taking his

eyes off his monitors. "Not enough. I've still got a long way to go."

Turning back to his own instruments, La Forge smiled. He was getting to know Simenon pretty well—he could tell when the professor had something on his mind. "Then what?" he asked.

A pause. "Tell me about the Romulans."

La Forge was a little surprised by the request. Then he remembered that the *Stargazer's* famous twenty-year voyage had taken place during the Romulans' decades-long period of withdrawal. Very likely, he realized with a bit of a jolt, Simenon had never even seen a Romulan—except in tapes, and even those were bound to have been pretty old.

Nor was it hard to figure out what had prompted the Gnalish's curiosity. When you were sneaking through enemy territory, it was only natural to want to know a little about the enemy.

"Tell you about them," the chief engineer echoed. "Where would you like me to start?"

"Start anywhere," Simenon instructed.

La Forge smiled again. "All right. For one thing, their technology has come a long way since their alliance with the Klingons. Their ships are bigger, faster, and deadlier."

"All very comforting," the Gnalish commented.

"And of course," La Forge continued, "no one schemes better than the Romulans. No one's more merciless." He thought about the *Enterprise's* various encounters with its Vulcanoid adversaries over the last few years. And of his personal experiences. "On the other hand," he went on, "they're people, with their own concepts of honor and loyalty, of right and wrong."

Simenon grunted. "Ah-hah. A ray of hope. Does that mean they refrain from shooting first and asking questions never? Is there a chance they'll believe our tale of woe and let us go?"

La Forge shrugged. "Depends on the exact circumstances."

"In other words, no."

"In other words, it's pretty unlikely."

The Gnalish sighed. "Sorry I asked."

Worf couldn't understand it. As he made his way down from deck eight in a parallel turbolift, his adversary didn't move out into the corridor. In fact, she didn't move at all.

She just maintained her position in the lift. And the lift maintained its position on deck eighteen.

But why? Had she been hurt in the course of Geordi's maneuver, or maybe in an ensuing melee with her guards—hurt so badly that she'd had only enough strength to go this far, and no farther?

Or was she up to something else entirely? Something he had failed to figure out?

The doors of Worf's lift opened and he swung out, breaking into a run. Nevins and Loyosha pelted along behind him.

All of them had their phasers at the ready—just in case.

"Computer," the Klingon barked one more time. "Location of Commander Asmund."

"Commander Asmund is in a turbolift on deck eighteen," the computer confirmed.

Worf's mind raced as fast as the rest of him. He had a vision of her standing there in the lift, doors open, a grim smile on her face—and then, when she heard him coming, closing the doors and watching the look on his face as she escaped him.

Was that it? Was she trying to humiliate him, knowing he would lead the search for her?

For what reason? Sheer spite?

Or was she truly mad now—not only homicidal, but out of touch with reality in other ways as well?

This time, when the Klingon arrived to confront the fugitive, he had plenty of company. Not only Nevins and Loyosha, but an additional trio of security officers approaching from the other end of the corridor.

Contrary to Worf's premonition, the lift doors were closed. He took in his people with a glance.

"Phasers on stun. Be prepared for anything."

Then, careful to keep his eyes on the doors, he touched the lift security override pad on the bulkhead.

Not that he expected the action to accomplish anything. With the technical expertise Asmund had demonstrated, Worf fully expected that she'd jammed the door-opening mechanism, which would force him to find an engineer capable of bypassing or otherwise nullifying her handiwork.

Much to his surprise, however, the override worked. The doors opened.

The security officers tensed, training their weapons on the interior of the compartment. As it turned out, it wasn't necessary.

There was no one inside.

Muttering a curse, Worf took a step forward—and noticed something on the floor of the lift. Grunting, he went in and picked it up.

A communicator. He turned it over in his hand.

Asmund had led him on a merry chase. And he had been too concerned with more complicated explanations for her behavior to consider the simplest one of all.

What was the expression humans used? About failing to see the forest for the trees?

The fugitive had asked the computer for Morgen's whereabouts and then programmed the lift for that destination—with a stop on deck four, just to prolong the chase. And while her communicator was buying her time, she was using it to serve her purposes.

He should have known she'd try something like this, the security chief told himself. He should have *known*.

He scowled. Asmund could be anywhere on the *Enterprise* now. Absolutely anywhere. He had no choice but to have his people comb the ship for her, inch by inch.

And Morgen . . . he had to contact the Daa'Vit, alert him to—

"Lieutenant Worf?"

The Klingon turned at the sound of his name. He was a little startled to see Morgen standing there, casting a curious eye over the proceedings.

"Is something wrong?" the Daa'Vit asked innocently.

Worf's scowl deepened. "That," he growled, "is one way of putting it."

The bleeding from her temple had stopped, but Asmund's head hurt mercilessly. Taking a deep breath, she leaned back against the cargo container and tried to put her thoughts in order.

By now, she thought, they would have found the communicator in the turbolift. And begun the search in earnest.

But it was too late. Avoiding the use of the lifts completely, she'd found an entrance to the cargo bays on deck thirty-eight and slipped inside.

Fortunately, the bay's manifest had told her it had the kind of cargo she needed. And the *Enterprise* crew had been every bit as efficient as it was reputed to be; the dolacite containers she sought were all in their proper locations.

Used extensively these days to line the insides of warp nacelles, dolacite was the only substance routinely carried on Federation starships that could foil internal sensor systems. By hiding among containers full of the stuff, Asmund had effectively rendered herself invisible to the ship's internal security systems.

She glanced at the phaser in her lap. Picking it up, she felt its reassuring heft.

Under other circumstances, it might have been a liability to her. After all, every phaser was hooked in with the ship's computer—to prevent the use of power levels at which a random blast could punch through a hull wall. And with that kind of hookup, it wasn't all that difficult to scan the *Enterprise* for phaser locations—there were only a few dozen of them on board.

It was certainly a lot easier than trying to find a single human bio-profile among a mostly-human population of more than a thousand individuals.

But the dolacite protected her from that kind of detection as well. Which was a good thing. She needed the phaser.

You've bought yourself some time, she mused. You'd better put it to good use.

If only her head didn't hurt so much.

All in all, Beverly decided, they'd been pretty fortunate. Not only had Simenon's strategy gotten them out of the slipstream, but they had avoided any truly serious injuries. The worst was a compound fracture of the leg, suffered by a man named Starros—one of the security officers who had been watching Idun Asmund. Nor had sickbay sustained any damage; there wasn't even a tricorder out of place.

Of course, Asmund had escaped in the course of the beating the ship had taken. And according to Worf, she was armed with a phaser and dangerous as hell.

But so what? They were also in Romulan space, in peril of being blasted to atoms or—if Fate was kind— merely becoming prisoners of the Empire.

Somewhere along the line, the doctor had decided it wasn't worth getting scared. And so, when the last of those injured in the attempt to break free of the slip-stream had been treated, she'd decided to return to her cabin, and enjoy some much-needed rest.

As soon as she stepped out of the lift, Beverly noted the beefed-up security presence in the vicinity of her door. She asked what it was about.

"Lieutenant Worf's orders," one of the officers on duty replied.

"I see. Then you've got squads like these by the captain's quarters as well? And Commander Riker's?"

"In every occupied residential corridor, Doctor."

Crusher nodded. "Good," she said. "I wouldn't want to be singled out for special treatment or anything."

The security officer looked at her. "I beg your pardon?"

"Don't mind me," the doctor told her. "I'm just asserting my right to be in as much jeopardy as everyone else."

And while the officer tried to decipher her last statement, Crusher walked by her and entered her apartment. It felt good not to be afraid anymore.

As she stepped inside, she saw a tiny red light shining at her from her bedroom. It was on the tape player—a reminder that the thing was on "pause." And a reminder as well that she'd made a promise to herself about listening to the end of the tape.

She let the light draw her on. Hell—if she was going to be space dust before long, she was at least going to hear the end of Jack's story first.

Without even ordering the lights to activate, she sat down on her bed and touched the display marked "play." Immediately, the tape picked up where it had left off.

"—there's Greyhorse and Pug Joseph and Simenon, who you've heard about also, and—hell, I'd better stop before I read off the whole roster. As I said, though, they're a good bunch."

Crusher sat back against her cushions. Maybe *that* was what had given her this spurt of resolve—the cumulative effect of hearing Jack's voice these last few days. Exposure to the courage that had spurred him to life—and ultimately death—among the stars. It was as good an explanation as any.

"And while we're on the subject of Greyhorse," Jack went on, "it seems there's more to him than meets the eye. He comes off pretty quiet, pretty studious. But the other day, I think I caught him in a compromising position . . . with Gerda Asmund, of all people. You see, Vigo and I were—"

Crusher's finger darted out and stopped the tape. In the dark of her bedroom, she could hear the thumping of her heart against her ribs—the sudden urgency of her breathing. Touching the mechanism's control display again, she rewound for a few seconds. Then she played it back again.

"—more to him than meets the eye. He comes off

pretty quiet, pretty studious. But the other day, I think I caught him in a compromising position . . . with Gerda Asmund, of all people. You see, Vigo and I were repairing to the lounge for a game of *sharash'di.* We didn't know there was anyone in there. And as we came in, we saw Greyhorse and Gerda sort of—well, sort of moving apart, as if they'd just been embracing one another. Anyway, I didn't want to embarass them, so I just ignored it, and so did Vigo. We went straight to the—"

The doctor shut off the machine. She had heard enough. *Oh my god,* she thought. *Oh my god.*

Heart hammering in her chest, she punched her communicator.

In the dim light he'd come to prefer, Carter Greyhorse sat in his quarters and considered the Klingon ceremonial knife. It was sheathed almost to the hilt in a black crust of dried blood—Ben Zoma's blood.

But not enough of it, apparently; the captain of the *Lexington* was still alive. The murderer cursed softly. He knew now that he should have inflicted a few more wounds before he fled. But if he'd stayed a little longer to do that, some crewman might have stumbled onto the scene.

And he couldn't afford to be found out. Not then— and not now. There was still so very much to do.

Turning the knife in his hand, he admired its cruel, cold lines, its sturdiness. It was a good tool; it had been made well. As well as the knives that Gerda had owned —but then, that was no surprise, considering Gerda and Idun had gotten them from the same source.

Idun . . . it was strange to see her again, after all these years. She was even more beautiful than he remembered

—just as Gerda would have been, if she'd lived. It made him ache to think about that. *If she'd lived . . .*

Straightening, he put the thought from his mind. There was no time for sentimentality. He had to think— to prepare.

What was that line from Robert Frost? *"Miles to go before I sleep . . ."* He smiled grimly. Rising, he crossed the room and slipped the blood-blackened blade beneath his mattress—pushing it in just enough so that it couldn't be seen.

Eventually, he knew, someone would suspect him and search his room. And the knife would be found. But by then, it would be too late for those who had wronged Gerda Asmund.

And he would no longer care what they did to him.

Picard was sitting in his ready room, reviewing all his options, when Beverly reached him.

"It's Greyhorse," she said without preamble. "Greyhorse is the killer."

Picard started. A chill climbed the rungs of his spine. "How do you know?" he asked.

Crusher's voice was trembling. "One of Jack's tapes. He and Vigo saw Greyhorse and Gerda embracing."

The captain thought about it. Gerda . . . and Greyhorse? "He never told me."

But then, he wouldn't have. That was why people had trusted Jack Crusher. He would sooner have died than given away a confidence.

"If Gerda and Greyhorse were involved—" the doctor began.

"Hold, Doctor." Picard didn't wait for the rest. "Lieutenant Worf," he called out.

"Worf here," came the reply.

"I want Doctor Greyhorse arrested and confined to his quarters. This assignment takes priority over all others—including the hunt for Commander Asmund."

Picard could imagine the confusion on the Klingon's face. But to his credit, Worf's hesitation lasted only a moment.

"Aye, sir. Worf out."

Picard was silent a moment.

"I thought I knew him, Jean-Luc," Crusher said. "I worked with him for a year at Starfleet Medical."

She sounded as if she were on the verge of tears.

"I thought I knew him, too," he said. "I thought I knew them all."

When the doors opened on the cargo deck where Asmund was hidden, the first thing she did was check the power charge on her phaser. Not that it was at all necessary—she already knew how many shots it had left. But her instincts compelled her to make sure.

The second thing she did was move forward into a crouch. Her legs hurt in a number of places—small injuries she must have suffered when she was thrown about the brig. But she had to endure all that now—just as she had managed to endure the pain in her temple for the last hour or so.

It was disappointing that they had thought to look for her here so soon. She hadn't had nearly enough time to consider what had gone before—to come up with even a halfway reasonable theory as to who the murderer might be.

Of course, it wasn't *necessarily* a security officer who'd just entered. It could have been a crewman coming down for supplies, or to make sure the environmental controls were working. After all, there were certain containers that carried temperature-sensitive cargo.

But Asmund had to be ready for the worst. She had to assume that Worf or someone else had outguessed her.

As the doors whispered shut again, she heard voices. *Two of them. Or more.* Leaning forward a little more, she strove to hear what they were saying.

But they had stopped. Definitely security, then. A couple of cargo handlers wouldn't have had any reason to become so quiet. She held the phaser a little tighter.

Then the silence was broken by the beep of a communicator. One of the security officers muttered something beneath his breath.

"Bednarik here," she heard someone say.

"Our orders have changed," said the voice on the intercom. Asmund recognized it immediately as Worf's.

"Changed, sir?" Bednarik was still trying to speak softly, though it must have been obvious to him that he'd lost the element of surprise.

"That is correct," the Klingon confirmed. "We are no longer searching for Commander Asmund. Our new objective is Doctor Carter Greyhorse."

Greyhorse. Asmund felt her teeth grind together.

"The big fella," Bednarik said.

"Precisely," came Worf's reply. "You are to report to deck twenty-four. Greyhorse has shown himself to be a consummate technician—he may decide to strike at the environmental support equipment."

"Aye, sir." A beep signalled the end of the conversation.

Bednarik's companion spoke up for the first time since they entered the cargo deck: "What about Asmund?"

There was a pause. "We forget about her," Bednarik said, "for now. But if we happen to run across her, I'll tell you what—I'm going to shoot first and ask questions later."

Asmund nodded. She wouldn't have expected anything else.

Then the cargo deck doors opened and closed again, and she was alone. She relaxed—though not completely.

Worf and his security people had given her what she'd been looking for—the identity of the murderer. If she just sat tight, they would eventually find Greyhorse and stop him. But the Klingon in her couldn't accept that as a solution.

The man had soiled her honor—tried to kill her comrades. It was *her* job to deal with him—no one else's.

She would get to him first. She promised herself that.

Carter Greyhorse was on his way to sickbay. He had some unfinished business there.

Once before, he'd visited sickbay to complete a job he'd started. But just when he thought he was alone with Cadwallader, just when he was about to slip the *ku'thei* pill between her lips, Beverly Crusher had come in and ruined everything.

This time, Crusher would not interrupt. The computer had already assured him that she was in her quarters. And with the murderer caught—or so everyone thought —it would be simple enough to smile his way into critical care. And pay Ben Zoma back.

As he would pay them *all* back. Each and every one—for taking from him the only person who'd ever made him *feel* anything.

Turning the corner, he entered the medical facility. It was crowded with those who had been injured in

Simenon's maneuver. None very badly, he saw—which was just as well. He hated to see innocent people get hurt; he was, after all, a doctor.

A few steps in, a nurse turned and looked up at him. She smiled. "Doctor Greyhorse," she said, recognizing him.

He smiled back in a perfunctory sort of way and kept going. She had no idea; his expression, as reserved as ever, hadn't given her a clue.

Critical care was just ahead and to the right. The barrier obscuring the area was still up, though it was meaningless now. The murder attempts were common knowledge. There was nothing left for Picard to hide.

As Greyhorse approached the barrier, he resolved to be patient. His lack of success in finishing off Cadwallader would not make him hurry. This was a slow game, this killing—slower than he had anticipated. But he would ultimately be the winner. All he had to do was keep going and not make any mistakes.

Then he saw that there was no one attending to Ben Zoma at the moment. My luck is changing, he thought. I will not need to be patient after all.

For a moment, he studied the readings on the monitor above the bed. Interesting. Ben Zoma was putting up quite a fight. It was a good thing he'd had the opportunity to come by—and change that.

Glancing around quickly to make sure they were still alone, he reached for the *ku'thei* pill. Fortunately, it left no traces. Nor was it a substance the transporter's bio-filter was programmed to red-flag. But then, he'd selected it on that basis. Working in the upper echelon of Starfleet Medical gave one some knowledge of bio-screening systems.

Sitting down in the chair at Ben Zoma's bedside, he

leaned over the patient. To an intruder, it would appear as if he were examining him. Ben Zoma's face was pale and waxy-looking; the only color in it was where the skin had been irritated by the tubes in his nostrils and his mouth.

Gilaad Ben Zoma, this is for Gerda Asmund. For the—

Suddenly, Greyhorse heard sounds of alarm outside the barrier. The *ku'thei* pill was poised just above Ben Zoma's parched lips. He had to do something—he couldn't allow himself to be found like this. Gripped by panic, he thrust the pill into the man's mouth as far as it would go.

That's when Dr. Selar came dashing around the barrier. One look at him was all she needed. Without breaking stride, she gripped him by the shoulder and spun him away from Ben Zoma.

She knows, he realized. The knowledge jolted him. But how? How can she?

And who *else* knows?

Shortly, they all would. No matter if he killed her now as she tried to get the pill out of Ben Zoma's throat. If she lived, she would spread the word—assuming it was not spreading already. And if she died, there would be witnesses to the fact that he had done it.

Better to escape while he still could. To follow the steps he'd outlined for himself if he should ever be found out.

Bolting through the space between the barrier and the bulkhead, Greyhorse flung himself through the gathering crowd. Someone tried to grab him by the wrist; twisting down savagely, he snapped the man's grip and left him screaming.

Then he was hurtling toward the exit, his mind locking down like a machine. Which, in the end, was what he was born to be. Not a man, but a machine. No more human, in all the ways that mattered, than the android Data. *A machine.*

In the corridor, people stopped to look at him. But that was all. Obviously, no one had warned them about him. They hadn't heard yet.

Taking advantage of the fact, he headed for the turbolift. A female crewman was in his way; he hurled her aside. Once he got to the lift, he knew, it would be impossible to stop him. His objective was only two decks away—a matter of moments.

As he passed a joining of the corridors, however, he saw something out of the corner of his eye. A flash of red and black. There was an impact, though he was too deep into his battle-state by now to feel it, and he was shoved sideways into the bulkhead on his right.

Recovering, he caught sight of his attacker's face— recognized the blue eyes, narrowed in determination. And of course, the beard.

Riker was quick. He got in a solid blow to the side of Greyhorse's head—a blow that jarred the big man but did not stop him. Before the first officer could follow up on his attack, Greyhorse retaliated.

First, he snapped Riker's head back with a well-placed *kave'ragh*—just as Gerda had taught him. Then, while the smaller man was still stunned, he lifted him off his feet by the front of his tunic and flung him hard into the bulkhead.

Before Riker slipped to the deck, Greyhorse was lunging for the turbolift again. A fraction of a second later, the doors opened and he was inside.

"Transporter room five," he said, breathing just a little harder than normal. Removing his communicator, he flung it on the floor. Then the doors closed and, though he couldn't feel it, the lift started to move.

* * *

"Captain? This is Doctor Selar."

On the bridge now, Picard glanced at Data before replying. "Yes, Doctor. What the devil is going on there?"

"Apparently, you were right to warn us about Doctor Greyhorse. He was putting something in Captain Ben Zoma's mouth when I interrupted him. A pill—poison, I would guess. Fortunately, I was able to retrieve it."

Picard swore softly. It had been close.

"Where is Greyhorse now?" asked the captain. "Were you able to detain him?"

A slight pause. "No, sir. My priority was the safety of the patient."

Picard nodded. "Of course. Thank you, Doctor."

"We must stop him, sir," Data said. He looked at the captain. "With what he knows about ship's systems—"

Before he could finish, Picard was calling Worf over the intercom.

"Aye, sir?" the Klingon replied.

"Mister Worf, we have located Doctor Greyhorse. He fled sickbay just a few moments ago."

The Klingon grunted. "I'll dispatch a team to the area—and limit the turbolifts to security use only."

"Very good," the captain said. He almost warned Worf about Greyhorse using his communicator to lay down a false trail—but he was sure the security chief was well aware of that tactic by now.

He stood and turned to Worf's replacement at Tactical.

"Get Commander Riker up here right away. And—"

"Captain?"

Picard responded without turning. "What is it, Commander?"

Data seemed to hesitate for just the smallest fraction

of a second. "Sir, we have made contact with the Romulans."

Picard turned and faced the main viewscreen—and his mouth went dry. Before him was a Romulan warbird —immense, powerful. And he knew without asking that all its disruptors were trained on the *Enterprise*.

CHAPTER 18

Picard stared at the image of the Romulan warbird. "Open hailing frequencies," he instructed.

A moment later the screen filled with a typically Romulan visage—finely chiseled, with hooded eyes and long, pointed ears. The man was seething with confidence—and why not? By now his scanners would have picked up the *Enterprise's* lack of warp drive activity—not to mention its inadequate shielding. He had the Federation ship at a disadvantage and he knew it.

The only thing he couldn't have divined was the set of circumstances that placed the *Enterprise* in Romulan territory. But then, he might not have cared. The fact was they were *there*.

The human decided to take the initiative. "I am Jean-Luc Picard, captain of the Federation vessel *Enterprise*. Whom do I have the honor of addressing?"

His mouth curling into a faint smile, the Romulan responded. "My name is Tav. I command the *Reshaa'ra.*" The smile faded. "You are in Romulan space. You will surrender your ship immediately."

No give in this one, Picard observed. No inclination toward satisfying his curiosity; he's going to go strictly by the book.

The captain frowned. He didn't have many tools at his disposal—just the truth, really. "We are not here by choice, Commander Tav. We were brought here by a subspace phenomenon which we only recently escaped."

The Romulan's eyes narrowed ever so slightly. "How intriguing," he commented. "Our engineers will no doubt be fascinated when they have the opportunity to debrief you. In the meantime, I repeat: you will surrender your vessel. The alternative is destruc—"

Picard never heard the end of Tav's threat.

Normally, Data's duties at Ops would have kept him from seeing what happened to the captain. However, the android had been halfway turned around in his chair, awaiting instructions, when Picard was enveloped in the scintillating pillar of light associated with molecular transport.

A fraction of a second later the captain was gone. It was as if he'd never been there in the first place.

There were curses and murmurs of apprehension from the other officers on the bridge. Data found that they were all looking in his direction, including Dr. Crusher.

Of course, he told himself. I am the ranking officer. They want to know what to do.

Using his control panel, the android cut into their link with the Romulan vessel. On the *Reshaa'ra,* it would appear to be a technical failure. With that done, Data turned and addressed the bridge contingent.

"Please remain calm," he said. "We must not let the Romulans know that anything has happened to our captain; it would only place us at a greater tactical disadvantage."

They understood. A moment later there was no trace of the confusion that had resulted from Picard's disappearance. Satisfied, Data restored the video portion of the link; after all, he didn't want the Romulans to think they'd been cut off on purpose.

Lastly, looking straight ahead at the Romulan called Tav, the android availed himself of the intercom system: "Commander Riker, please respond . . ."

It had been a long time since someone had handed Riker as bad a beating as Greyhorse had. As the first officer slowly got to his feet, he found he hurt in a dozen places. Could've been worse, he thought. He'd had no idea the doctor was so strong—though his size should have been a clue.

"Commander? Are you all right?"

He turned and saw Pug Joseph making his way through a gathering crowd. The man's face was lined with concern.

"Fine," the first officer replied, dusting himself off. He looked about, saw that the woman Greyhorse had flung aside was recovering too. A couple of crewpeople were helping her up. "You didn't by any chance see what happened to Dr. Greyhorse, did you?"

Joseph's brows came together. "Greyhorse? *He* did this to you?"

Riker nodded. "I'm a little stunned myself—no pun intended."

"I don't get it. What's the matter with him?"

The first officer met the other man's gaze. "Greyhorse is the murderer, Mr. Joseph."

Pug just stared at him.

By that time Worf was approaching from one end of the corridor, trailed by a couple of security people. The Klingon navigated briskly through the clot of onlookers, his expression one of urgency.

"He was here," Riker said. "Unarmed, as far as I could tell."

Worf took in the scene at a glance, finally turning back to the first officer. "The turbolift?" he asked.

Riker was about to plead ignorance when someone in the crowd spoke up: "Yes. He went into the lift."

"No doubt," Worf said, "before we restricted access to them." He had begun to bark out a security clearance code to open the lift doors, when another voice cut in—over the intercom.

"Commander Riker—please respond." It was Data. And though Riker knew it was an impossibility, the android sounded . . . agitated.

He tapped his communicator. "Riker here."

"We have encountered a problem," Data informed him.

"What *sort* of problem? Not the Romulans?"

"Aye, sir—the Romulans."

The first officer cursed inwardly.

"But that is not all, Commander. The captain has disappeared."

Worf looked at Riker. "Disappeared?" he echoed.

"That is correct," the android said. "Shortly after he established communications with the Romulan commander, he vanished—in what seemed to be a transporter effect."

The first officer's mouth went dry. "Speculation, Data."

"We cannot rule out the possibility that the Romulans have captured him," the android explained. "But with our shields up, even at partial strength, it seems highly unlikely."

True. The Romulans didn't have the technology to transport through shields. Hell—neither did the Federation.

Then, what—?

Like sequenced grippers in a perfect docking maneuver, everything seemed to fall into place. Riker's conclusion hit him even harder than Greyhorse had.

"All hands!" the first officer called suddenly—thereby opening the entire intercom system to his message. "Remove your communicators immediately! I repeat—remove your communicators!"

It took those around him a couple of seconds to follow his line of reasoning—but follow they did.

"Greyhorse," Worf spat out, complying with Riker's order.

"He's gotten hold of a transporter," Joseph expanded, complying also.

"That's right," Riker said, taking off his communicator and tossing it onto the deck with everyone else's. Before his eyes, one of the badges—it was hard to know whose—shimmered with an unholy radiance and vanished. The sight sent a shiver through him.

Not a moment too soon, he reflected. If they'd waited any longer, one of them would have been Greyhorse's prisoner. Or worse—transporter soup.

"Data," he called, opening up a channel through the intercom grid. "I'm coming up to the bridge. Just stay where you are—don't do or say anything." He turned to Worf. "Find out what transporter room Greyhorse has occupied. Cut off his power, jam his annular confinement beam—whatever. Just stop him before he starts transporting away pieces of the hull."

The Klingon looked at him. "What about the captain?"

Riker frowned. What he was about to say went directly against his grain as first officer. "If he's still alive, try to keep him that way. But as long as Greyhorse has an operative transporter in his possession, Captain Picard is not the priority."

Worf looked as if he'd swallowed something rancid. But he obeyed, turning and leading his officers back through the crowd. Riker needed the nearby turbolift; the Klingon would find another one.

"I'm coming along," Joseph insisted, falling in behind the security team. He sounded determined.

Nor did Worf protest. Apparently, he was willing to accept all the experienced help he could get.

Riker turned to the lift and freed it with his own clearance code. As the doors opened, he got inside. "Bridge," he commanded.

And tried to figure out what in blazes he was going to say to the Romulans.

One moment, Picard was on the bridge; the next, he was somewhere else. And before he could determine exactly *where,* he felt something hard smash into his chin. Staggering under the impact, he was hit a second time, even harder. And a third. Finally, he fell, his legs refusing to hold him up any longer. As he lay there fighting off the lurching blackness that was threatening to engulf him, he felt the floor start to slide by.

His head felt like a block of stone, but he managed to lift it—to look around. He saw that he was in the transporter room, being dragged by someone—someone massive, who had a handful of the captain's tunic in his fist. After a second or two, he realized that it was Carter Greyhorse.

They were headed for the transporter controls. Why? Picard had no idea. His brain was too sluggish—he couldn't seem to pull his thoughts together. But instinctively, he knew that he had to stop the big man from reaching his destination.

Grabbing Greyhorse's wrist and swinging around at the waist, he fought off a black wave of vertigo and wrapped his legs around the man's ankle. Then he twisted his hips as hard as he could.

Caught unawares, the doctor reeled wildly. When Picard twisted a second time, he toppled altogether.

With an effort, the captain rolled away, already anticipating retaliation. But the big man was much faster than he seemed. Before he could scramble to his feet, Greyhorse whirled and kicked him in the ribs.

The pain was excruciating. Somehow, Picard weathered it and kept his legs underneath him. But it only made him an easier target. Putting all his weight behind the blow, Greyhorse leapt and kicked again. It was like being hit with a phaser set on heavy stun.

The captain skidded backward across the deck, the breath knocked out of him. As he wheezed and struggled to fill his lungs, Greyhorse advanced on him purposefully. A second time, Picard rolled in the opposite direction —it was all he could manage. Lights exploded behind his eyes; his pulse thundered in his temples. But he hung on to consciousness, greedily gulping each painful breath.

"You're as much a fighter as you ever were," the doctor said. He sounded as if he were speaking to him from a great distance. "But it won't help. Your crimes have finally caught up with you."

And with uncanny ease he lifted Picard's limp form and flung him across the room. The captain felt himself hit the deck, tumble, and finally come up hard against the base of the console. When it was all over, the taste of blood was strong in his mouth. He spat it out, lifted his head.

The transporter platform was being activated again. Dimly, through the layers of wool in his brain, he realized what Greyhorse might have been up to—and curling his fingers over the lip of the control console, digging his heels into the carpet, he slowly dragged himself to his feet.

Too slow, he told himself. *Too slow.* With each passing second, Greyhorse was destroying another life.

But as Picard inched up high enough to see his adversary, he knew that he hadn't been too late after all. Something had gone wrong for Greyhorse.

He could see it in the man's eyes—trained on him now instead of on the controls. They were fierce and dark, full of unbridled fury. His lower lip trembled savagely.

"Damn you!" Greyhorse rasped. He pounded on the transporter console with his huge right fist; it shuddered beneath the blow. "They're on to me! They've taken off their communicators."

A wave of relief swept over the captain. Someone had seen Greyhorse's strategy in time.

The big man reached over the console and took hold of the front of Picard's tunic. *"You.* You delayed me, or I would've killed them all by now—scrambled them in transit." His lip curled. "I wanted you to watch, Captain. I wanted you to see your friends die—that was the worst thing I could've hoped to do to you." His face was just inches from Picard's. It was a shaman's mask of pure, writhing hatred. "I never should have cut it so close. I should have scrambled you too, and been done with it. I just didn't think you'd fight so hard."

Trembling with rage, Greyhorse let go of the captain with one hand and started resetting the transporter controls. Picard grasped the man's wrist with both hands, but he couldn't seem to break that monstrous grip.

"Maybe I can't scramble *them,*" the doctor muttered. He looked up, his eyes suddenly alight. "But I can still scramble *you.*" He turned his attention back to the board. "And don't expect anyone to stop me from outside; I made sure they couldn't interfere once I got started."

Picard believed it. He knew what kind of technical expertise Greyhorse had demonstrated in his other attempts at violence.

"Carter," he gasped, still fighting to get air into his lungs. He needed time—to get his strength back. To make the room stop spinning. "Carter—*why?*"

The big man sneered at him. "Why? You have the gall to ask that—after you stripped Gerda of her honor? Of her life?"

The captain shook his head. "No," he got out. "I only stopped her . . . from killing Morgen . . ."

"Lies!" the doctor cried. With one hand he pulled Picard halfway up over the transporter console. His other hand curled into a claw and hovered just over Picard's face. "You dishonored her! You deprived her of her right to suicide! And then you dishonored *me*—by

making me the instrument by which you saved her!"
Spittle clung to the corner of his mouth. "Do you know
how she looked at me afterward? How she *hated* me? For
that alone you deserved the worst torture I could devise.
But her hatred wasn't the worst of it—the worst was
what happened in that rehab colony." His large brow
rippled painfully with the memory. "Klingons aren't
humans. They're not *meant* to be put in cages like
beasts—day after day, month after month. It deprives
them of everything that makes them Klingon . . ." He
swallowed hard. "It *changes* them."

Picard knew it would be no use arguing that rehab
colonies weren't cages. Greyhorse was mad—truly mad.
He felt another surge of vertigo wash over him and
fought to keep himself from succumbing.

"I saw her after she came out," the big man went on.
His upper lip curled back. "She wasn't the same. She
wasn't Gerda. I wanted to hold her, to help her after all
she'd been through—but she told me to just go away, to
just get the hell away from her." A sob came up from
deep in his massive chest. "She said I was no good for
her. That she'd paid for what she'd done, and she didn't
want to be reminded of it."

Another sob, worse than the first. He shook with it. "I
thought that she'd change her mind—get over it—and
we'd be together again. And then . . ." His eyes went
blank. "And then she died, and there was nothing left for
me to think about—except what I would do to the ones
who hurt her."

Past Greyhorse, Picard saw something happening to
the transporter room doors. They were glowing in a
couple of places—with a distinct pinkish radiance.
Phasers, he realized. Of course. Security was trying to
burn its way in.

But he couldn't let Greyhorse know—not until it was too late. Quickly, he looked away.

How long would it take for Worf to cut his way in? At one of the higher settings, only a few seconds. But there was less control that way. He might burn through and hit someone inside—someone like the captain—so he'd be using a lower setting.

And how long then? A minute? Maybe two? Could he stall Greyhorse that long?

As if in response to Picard's silent question, the doctor punched in the balance of the transporter's instructions and came around the console—jerking his captive along with him. They were headed back to the platform. And Picard could see that one of the disks was live—hungry for an object to transport.

The captain took a second to gather his strength and tried the same maneuver that had worked before. But this time he was too slow, or else Greyhorse was ready for him. Before he could get a good grip on his tormentor's wrist, the doctor stopped and swung him forward with all his strength. Unable to stop himself, Picard tumbled end over end, finally coming to rest against the base of the transporter grid.

When he looked up, he saw Greyhorse advancing on him. But behind the doctor, the phaser glow was getting darker.

"Carter," Picard gasped. "Don't do this. I hated what happened to Gerda too—but there was no other way."

The big man stopped, towering over him. He grunted scornfully. "That's it," he said. "Go ahead. Beg." He got down on his haunches, came closer than he should have. "I *want* to hear you beg."

The captain knew he wouldn't have another chance. Planting his heel against the side of the platform to get his whole body into it, he launched a blow at the center of the doctor's jaw. It landed more solidly than he might have hoped, jarring him all the way to his shoulder. There was a sound as of cracking ice and Greyhorse fell backward.

Pressing his advantage, Picard staggered to his feet and made for the door, where the hot spots were getting angrier than ever. I can make it, he told himself. I can—

Then he felt something grab his ankle, and his feet went out from under him. He hit the deck and Greyhorse whipped him around again toward the transporter platform. Clawing at the carpet, the captain managed to stop himself short of the live disk.

But the doctor had other ideas. Again, he drove a booted foot into Picard's ribs, robbing him of what sense had been restored to him. Then, picking the captain up like a rag doll, he took a step backward, preparing to hurl him to his death.

He was stopped short by a sound like all the banshees of hell as the doors to the room burst open. Greyhorse whirled to see what had happened and the captain groped for the big man's shoulder, trying to anchor himself against being flung into the transparent beam. But with what seemed like no effort at all, Greyhorse lifted him even higher.

The room was filling with a flood of security officers, led by Worf. To Picard's surprise, Pug Joseph was right beside him. They pointed their phasers, but stopped short of using them on Greyhorse once they saw the situation. Numbed, battered, the captain could only watch.

"Go ahead," cried the doctor. "Shoot me. And before I fall, I'll see to it that Picard's atoms are scattered through the void."

Worf stuck out a hand to hold his people back. "Put him down," he said, "and we will talk."

Greyhorse laughed. "What is there to talk about? A rehab colony—maybe the same one where Gerda lost her soul?" He shook his head. "I don't think so."

"Carter," Pug interjected, taking a step forward. "What are you doing? He was your captain, for godsakes. He was your friend."

The doctor's mouth twisted. "My *friend?* Then why did he kill the only person I've ever loved—the only one who ever made me feel *human?"* He glared at Joseph. "Why did *you?"*

The security chief shook his head. "I didn't kill Gerda, Carter."

"Didn't you?" the doctor asked. "You stood by like all the others and watched as they took her away. You—"

Picard wasn't quite certain what happened next. But somehow, it seemed that Greyhorse was hit from behind. The deck rushed up and hit the captain hard, and a moment later Pug was kneeling at his side.

Twisting his head, Picard tried to see what was going on. What he saw was Greyhorse, crouching like a beast at bay—held there by a figure in black and gold wielding a phaser. It took the captain a moment to realize that the figure was Idun Asmund.

She glowered at the doctor. "You forgot to lock out the other disks," she said. "You remembered everything else—but you forgot that."

"Traitor," he spat out. "How can you side with them? They killed your sister!"

Asmund's eyes narrowed. She raised the phaser just slightly.

Picard saw that it was set for "kill." The woman took a couple of steps toward Greyhorse.

"Idun," the captain said, "stop and think." With his arm slung over Pug's shoulder, he got to his feet. "You don't really want to do this."

Worf was just a few feet behind Greyhorse. He had his phaser in his hand as well. Set on stun, it was pointed at Asmund's breast—but he seemed unwilling to press the trigger. "It's over," he told her. "Your name has been cleansed."

"No thanks to him," she replied, taking another step toward the doctor. She was almost close enough now to reach out and touch him. "He would have stripped me of the only thing left to me—my honor. Knowing how hard I'd worked to disassociate myself from Gerda's crime, knowing what it meant to me to be trusted and respected again . . . he would have obliterated that without a second thought."

"Yes," Greyhorse agreed. "That and more. For Gerda. Someone had to *remember* her—*avenge* her."

The muscles in Asmund's jaw worked. Her eyes narrowed a notch.

"Commander," Worf entreated, "you *have* your honor. It is *intact.* Don't blacken it now. Don't finish the job he started."

For a long moment she stared at her former comrade. Then, suddenly, she replaced the safety on her phaser and tossed it to the Klingon. Worf caught it in midair.

Greyhorse grinned derisively. "Your sister had more courage. *She* would have killed me."

Asmund appraised him, her dark blue eyes as hard as stone. "No," she decided. "Gerda was too honorable to kill a madman."

Without another word, she walked over to Picard and took his other arm. "Let's go," she said, "Captain."

Picard looked at her and squeezed the hand that held his. "Yes," he responded. "By all means. We have some Romulans to deal with."

And as Worf and his security people surrounded Carter Greyhorse, the captain let his two former officers escort him out of the room.

"You are not Captain Picard," the Romulan commander observed.

Riker stood before the command center, where Beverly Crusher sat on the edge of her seat and sized up his adversary. He still had no idea of how he was going to get them out of this one.

Clearing his throat, he said: "I am Commander William T. Riker, first officer. The captain has been called away to deal with an emergency."

That elicited a certain degree of interest from the Romulan. "An emergency," he repeated. He made a derisive sound—loud enough to be heard over the communications link. "Something more pressing than a Romulan warbird with its talons around your throat?" He shook his head. "You take me too lightly, Commander. Perhaps I need to remind you where the *true* emergency lies."

Looking back at one of his officers, the Romulan barked an order. As the officer complied, his fingers dancing over his console, Riker had a feeling about the kind of reminder the commander had in mind.

And there was no way they could escape it. Not at impulse speed.

A moment later the bridge of the *Enterprise* shuddered. The first officer's teeth ground together; he hated being so helpless.

"Shields at eighteen percent," Data reported. He turned to face Riker. "One more such assault will result in extensive damage to the ship."

Riker nodded, still staring at the screen—and the Romulan. He cursed softly. Come on, Will—*think!* Do something—before it's too damned late!

The Romulan raised an eyebrow. "Now," he said, "will you surrender—or must I incapacitate you first?"

The first officer's mind raced, but to no avail. He was drawing a blank at the worst possible time.

Ironic, wasn't it? They couldn't move fast enough to even give these Romulans a run for their money, when not too long ago they were breaking every speed record in the—

Blazes! That was it!

Frowning at his adversary, he said: "I can't hear you, Commander. Your transmission is jumbled."

Of course, that wasn't the case at all—Riker could both see and hear the Romulan much better than he cared to. But he needed a minute to work on his idea.

The commander's head titled ever so slightly. He was trying to decide whether to believe the human or not—particularly in light of the apparent glitch that had occurred earlier.

Riker didn't have the luxury of waiting to see the outcome. Turning toward Tactical as if he wanted to know what had happened to communications, the first officer subtly drew a forefinger across his throat—a signal that Picard had used in the past. It meant *cut transmission.*

Recognizing the gesture, the Tactical officer complied. Nodding to Riker, he said: "Done, sir."

"Good," the first officer told him. He glanced at the viewscreen, where the Romulan was consulting with another of his officers. He looked skeptical—but at least he wasn't firing on them. Not yet.

Lifting his eyes to the intercom grid, Riker called on Geordi La Forge.

"Aye, sir," came the chief engineer's response.

"We've got trouble," Riker advised. "Romulans. I need warp one—and I need it now."

For a moment Geordi hesitated. The first officer's heart sank. If they couldn't rouse the warp engines even *that* much, his plan was useless.

"All right," La Forge said finally. "We can give it a shot. But I've got to warn you—we're probably not far enough from the slipstream yet. Even if we can get the warp drive to respond, it's probably only going to get us stuck in subspace again."

Riker smiled. "I'm counting on it." He turned to Wesley. "Heading one four five mark nine oh, Mr. Crusher. Warp one—on my order."

"Warp one," the ensign confirmed, locking in the new information.

Riker looked at the viewscreen. The Romulan commander was glaring at him, considering his options. He still appeared confident; he wouldn't act hastily. Not unless something changed.

Something like the powering up of the *Enterprise's* warp engines.

"Got 'em going," said Geordi over the intercom. "But we'd better move quickly—I don't know how long they'll last."

A split second later, the Romulan received the news. His brow furrowed as he saw the possibility of his prey slipping through his net. He whirled to address his weapons officer—

And the viewscreen reverted to an exterior view of the

Romulan vessel. The enemy had made the communications blackout mutual.

"Engage," shouted Riker, bringing his hand down for emphasis.

Wesley carried out the order.

The first officer steeled himself against the jolt of the Romulans' barrage. A second ticked off. Another . . .

No impact. That could mean only one thing . . .

"Proceeding at warp one," Wesley announced. He made no effort to disguise the mixture of relief and uncertainty in his voice. "At least, that's what the engines are—"

Before he could finish, there was an abrupt surge in speed. They could hardly help but notice it. And the starstreaks on the viewscreen began darting by with frenetic intensity.

"Commander—the Romulans are giving pursuit," the man at Tactical reported.

Riker nodded. Now, if there was any justice at all in the universe . . .

"What's their speed?" he asked.

The Tactical officer was prompt. "Nine point nine five, sir. The same as ours."

"Commander?" It was Geordi.

"It worked," Riker told him. "We're back in the slipstream. And so are they."

"Which is just the way you wanted it."

Geordi had caught on. And judging from the look on Dr. Crusher's face—a mixture of admiration and relief—Geordi wasn't the only one.

"That was the plan," the first officer agreed.

Of course, he'd taken a big chance. They were still sitting ducks if the warbirds decided to fire. But by now the Romulans were no doubt discovering they had more important matters to worry about.

"How's the warp drive?" he asked Geordi.

A pause. "Better than I figured it would be."

"Have we got enough juice to try your shield maneuver again?"

Another pause. "Not yet. Can you give me an hour?"

Riker said just what the captain would have said. "Take a *half.*"

Geordi said he'd see what he could do.

The first officer returned his attention to the forward viewscreen. After all, his work wasn't over.

"Raise the Romulan commander," he told the Tactical officer.

Seconds later, his adversary's face filled the screen again. But this time that air of confidence had been replaced with suspicion.

"What have you done?" the Romulan asked angrily.

"I have lured you into a trap," Riker explained. "The same one that forced us into Romulan space. Of course, we've since discovered a way out of it—which we'll be employing shortly."

The commander's eyes narrowed. "Do not taunt me, human. I still have my weapons trained on you. And your shields are at low power."

"True," the first officer conceded. "But we're your only hope of escape. If you destroy us, you'll never see your homes again." He smiled affably. "Sometime prior to our departure from subspace, we'll give you the data you need to follow us."

The Romulan looked incredulous. "What kind of fool do you take me for? If you truly know a way out, why would you share it with us?"

"Because we have no reason to do otherwise. It will take you some time to decipher the information—and by the time you do, we'll be safely out of Romulan territory."

The commander mulled the matter over. "There is a way to insure that you do not leave us here. We could take hostages."

Riker shook his head. "I'm afraid not. Any attempt to board us will force us to try to escape prematurely. If we succeed or fail, you will be left here alone—without the information you need. And if we fail—we will be destroyed," he lied. "Again, leaving you here alone, with no inkling of how to extricate yourself."

The commander's mouth became a hard, taut line. How much did he know about the Federation? About human attention to such things as honor? About a poker-faced bluff?

At last, he uttered a curse—one the computer had trouble translating—and relented. "We will allow you to prepare whatever maneuver you have in mind. At the slightest hint of treachery, however, I will not hesitate to destroy you."

That was fine with Riker. He had no intention of being treacherous. Or, for that matter, even giving the *appearance* of treachery.

In the next moment, the Romulan's image blinked out again, to be replaced by the streaking stars of the slipstream. The first officer took a sobering look at them, then remembered that the Romulans were only half his problem.

"Lieutenant Worf," he called. "What's going on down there?"

The Klingon's answer wasn't long in coming. "Dr. Greyhorse has been taken into custody."

Riker swallowed. "And the captain?"

The words were hardly out of his mouth when the turbolift doors opened and Picard emerged. His face was swollen and bruised, his uniform was torn in a number of places, and there was a decided limp in his gait. But he was alive, damn it—he was alive!

A moment later, Asmund and Joseph stepped out of the lift as well. The blond woman had the look of one who'd just been exonerated.

"The captain is on his way up to the bridge now," replied the security chief.

"Actually," the first officer responded, "he's just arrived. Thank you, Mr. Worf."

Out of reflex, Crusher had started out of her seat—but Picard waved her away. "It's all right," he said dryly. "I'm much better than I look."

Riker smiled. As Picard made his way to the command center, he said: "It's good to see you, sir."

The captain nodded stiffly. "Good to see *you*, Commander. He glanced at the viewscreen and saw the telltale effects of the slipstream. *"Mon Dieu,"* he muttered. And turning again to his next in command, he asked the question with his eyes.

"It was the only way to escape the Romulans, Captain."

"We left them behind?" Picard asked.

Riker straightened. "Not exactly, sir. They entered the slipstream behind us."

And then the strangest thing happened. Slowly, gradually, a grin spread over the captain's battered visage. He regarded his first officer.

"Clever move, Number One."

Riker smiled again. "I try, sir."

CHAPTER 19

Picard leaned back in his ready-room chair, trying to ignore the damage Greyhorse had inflicted on him. Unfortunately, as his mind cleared, he was becoming that much more aware of the pain.

His former shipmates—Idun and Pug—apparently intended to wait with him until Dr. Selar arrived. Beverly Crusher had wanted to stay as well, but Picard had assured her again that his injuries were not all that serious, and that she was needed more down in sickbay. After all, should past prove to be prologue, she would have her hands full with slipstream-exit victims.

That is, he told himself, *if an exit is even possible. The fact that we did it once is no assurance we can do it again.*

No—he stopped himself. There was no point in entertaining morbid thoughts. The finish line was in sight; all they needed was a little luck and they'd win this race.

"You know," Pug said, "there are a couple of things you still haven't told us." He was standing by the captain's desk, addressing Idun, who was halfway across the room gazing into the captain's aquarium.

The blond woman looked back over her shoulder. "What's that?"

"How you knew where Greyhorse would be holed up. And how you managed to show up when you did."

Picard nodded, reminded that Idun hadn't finished the story she'd begun in the turbolift. "Yes," he said, his curiosity aroused, "how *did* you accomplish all that?"

She shrugged, turning to face them. "It really wasn't all that difficult. I was tipped off by Commander Riker's warning over the intercom—the one that instructed everyone to remove their communicators. I asked myself why that might be necessary—came up with the fact that the communicators are used to establish beaming coordinates—and realized that someone with danger- ous intentions must have gotten hold of a transporter."

Pug grunted. "Good thinking."

"Indeed," the captain said. "But to beam yourself into the room which Dr. Greyhorse had taken over—" Suddenly he stopped, realizing the implications.

"That's right," Idun told him. "I had to find another transporter room and stun the operator on duty. Like- wise, the security officer who came to provide rein- forcements—no doubt following Mr. Worf's orders." There was a tinge of regret in her voice. "In any case, they should have regained consciousness by now."

Picard frowned. That wasn't exactly the kind of thing he liked to hear about—even if it *had* been a prelude to saving his life.

Pug, on the other hand, shook his head in apprecia- tion. "Beautiful. And once you had a transporter, you could use it to trace other transporter activity in the ship. So when you found something going on in room one, you just set the controls, stepped on the platform, and beamed over."

"Yes," Idun said. "Fortunately, Greyhorse planned to use the entire platform in working his revenge on us, so all the stations were operational. Which was a good thing, because I couldn't have beamed over with any assurance of success otherwise. Having never been on a Galaxy-class ship before, I would only have been guessing at the coordinates." She cast a glance at the captain. "Of course, Greyhorse might have realized the stations were open and locked them down—if he hadn't been distracted." A faint smile took shape on her lips. "I'm willing to wager you provided *more* than a small distraction."

Picard harumphed. "Not *much* more, I'm afraid."

"Don't sell yourself short, Captain," Pug told him. "I never thought of Greyhorse as a fighter, but anybody that big . . ." He left the conclusion hanging in the air.

"And if he was . . . *involved* with Gerda," Idun added, "he knew how to use his size to good advantage. Klingons are taught that at an early age."

For a moment, her dark blue eyes seemed to lose their focus; she folded her arms over her chest. Was she thinking about her sister and the relationship Gerda had kept secret—even from *her?*

"Be that as it may," Picard said, cutting into the silence, "I—"

His sentiment was interrupted by a beeping at the room's single entrance.

"Come," he instructed, expecting Selar. But as the doors parted, it was Worf who entered instead.

"Sir," the Klingon said. He acknowledged Pug and Idun with a couple of brief nods.

"You've attended to Dr. Greyhorse?" the captain

surmised. His discomfort was getting worse—harder to put aside.

"I have," Worf replied. "As a precaution against his escaping from the brig the way Commander Asmund did"—he shot Idun a sidewise look as he said this—"I've stationed additional personnel at the site. They have grappling devices to secure them against turbulence. Also, the brig's restrictive barrier has been repaired and placed on battery power, so it should not be affected by any damage to ship's systems."

"Excellent," Picard told him. "What about the possibility of suicide?"

"I have scanned the doctor's person. He will have no opportunities to take his own life."

"And my knife?" asked Idun.

Worf turned to her. "It was discovered in his quarters. It will be necessary to hold it as evidence."

Idun frowned, but she seemed to accept the necessity.

Turning back to the captain, the Klingon said: "Our search of Dr. Greyhorse's quarters also revealed a small supply of *ku'thei* pills. It was one of these that he used in his attempt to finish Captain Ben Zoma."

"I see," Picard responded. However, his attention was starting to wane as the pain mounted—particularly in his side, where Greyhorse must have fractured a rib or two when he kicked him. Where in blazes was Selar?

Coincidentally, his door chose that moment to beep again.

"Come."

This time it was the Vulcan. And she had her medical tricorder with her, slung by its strap over one shoulder. Also, what Picard recognized as a small case full of commonly used drugs.

Snatching a chair as she came in, she pulled it with her

as she approached him. "I assume," Selar said in a very businesslike tone, "that the captain would prefer to be examined in private."

Picard started to protest to the contrary, but his guests were already on their way out.

"Commander Asmund," he called, stopping her in her tracks. She regarded him.

"Aye, sir?"

"There is something I would like to say to you." He looked to Selar. "If you would give us a moment, Doctor—"

"No." Idun shook her head. Her posture was as stiff as ever—but there was an uncharacteristic vulnerability in her eyes. "There's no need, sir. I *know.*"

And before he could insist, she was out the door and on her way.

Picard sighed. He was glad he had been wrong about Idun Asmund. Very glad. He only hoped that she would finally get what was coming to her—the friendship and admiration of her *Stargazer* colleagues.

It was long overdue.

Before he had completed the thought, Selar was running her tricorder over him and making those discouraging sounds that doctors seemed so good at. Sighing, he submitted to the scrutiny.

It was Eisenberg's turn to monitor Ben Zoma when the captain's warning came over the intercom. They would be trying that maneuver again—the one that had gotten them out of the slipstream once before. And it would probably shake them up as much as it had the last time.

That was all right. Sickbay had fared pretty well once; there was no reason to believe it wouldn't do so again.

As he checked Ben Zoma's readouts for the umpteenth time, he thought about what O'Brien had told him in Ten-Forward—about "ringside seats" and "the greatest show in the galaxy." For a little while there, the transporter chief had made it seem so exciting, so heady. But if the stars were a little more tame next time he visited Ten-Forward, Eisenberg wouldn't be too upset.

And neither, he expected, would O'Brien—despite his brave talk and his toasts to "warp nine point nine nine five."

Completing his review of the readouts, the med tech started around the divider that separated Ben Zoma from their other patient—Cadwallader, no longer a critical-care case. But before he could reach the woman's beside, he caught a glimpse of a couple of cranberry-colored uniforms coming his way.

Instinctively, he turned to see what had occasioned a visit from the captain and his first officer—especially when the maneuver was to take place in a matter of minutes. Then he realized that it wasn't Picard and Riker at all. It was Captain Morgen and Commander Asmund. And right behind them, Lieutenant Joseph, and the Gnalish—Professor Simenon.

As Morgen led his companions past the curiosity-ridden med tech, he saw Cadwallader get up on her elbows and smile.

"To what do I owe the pleasure?" she asked.

"Our fear," remarked the professor. "We heard that it was safer here than anywhere else on the ship."

Cadwallader chuckled dryly. "You know," she said, "I think I believe you."

"Don't," Morgen told her. He laid his great bony hand

on her bed. "I just thought it was time you received a visit from your friends." He regarded Asmund. *"All* of them."

The blond woman nodded, returning the Daa'Vit's gaze. "That's right. Or at least, that's the reason he gave *me*. And when the ruler of the Daa'Vit Unity summons you, you don't dare disobey."

Morgen laughed and turned to the patient again. "For the record, it was actually more of a *request.*"

Cadwallader's smile got a little broader. "That's all right. Frankly, I don't give a damn why you're here. I'm just glad that you are."

"Guttle's Maw," the professor spat out. "What's next? Hugs and kisses all around?"

"What's going on here?" Morgen followed the voice to its source, and saw Dr. Crusher standing at the threshold of her office.

"I thought Commander Cadwallader might want some familiar faces about her—particularly now." The Daa'Vit smiled charmingly. "Won't you join us?"

Crusher seemed surprised—pleasantly so. "I'd be delighted."

Joseph turned to Morgen. "If it's all the same to you," he asked, "I'd like to be with Captain Ben Zoma." He glanced at Cadwallader. "You understand, Cad?"

"Of course," she told him.

"Wait," Asmund said. She looked at the doctor, indicating with a jerk of her thumb the divider that hid Ben Zoma from view. "Can we remove it?"

Crusher thought about it for a moment. "I don't see why not," she said at last.

Simenon snorted. "This is getting more sickly sweet all the time."

"Hush, you," Cadwallader told him as Crusher got two burly nurses to move the divider aside.

When Ben Zoma was revealed, they all stared at him for a moment. Then Joseph went to stand by his bed, and Asmund as well.

Morgen nodded approvingly. Old comrades banding together against the tide of events—no matter where that tide might take them. He was mightily glad he could call these people his friends.

Then he realized that it was almost time for the maneuver to begin, and the Daa'Vit held on to a convenient projection from Cadwallader's biobed.

This time things were a little different. On the downside, they didn't have full warp speed capability. On the upside, they knew what to expect.

Hunched over his engineering console, Geordi ran a couple of last-minute checks. Satisfied that all was in readiness, he turned to the command center.

"Ready to go," he told the captain, who'd been standing in front of his chair and looking back at the chief engineer, waiting patiently for just those words.

Picard looked just slightly the worse for wear—a big improvement over his condition a little more than half an hour before. Or so Geordi had been told, and by no less dependable a source than the first officer himself. Of course, Dr. Selar's ministrations had helped the captain regain some of his form—and a change into a new uniform hadn't hurt either.

"Thank you, Commander," said Picard. With perfect aplomb he sat down in his chair. "You may commence."

Without further ado, Geordi turned back to his monitor, where the blue-line representation was once again in effect. Rather than approach the desired configuration by stages, as he had before, he went right to the final product: two flat surfaces, one fore and one aft, each pitched at an angle of thirty degrees to the ship's long axis.

After all, they had no time to fool around. Geordi was confident that their current warp capability would be enough to hold the shields in place for the duration of the maneuver—but maybe not much longer than that.

For just a second before he input the change, he paused to consider the possibility that they had pushed their luck a bit too far—that this time the maneuver wouldn't work, or that they'd be torn apart in the process. Geordi looked around at the familiar figures on the bridge—defined in electromagnetic patterns that only he and his VISOR could decipher. Even in that tiny tick of time, he was able to consider them one by one: Picard. Riker. Troi. Worf. Data. Wesley.

The chief engineer smiled. If the maneuver failed this time, if they had miscalculated, it had at least been one hell of an adventure.

Steeling himself, he gave the computer its marching orders.

Idun Asmund studied the face of Gilaad Ben Zoma. It was gaunt and bloodless, so different from the handsome, smiling countenance that had been the man's trademark. It was painful for her to look at him—but being a true Klingon, she forced herself to do it anyway.

After all, he was dying. Not quickly, not without a fight, but he was dying nonetheless. And there might not be too many more opportunities to see him while there was still breath left in him.

Asmund looked at Pug. He knew also that Ben Zoma wasn't long for this world. She could see it in his eyes. It occurred to her that Pug might even feel responsible for what had happened. After all, he was a security chief—one of a breed that would sooner die themselves than see something happen to their commanding officers.

She sympathized, feeling responsible as well. Hadn't it been her knife that had stabbed Ben Zoma? And wasn't it her lapse of vigilance that had allowed Greyhorse to obtain it?

Asmund recalled the first time she'd ever seen anyone die. Though she and Gerda had been too young to understand at the time, her family was embroiled in a feud with another clan. There had been threats, then violence. And finally, in the middle of the night, two men had brought her father's older brother into the house.

She remembered her mother closing the door against the billowing mists. She saw her father again as he helped lay his sibling on a table—as he tore aside Lenoch's cloak and inspected his wounds. And she felt anew the mixed sense of fear and fascination—the guilt that had taken hold of her as she and Gerda peeked into the room all unnoticed by the adults.

Like Ben Zoma, Lenoch had been stabbed over and over again. Even in the dimly lit foreroom of her father's house, even against the dark hues of Lenoch's clothing, she had been able to see the blood—a lot of it and in many places. Her father had cursed at the sight.

The rest was a blur. She had a vague impression of being discovered by her mother—of being sent back to bed. Not that she and Gerda had been able to sleep. They'd lain awake all night gazing at each other, wide blue eyes a-glitter with moonlight, listening to the guttural exchanges in the rooms below them. Listening and wondering—until the night was shattered by the sound of a half dozen voices bellowing all at once. Like the cry of the *taami*-wolves that roamed the hills back on Alpha Zion, but with a tinge of something distinctly Klingon. And by that howling, they knew that Lenoch was dead.

But there was more—wasn't there? Before she and her sister had been shooed upstairs, hadn't she seen something else? Something that Gerda had remarked about once they were alone in their bedroom?

She frowned. It bothered her that she couldn't remember. *Gerda* would have remembered—but Gerda wasn't around to be asked. Idun forced herself to concentrate.

What was it? What had they seen?

Suddenly, the deck beneath her feet shuddered and shifted, forcing her to hold on to Ben Zoma's biobed in order to maintain her balance. It lasted only a couple of seconds, however. Idun looked around.

Certainly, the lack of a more violent tremor was encouraging. But no one was saying anything. At least, not until they received official word.

Then it came: "Attention, all decks. This is Captain Picard. We have returned to normal space with minimal damage to the warp drive and other systems."

There were murmurs of approval, sighs of relief. One doctor slapped another on the back.

"Please note," the captain's voice resumed, "that the crisis is not yet over. Our emergence from the slipstream phenomenon has deposited us once again in Romulan space. However, we are much closer to the Neutral Zone this time." A pause. "We will maintain yellow alert status until we leave Romulan territory—which, if all goes well, should be a matter of just a few hours. I thank you all for your cooperation."

Of course, Asmund thought, there was still the possibility of an encounter with another Romulan ship. But at least it wouldn't be the *Reshaa'ra*. It would take Commander Tav some time to unravel Picard's encrypted directions for emerging from the slipstream. And in the meantime, the Romulans would get a taste of—

Idun could feel the blood rushing to her face. A *taste* . . .

That was *it*—the thing she couldn't remember. Before their mother had chased them upstairs, she and Gerda had seen their father *taste* Lenoch's wounds!

But why? Why would he do that?

Unless . . . he suspected them of being *poisoned.*

It was a dishonorable thing to do in the course of an assassination. But then, whoever attacked Lenoch might have been a dishonorable individual.

Suddenly, a connection snapped into place. She looked down at poor, haggard Ben Zoma and wondered: what kind of person was *Greyhorse?*

"Dr. Crusher," she snapped—before she'd even completed her chain of reasoning.

Crusher rushed over. "What's wrong?" she asked.

"Poison," Idun said. "I think Ben Zoma's been poisoned."

The doctor shook her head. "No. Greyhorse never got that pill into him. Besides, I administered the antidote for *ku'thei*—just in case."

"I'm not talking about a pill," Idun insisted. "I'm talking about the *knife* Ben Zoma was attacked with."

Crusher's brow creased. "You think there was poison on the blade?"

Idun nodded. "Not enough, perhaps, to do the job as quickly as Greyhorse desired. But in the long run, enough to kill him."

Crusher glanced at her patient—and recognized the possibility that Asmund was right. "I don't suppose you know *which* poison?"

Idun shook her head. *Ku'thei* was widely used, but hardly the only option. Klingons used a number of untraceable toxins.

Nor could the doctor administer the antidote for each and every one—not all at once, or their interaction would prove as fatal as the poison itself. And Ben Zoma didn't have that much time.

Both she and Crusher knew all this. But how could they narrow it down?

"Idun," the doctor said, "Greyhorse never treated a Klingon in his life. Much of his knowledge of Klingon medicine must have come from Gerda."

So the question became: What poison would *Gerda* have used? Given what they'd seen the night of Lenoch's death, there could be only one answer: the poison their father had tasted. But what was it?

Idun bit her lip. She tried to picture her father again, dabbing his fingers in their uncle's wound. Lifting the fingers to his mouth. He'd said a word—hadn't he? A single word.

"Choc'pa," she told Crusher. "Try the antidote for *choc'pa.*"

CHAPTER 20

The stars outside were back to normal once again.

Guinan was surveying the newly restored Ten-Forward lounge, such as it was, when the doors to the place opened and revealed Pug Joseph. As he had the last time she saw him, he hesitated just inside the entrance.

This time, however, he wasn't drunk. She noticed that right away. But he looked off-balance, confused, as if he'd been staring at the sun for too long.

When he saw her standing behind the bar, he didn't get angry. He didn't turn tail, either. He walked right up to the bar and confronted her.

"Nice to see you again," she told him.

"Sure it is." For a while, he just stood there looking at her. Looking through her, she thought. Then he spoke up: "Listen, you were right. I've got a problem."

Guinan was genuinely surprised. She hadn't expected him to come around so quickly.

He smiled, though there was no humor in it. "You didn't expect me to say that, did you?"

She had to be honest. "Frankly, no, I didn't. What made you change your mind?"

He wet his lips. "A lot of things," Joseph said. "My captain was attacked—nearly fatally. And a good friend —make that two good friends—were seriously injured. All by a man I thought I knew." He breathed in once, out once. "I didn't know anything! I didn't know where my captain—my responsibility—was, or where he was going. I couldn't see the hurt that Greyhorse was carrying inside him, the hurt that twisted and changed him. I was too busy getting soused for anything else."

Guinan nodded. So that was it. Well, it wasn't the kind of therapy she'd have wished for, but it seemed to have done the trick. Admitting that a problem existed was half the battle.

But now that he had made the admission, there was no need for him to torture himself. "This isn't the *Lexington*," she reminded him as gently as possible. "You're not in charge of security on this ship."

"Doesn't matter," replied Joseph. "At the least, Ben Zoma was my captain. My responsibility." He looked down at the bar. "The last thing I wanted was to be the cause of someone else's death."

His emphasis on "else's" sent a chill up her spine. "You mean this happened before?" she asked softly.

"That's right. A long time ago." He raised his head until their eyes met. His were like black holes. "That's what I carry around inside of me. That's the reason I drink the way I do. Because I killed somebody, somebody who depended on me." A pause, as he wrestled silently with his demons. "You don't know what that's like. No one does—except ol' Pug." His face twisted. "So what do I do? What does anyone do when he has that hanging around his neck?"

Guinan's heart went out to him. She'd been right about this one, about his self-hatred. But like Troi,

she'd thought it was rooted in disappointment—
with his career, with the way his life had turned out.
She hadn't had any idea how heavy his burden really
was.

"You could start," she said, "by talking about it."

Joseph shook his head. "It's not a real nice story." His
expression suggested that he meant it.

"No problem," she insisted. "I hear all kinds."

That was all he really needed—those few words of
invitation. Slowly, painfully, he began to tell her what
had happened.

Normally, she would have heard him out—listening
ever so carefully, speaking only if he needed a push to
keep going—until he had purged himself of whatever
was plaguing him.

But this time was different. It was wrong.

"Stop," she said.

Joseph looked at her, a little shocked.

"I'm not the one who should be hearing this."

The man's eyes opened wide. He knew exactly what
she meant.

"No," he told her. "I can't."

Guinan smiled her most serene smile—the one she
used only when absolutely necessary. "You can," she
assured him. "What's more, you have to. It's the only
way."

Beverly wasn't expecting any visitors, so she was more
than a little surprised when she saw Pug Joseph in
sickbay, heading in the direction of her office.

As he filled her doorway, the *Lexington*'s stocky
security chief appeared uncomfortable. Fidgety. Or at
least that's how it seemed to the doctor.

"Pug." She smiled. "Hi. Care for some coffee?"

He shook his head. "No. Thanks."

"How about a seat, then?"

He nodded, pulled the chair out from the other side of the doctor's desk, and sat. For an awkward moment or two he just looked at the floor. When he raised his eyes, they looked . . . what? Haunted?

"How's the captain?" he asked.

"Fine. He'll be out of bed in no time."

Joseph bobbed his head. "Good." He glanced fiercely at something on the wall, and then at something else on her desk. But not at her—not exactly.

The doctor was acutely aware of sounds that she hardly ever heard otherwise . . . the murmur of physicians and nurses as they discussed some minor-injury case . . . the hum of an overhead light fixture that hadn't worked right since Simenon squeezed them out of the slipstream . . . the sharp clatter of a tricorder as it dropped onto a tabletop.

And still Joseph looked around, not quite facing her and not quite facing away—anger and hurt passing over his face in waves.

Beverly leaned forward. "Pug—is something wrong?"

He looked directly at her now, and his mouth became a taut, hard line. "Yes. Something's wrong," he got out. He swallowed. "It's been wrong for a long time."

She returned his gaze, not having the least idea what he was talking about. "I don't understand."

"No," he said. "I guess you wouldn't." He sighed deeply. "You've heard the story about how Jack was killed, right? About the problem with the nacelle, and how we had to go out there and sever it? How the energy buildup overcame us, and Jack died in the explosion?"

Crusher nodded. "Of course."

"Well, it didn't exactly happen the way you heard."

The doctor felt the blood drain from her face. "What do you mean?"

Joseph thrust his chin out. "I mean, Jack didn't have to die." He paused. "It was because of me that he got killed. Because of *me.*"

Crusher felt as if someone had hit her in the stomach. Clutching the armrests of her chair for support, she stared at Joseph. Watched him hang his head, watched his shoulders rise once and sag.

"It was hard work cutting through the nacelle assembly," he told her. His voice was distant. "We were drenched with sweat despite the cooling systems in our suits. And as hard as we worked, it didn't seem we were making much progress. Being out there, being so focused on what you're doing, you lose track of time. You feel like you've been hanging out over the edge forever, your whole life.

"And all the time, the energy is cycling through the warp field generator. Building and building, getting ready to explode. And you don't know when—you just don't know. Any moment could be the one." He shook his head. "It gets to the point where you believe you can feel the explosion—the heat, blistering your skin. And the impact—like someone's taking a hammer to all your bones at once. And the shrapnel—the tiny pieces of hull ripping through you like razors.

"We thought about that. I did. Jack did too—you could tell by the expression on his face, by the feverish look in his eyes. He was just as scared as I was. But he didn't panic. He just kept at it, slicing away with his phaser rifle. Talking with the captain every now and then, putting on a show of confidence despite the emptiness he felt in his gut.

"Getting into the transfer tunnel was the worst part.

The *worst.* We could imagine all the energy jumping around inside. Lightning in a bottle. And yet we were pouring on all that phaser fire—like lighting a giant fuse. It was crazy. We knew that, I was *telling* myself that, but we kept firing at the tunnel as if we were too stupid to accept it.

"Suddenly, we were in. We were in and we hadn't blown up. Jack told the bridge and everyone was happy. I was happy too. I was giggling like a madman." A muffled groan. "I think I lost it then. I used up all my nerve getting into the transfer tunnel. After that I had nothing left—nothing. I fired away, I did what I was supposed to, but it wasn't me that was doing it. It was somebody else's arms holding the rifle, somebody else's eyes staring into that mess of tangled metal and circuitry and hellfire. And after a while, that someone didn't have the brass to stick around."

He raised his head, looked at her. If Crusher had thought his eyes were tortured before, she knew now that that had been nothing—compared to *this.*

"At one point Jack was grabbing my arm. He tried saying something to me, but our communicators were dead—silenced by all the energy running wild around us. And even if they'd been working, I don't think I would have heard him. I was too rattled by then. Too intent on just getting out of there, getting back inside the ship. Getting *safe.* I let go of my rifle and started back for the hatch. And I screamed—I think—for him to do the same thing.

"He didn't. He stayed out there, cutting at the assembly—trying to do it by himself. More than halfway to the hatch, I looked back and saw him." Joseph's brows came together into a twisted knot. "I'll never forget it. There he was, blasting away like he couldn't stop." Pug's

330

eyes went wide. "And the energy leak from the nacelle was getting worse. It looked like something alive, something fierce—like the bloody Angel of Death or something. But he'd done some damage. It looked as if he was close to severing the nacelle entirely. Maybe with a little help from me, he would have.

"Suddenly, without warning, the energy leak began accelerating—growing like crazy. It was obvious that something was going to blow. But Jack didn't budge. He kept firing his rifle, even though you couldn't even see the phaser beam anymore for all the radiation pounding at him. He must have known how near he was to accomplishing his mission. And while he was trying to blast away the last of the assembly, I started moving again toward the hatch—even more out-of-my-head frantic than before. As fast as I was going, I should have gotten tangled up in my grapples. Somehow, I didn't."

Joseph bent his head again, ran his fingers through his closely cropped hair. "Then I saw the captain coming from the other direction, and I realized what I'd done. And I knew what the others would say about me—how I chickened out, how I lost my nerve. I couldn't stand the thought of that, I couldn't. So I just went limp, just pretended I was unconscious. It was all I could think of.

"I didn't expect him to drag me back. I thought he'd go after Jack—after his friend. But I was closer, I was a sure thing. A part of me wanted to tell him I didn't need his help, that he should have gone after the other guy to talk some sense into him. But then he would have known I was a coward, and he would have told everyone else. So I stayed quiet.

"When the energy pocket exploded, we were sheltered from the impact. All I saw of the blast was the radiation from it, and then the nacelle, or what was left of it, spiralling off into space. And I knew Jack was gone. The captain knew it, too; I could see him—"

Joseph's voice broke and he had to stop. "Howling," he whispered, shaking his head from side to side. And then a little stronger, as he drew on some inner reserve of strength: "Howling on the inside of his damned face plate, as if it was him that was dying, and not Jack. But just for a second or two. Then he pulled himself together and got me to safety."

A muttered curse. "That's when I told everyone the story—about how we'd blacked out from all that energy coming out of the transfer tunnel. About how we'd done our best, but it was just too much for us." Now the sobs came, wracking him, shaking the man like a rag doll. "And they believed me," he rasped angrily. "God help me, how they believed me."

Crusher sat there in her chair, not sure what to feel. Should I be angry, she wondered? Bitter? Should I pity him—or should I pity *me?*

Slowly, she got up and came around her desk. Pug wouldn't—or couldn't—look up at her. He was too ashamed—and not only of the tears that had to be in his eyes. He covered his face with his square, powerful hands.

How long ago was Jack killed in that accident? It seemed like forever. And Joseph had been carrying this secret—this burden—all that time. Until now he probably thought he'd be carrying it to his grave.

Tentatively, she reached out—and placed her hand on his shoulder. It was like a rock, clenched against the pain. She could feel it.

"It's all right," she said mechanically. And then she realized—it *was* all right, wasn't it? Whatever crime this man had committed, if one could call it a crime, was a

332

long time ago. And he had been her husband's friend; Jack wouldn't have wanted to see him this way, no matter what. She said the words again, with more conviction this time: "It's all right, Pug. *I forgive you.*"

Joseph looked up at her, his eyes red-ringed and swollen. Taking her hand off his shoulder, he held it against his cheek. And shamelessly cried some more.

It wasn't really Cadwallader's fault that she was running a few minutes behind schedule. After all, they hadn't let her see Ben Zoma until just a little while ago, and she hadn't wanted to leave sickbay before welcoming her captain back to the world of the living. Hell, she'd have done that much even if he'd been only her commanding officer—and not her friend as well.

Nonetheless, she hated like the devil to be late. Especially when it came to something as mysterious as the dinner experience Will Riker had created for her. Despite her protests, he'd told her nothing at all of what was in store—advising her only to wear "that dress" he'd seen the evening of their *last* scheduled appointment.

Finally, a little out of breath, she turned the corner and came in sight of their rendezvous point—the entrance to holodeck one. But Riker was nowhere to be seen.

Oh, come on, she remarked silently, slowing down as she approached the place. I'm not *that* late. And even if I were, he owes me one after the way he—

Abruptly, the doors to the holodeck opened and Riker stepped outside. He was wearing a fitted black suit, the kind worn on Earth for formal occasions. The first officer smiled and extended his hand to her.

She looked past him into the holodeck. What she saw

looked like a patch of lush green fir forest, with shards of deep azure sky showing between the needled branches.

"Don't just stand there," Riker said. "Come on in."

She turned to him. "Are you, um, sure I'm *dressed* for it?"

He nodded reassuringly. "You couldn't be dressed more perfectly."

Laying her hand in his, Cadwallader let him draw her into the holodeck. As the doors closed behind her, she got a better idea of her surroundings.

They were perched on a steep mountainside—or more specifically, on a wooded ledge jutting *out* from a steep mountainside. She could see other mountains all around them—a chain stretching in every visible direction to the horizon. And above them was a perfect dome of blue heaven, uninterrupted by even a single wisp of cloud. It looked like the kind of place that should have been quite cold, but the sun was hot and strong, and the trees protected them from the winds.

"You approve?" Riker asked.

She nodded. "Where are we?"

"Alaska," he told her. "Not far from where I grew up." He tapped his foot on the moss-covered ground. "I got a chance to see this place only once—just before I left for the Academy."

"Helipod?" she guessed.

"Nope. I *climbed* up. Took three whole days and a lot of bruised body parts, but I made it."

Cadwallader looked down into the valley below. She whistled.

"And it was just as beautiful as I thought it would be," he went on. "Only one problem. There was nobody to share it with."

She chuckled, amused. "I think I get the picture. But wasn't this supposed to be a *dinner* date?"

Riker snapped his fingers. Suddenly, a gas-fired stove materialized in front of them. There were a couple of pans on the cooking grill. The aroma that came to Cadwallader was spicy and faintly fishy.

"Smells good," she said. "What is it?"

"Trout remoulade," he replied. "An old family recipe."

He snapped his fingers a second time, and a red-and-white checkered tablecloth materialized not far from the stove. It sported a basket of bread and a couple of glasses of wine.

This time, Cadwallader actually laughed. "You think of everything, don't you?"

Riker shrugged. "When I'm inspired."

She turned to him. "And when it gets dark?" she asked. "What do we do to keep warm?"

"I don't think that will be a problem," he told her.

"Really? And why is that?"

He was completely deadpan as he said it: "You'll have to wait until *after* dinner to find *that* out."

Today, there were only two of them at Ben Zoma's bedside—Troi and Commander Asmund. Of course, the empath had a professional reason for remaining there. It was disconcerting to regain consciousness and find that so much had changed while one was unaware. Often, a ship's counselor could smooth the transition.

But not all Troi's reasons for visiting were of the professional variety. She also *liked* Ben Zoma. Hell—it was difficult not to.

And to be honest, she felt a little guilty for having had

to deceive him when he confronted her that time in the corridor. She was glad the time had come when she could drop the pretense and be honest with him.

Just as she was glad she didn't have to lie to Idun Asmund anymore. Or to probe her emotions for evidence of murderous intent.

"How long until we reach Daa'V?" Ben Zoma asked softly. With the poison completely neutralized, he was considerably stronger than he had been the day before. He'd even gotten most of his color back.

"Another four days," Troi told him. "And that's at warp nine."

Full warp capability was a luxury she'd never take for granted again. Not after crawling into and halfway through the Romulan Neutral Zone at warp one.

He thought for a moment, then seemed surprised. "We'll be on time."

"That's right," she said. "Even with all that's happened, we'll be on time. Thanks to Geordi and his engineering staff—and a little help from your friend Simenon."

Ben Zoma smiled. But a moment later the smile faded.

"It's too bad. About Greyhorse, I mean."

She nodded. "We all feel bad. Perhaps with some rehabilitation . . ." She shrugged. "One can only hope."

He turned to Asmund. She returned his gaze attentively.

"Funny," he said, "isn't it—that the one we were most eager to pin the problem on . . . should be so instrumental in the solution. And in saving my life to boot."

Idun grunted. "Remember Beta Gritorius Four?"

After a second or two it came to him. "So I do. Then we're even?"

The blond woman shook her head. "Not at all. It's just *your* turn again to save *my* life."

Ben Zoma laughed—which turned out to be a bad move, as it drew the attention of Dr. Selar. The Vulcan was suddenly standing at the foot of the biobed.

"I think we should be going," Troi said, rising.

Asmund stood too. "If we must. But I'll be back," she told Ben Zoma.

The captain of the *Lexington* pointed at her with mock-solemnity. "I'm depending on it, Commander."

Troi grinned—and not just at Ben Zoma's antics. She saw the look on Idun Asmund's face, and she knew that she was happy. For the first time in years the woman felt as if she *belonged*.

One didn't always have to be an empath to know what was going on in people's hearts. And to rejoice with them.

Worf looked at the entrance to his quarters, where the alarm was beeping insistently. "Enter," he said.

As the doors opened, Morgen's angular frame filled the gap. "I hope I am not interrupting anything," he remarked, his yellow eyes glinting.

Worf made a point of not paying excessive attention to the long, leather-wrapped object tucked under one of the Daa'Vit's arms—though when this voyage began, he would have been more than a little leery of it. "No," he replied evenly. "Not at all. Come in."

Morgen walked directly to the chair he sat in last time. Momentarily, the Klingon considered placing himself on the other side of the room, as he had before. Then he thought again and took a seat much closer to Morgen's —separated from it by only the width of a low, *s'naiah*-wood table.

Their eyes met and locked. Klingon and Daa'Vit—
though no longer *just* Klingon and Daa'Vit. With a hint
of ceremony, Morgen laid the leather-wrapped object on
the table.

"Open it," he instructed. His inflection rendered it
more of a request than a command.

Worf picked it up and unwrapped the thing. Before he
was entirely finished, he saw the curved, razor-sharp
blade. It gleamed even in the subdued light. The Klingon
regarded his visitor.

"Go ahead," Morgen said.

Carefully, Worf unwrapped it the rest of the way. He
noted the grim elegance of the weapon, its surprising
lightness, the intricately woven leather of its pommel.
He nodded appreciatively.

"I only regret," the Daa'Vit told him, "that it could
not be a real *ka'yun*. But I was quite pleased with the
job your ship's computer did in fabricating this one.
You'll find it handles slightly better than the one *you*
gave *me* when we participated in your 'calisthenics'
program."

The Klingon looked at him and suppressed a frown. It
was only reasonable to expect that a Daa'Vit would
make a superior *ka'yun;* they were trained to do so from
the age of three.

"The hardest part was convincing your captain to
authorize a bypass of the computer's security restric-
tions. As you know, it will not create a weapon without
the prior approval of either the captain or the security
chief." Morgen smiled. "And I could hardly have asked
you—not if I wanted it to be a surprise."

Worf rewrapped the *ka'yun* and set it down again. He
didn't know what to say. It was the first time in the
history of the universe that a Daa'Vit had ever offered a

Klingon such a gift. "I am honored," he managed to say at last.

"Of course you are," Morgen quipped. "But you understand—it's only a temporary thing."

The Klingon's forehead ridged over. "Temporary?" he echoed, not understanding at all.

"That's right," the Daa'Vit informed him. "When my coronation is over, I'll beam you back with a real one."

Worf shook his head. Now he *really* didn't understand.

Morgen leaned closer. "Unfortunately, I have a couple of vacancies in my escort. Dr. Crusher has graciously agreed to fill one of them. I am asking you to fill the other."

The security chief looked at him. "A Klingon . . . on Daa'V . . . ?"

Morgen waved aside the objection. "I'm not saying it will be easy, Lieutenant. Not for you—and not for me. But I'm willing if you are."

Worf sat back in his chair. "You will be denounced as a traitor. Your throne will be forfeit."

"Does that mean you're turning me down?" the Daa'Vit asked.

The Klingon attempted a grin. "No," he said. "Once again, I am honored."

"And perhaps a little crazy," Morgen suggested.

Worf nodded. "That as well."

As the holodeck doors opened, Wesley recognized the scene. It was just as he remembered it—a scarlet forest set ablaze wherever a sunbeam pierced it. The flying things were there too, hurrying from one overhead branch to another, making their deep-throated cries and dropping their beautiful, deadly feathers.

As the ensign entered, he remembered also to adjust for the strange springiness of the turf—and to look for the path that cut through the woods.

Simenon was just where Wes had expected to find him. This time, however, he was dressed in regulation Starfleet attire—not the casual robe he'd been wearing when they last visited this program.

As Wesley approached, the Gnalish was picking up a stone from the pile. "Greetings," he said without turning around. Then, pausing—as if savoring the moment for as long as he could—he pulled back and let fly.

The stone sailed effortlessly over the bright, placid water. It skipped once, twice, and then three more times in quick succession. Brushing his hands against each other, Simenon turned to his young companion.

"It's like piloting a shuttle," he said. "Once you've got it, you never lose it."

The ensign smiled. "I guess you're right."

The professor trained his ruby eyes on him. "Come to polish your technique?"

Wesley shook his head. "To wish you luck."

Simenon snorted. "What sort of luck will I need on Daa'V? One diplomatic mission is much like another." His tail switched back and forth; his expression eased just a bit. "But thanks for the thought."

"You know," said Wesley, "I'm hoping to get to the Academy one day. As soon as possible, in fact."

The Gnalish tilted his head as he regarded the human. "And?"

Wesley shrugged. "I don't know. I guess I'm looking forward to seeing you there."

"I see." He bent and picked up another rock, appraised it. "I should tell you—I'm not the most popular fellow in the place. Cadets see me and run the other way."

"Then they're not very bright," the ensign told him. "I've already attended one of your classes." He glanced at the pile of flat rocks at Simenon's feet. "I wouldn't mind at all taking another."

The professor snorted again—more softly this time. "That's what you say *now*. Just wait until exam time."

Wesley laughed. And after a moment Simenon joined him.

Beverly Crusher smoothed out her dark blue and black dress uniform and considered herself in the mirror. She looked fine. But then, her appearance wasn't the source of her dissatisfaction.

Her door mechanism beeped. The captain, no doubt. Right on time, as always.

"Come in," she said, and left her bedroom to meet him in the apartment's reception area.

Picard was idly taking in the furnishings when she emerged. He smiled at the sight of her.

"Very becoming," he said. "Very becoming indeed. It has been some time since you've worn your dress uniform, Doctor."

She smiled back. "Thank you. And yes, it has."

He held his hands out, palms up. "All ready?"

Crusher nodded. "I guess so."

The captain regarded her. "Is something wrong, Beverly?"

She sighed. "I just wish I'd had more time to prepare for this. Ever since Morgen asked me to be part of his escort, I've been studying Daa'Vit culture. But there's still a great deal I don't know."

"And you are afraid you will do something to embarrass Captain Morgen—or even jeopardize his ascension to the throne."

"Exactly," Crusher said.

Picard shook his head. "No need to worry. Unlike you, I have had time to veritably immerse myself in Daa'Vit custom. And I can tell you there are no hidden traps to catch you by surprise."

She looked at him. "You're sure?"

"I'm sure. Do you feel better now?"

"As a matter of fact," she told him, "I do." Taking a quick survey of her quarters, Crusher turned and headed for the door. The captain followed her out.

Once in the corridor, they headed for the nearest turbolift. There was a spring in Picard's step that the doctor hadn't noticed for days. She approved—and not just in her capacity as chief medical officer. It was good to see the man feeling so chipper after all that had come before.

Maybe his good spirits were contagious, she mused— because by the time they reached the lift, she felt pretty chipper herself.

"You know," she said, surprising herself a little, "I was actually dreading seeing the people from the *Stargazer.*"

The captain shot her a glance. "Oh?"

"It's true. I didn't even want to come out of my quarters."

He grunted. A moment later, the lift arrived and the doors opened. They stepped inside.

Once they were in the privacy of the conveyance, Picard cleared his throat. "To be perfectly candid," he said, "I was a little apprehensive myself."

Crusher saw him in a new light. "*You* were apprehensive? For godsakes, why?"

He turned to look at her. "I thought our visitors would bring back memories. Matters I hadn't quite laid to rest."

And suddenly, she understood. She'd been so wrapped up with her own ghosts, she'd forgotten the captain had some of his own.

"What about now?" she asked.

"Now," he said thoughtfully, "I am glad I had a chance to see my old friends again. *All* of them—living and dead."

She took his arm and squeezed it affectionately. "I know the feeling, Jean-Luc. I know it quite well."

That was how they emerged from the lift—with her arm tucked into the crook of his. And it was still there when they entered the transporter room, where they found the others already waiting for them.